"Would you like to live forever . . . ?"

His hands were on my shoulders, drawing me to him. He pressed his lips against mine. My tongue felt something sharp and out of place in his mouth, but I was unable to imagine what or even care. . . . I can remember wondering: What is happening to me? Magical, frightening, irresistible, sensual. It was all these things and more. Words do not exist to frame the pleasures and passions one enjoys with a vampire—and as one. Imagine hearing all the world's greatest symphonies at once, not as a jumble of noise but as a single explosion of bliss that fills you with total ecstasy. . . . There, trembling in the arms of a simple serving man, the universe was about to open itself to me. I was about to hear the music of the spheres, those first faint measures the tantalizing promise of what was to come.

And then, without a word of warning or reassurance, he sank his teeth into my neck. . . .

By Michael Romkey
Published by The Ballantine Publishing Group:

I, VAMPIRE
THE VAMPIRE PAPERS
THE VAMPIRE PRINCESS
THE VAMPIRE VIRUS
VAMPIRE HUNTER
THE LONDON VAMPIRE PANIC

THE LONDON VAMPIRE PANIC

Michael Romkey

BALLANTINE BOOKS • NEW YORK

A Ballantine Book
Published by The Ballantine Publishing Group
Copyright © 2001 by Michael Romkey

All rights reserved under International and Pan-American Copyright Conventions. Published in the United States by The Ballantine Publishing Group, a division of Random House, Inc., New York, and simultaneously in Canada by Random House of Canada Limited, Toronto.

Ballantine is a registered trademark and the Ballantine colophon is a trademark of Random House, Inc.

www.randomhouse.com/BB/

Library of Congress Catalog Card Number: 00-193410

ISBN 0-449-00573-9

Manufactured in the United States of America

First Edition: April 2001

10 9 8 7 6 5 4 3 2 1

For Carol, Ryan, Matt, and Drew

And with special thanks to Dr. Michael R. Davis of Cannock, U.K., and Lisa and Nicholas Labnon-Mohacsy of Naples, Florida, for their invaluable help with information about Britain and Hungary, and for their long-distance friendship.

Prologue

Annie Howard

THE WIND IS blowing off the Channel, a January gale cold as a workhouse, bending back the bare trees, scouring dead leaves from the hiding places where they lie rotting.

From the window seat in my lady's room, I watch a single carriage's progress up the street. The horse shakes his head against the reins, angry at having been led from his stall on such a day. He arches his neck and strains against the traces like a demon in harness, plumes of smoke exploding from his nostrils with each snorted breath. I cannot see the passengers. The carriage windows are closed tight, the curtains drawn against the cold. The driver has heaped a mountain of rugs about him to keep from freezing. He wears a scarf wound so high around his head that he could be a Muslim lifted from Persia by some spell and dropped onto this ice-blasted London street.

Despite the cold, I would be outside in a flash, if I could, but I cannot leave this house. Such are the rules governing my life, if one can call it a proper life—and I don't suppose one can.

The door across the street opens. A man comes out and pulls it quickly closed, as if he is in a very great hurry. It is the Carlsons' butler. He is a Scot, I think, although I no longer remember his name. He draws the snapping cloak

1

more tightly about him and leans into the storm. The wind pushes back, standing him up. For a moment it seems he will blow away like a discarded newspaper, tumbling to the end of the street, catching finally on the iron fence that surrounds the Earl of Stemple's house, squeezing through the black forged bars, flying on toward Hyde Park, the heath, and whatever else is beyond, driven all the way to the Atlantic by this heartless wind.

Invisible forces surround us. We mostly ignore them, while we are alive.

The storm would be the end of me if I could go out, which must be part of the reason I am bound to this house. There was never much to poor Annie Howard, and now I am as insubstantial as the whiff of smoke that rises from an extinguished candle. This tempest would blast me into nothingness with its kiss, and I would no longer haunt this house. The cook would not glimpse a shadow going up the stairs in the dark. The peculiar scent of soap would not rise mysteriously in the parlor on certain evenings. Soft footsteps would be heard no more in the hall outside the child's room. And the rocking chair beside his bed would not move gently back and forth in the middle of the night, as if of its own accord, unless some living soul were seated in it.

This wind!

I used to love the feel of the wind. On my free days last summer I would go for long walks and take off my hat to better feel the sun against my face and the wind playing in my hair. Sometimes I went as far as Hyde Park, if I had a friend. (A girl, of course, one of the other servants from Mayfair.) I remember one time sitting beside the Serpentine when a raven's feather, blue-black and shiny, came floating down out of the sky and practically landed in my lap! Once I watched a tiny spider laboring in the grass, patiently building a silver web to catch the dew. There were two boys in a rowboat that afternoon. They raised their straw hats and waved. We ran nearly all the way home, laughing inside with the secret joy.

There are so many things you do not have the opportunity to do and know when you die young. I never had a beau. I never was in love. I regretted this very much at first, but now the disappointment has faded. Time passes and things that once mattered no longer seem important.

I was fortunate to find a position at Moore House, a girl without family, who possessed little more than the tortoise-shell comb I won for being the first in my form to learn the catechism. When I came here, this big house overpowered me. I sometimes got lost: There were so many rooms, all richly appointed, with ornate moldings and wood paneling. The furniture was exquisitely carved and inlaid, and I polished it until the air smelled of warm beeswax. The oil paintings on the walls, turned dark with age, showed men and women from long ago—people with stern looks and strange, antique clothing. The portraits frightened me a little bit, to be completely honest. But the chandeliers! They glittered at night like constellations of diamonds on fire in the sky. When I was alone, I used to stand and stare up at them. The chandelier in the entry hall was the most beautiful thing I had ever seen.

I hardly notice these things now, and they give me no pleasure. I am losing interest in the world and its people. Sometimes I sit and listen to their conversations, but the words have become difficult for me to make out, a soft, drowsy muttering that seems spoken in a language I have mostly forgotten. I have trouble remembering all their names—except for the child. I will *always* remember him, and adore him. He is my special one, my golden boy, my beloved Andrew. Nothing could change that, not even my death.

He is the reason I linger between two worlds. I do not know how I can protect him, but I cannot continue on my way until the danger has passed. Who understands this better than I, who watched over the boy and happily gave him everything?

I wonder what became of my body. I hope it was buried

in a nice place, where grass will grow in spring. I picture myself going to my rest in my Sunday dress, with the tortoiseshell comb holding my hair up. It is pleasant to think of myself sleeping peacefully in the ground, even with my grave covered with a blanket of black earth. In spring the sun will return, the soft rain will fall, and the grass will grow. There is a time for all things, and a season, and when our time has passed and our work here is complete, we move on to God.

Soon, perhaps, when I no longer have to fear for the boy.

I close my eyes and think of the wind brushing across the frozen dirt on my grave as it once played in my hair. The cold no longer bothers me. I am beyond the cold now.

Even though I am dead, I begin to dream . . .

PART I

✦

Front Papers

1

Letter to a Consulting Historian

February 15, 2000

Penelope Newton-Medwick
M.A., D.Phil., Professor and Tutor of History
Balliol College
Broad Street
Oxford, Oxfordshire OX13BJ

Dear Dr. Newton-Medwick,

Enclosed is the Dr. Posthumous Blackley memoir I spoke to you about on the telephone. The history and its related documents have been kept in our office's vaults since Dr. Blackley's death in 1920. The file was opened this past January, in accordance with Dr. Blackley's instructions that his papers remain sealed until the year 2000.

Dr. Blackley was evidently a person of some standing in Victorian and Edwardian times. The image of him arising from the memoir is that of a candid—indeed, unusually so—observer unafraid to confess his own weaknesses and foibles.

I leave it to you, Professor Newton-Medwick, to determine

whether this is an authentic account, an elaborate hoax, or the product of a clever but unsound mind. If there is enough evidence in the record to indicate the disturbing things Dr. Blackley has to say are *true*, we shall have to determine how best to proceed.

Keep this information in the strictest confidentiality. I do not wish to ignite a *second* London vampire panic. I also do not want to embarrass the royal family. They have troubles enough on their own without us adding to the balance.

I can only provide a few details about Dr. Blackley beyond what you will read in his history. He was a prominent London physician, well-born and wealthy, a lifelong bachelor who died in 1920 at age eighty. He left his estate to the child of an unmarried Irish serving girl who was in his employ at the time of his death. The implication is that Dr. Blackley fathered the boy in the final years of his life. The child—his name was *Posthumous* O'Connor—died piloting a Spitfire during the Battle of Britain, leaving no relatives. Therefore, Amberfield & Porter, executor of Dr. Blackley's estate, retains sole ownership and authority over Dr. Blackley's history.

I am including a check for one thousand pounds as your retainer. Please do not hesitate to contact me if I can be of any assistance, or if it is necessary to secure additional funds for research. I am most anxious to learn your conclusions at the earliest possible date.

I remain most sincerely yours,

Lygeia Wickersham, Q.C.
Amberfield & Porter
50 Bishopsgate
London EC2N4AJ

2

✧

A Note to the Future

Beloved Reader,

It is sometime in the new millennium if you are reading this, which means your devoted author has been dead eighty years, give or take a few odd turns of the calendar. Pray do not waste time mourning the handful of coffin dust that was once the devilishly handsome Dr. Posthumous Blackley. I have had as full a life as it is possible for any man to live. For eight delicious decades I have sampled pleasures both high and low, and now I find myself exhausted and quite ready to die. I have not the least desire to live beyond my time, or to pursue the fountain of eternal youth that has only recently been made known to me.

After reading this memoir, and the related documents I have gone to a certain degree of trouble and expense to collect, you will understand why I ordered it kept under lock and key for the better part of a century. Moreover, perhaps the passage of time will improve the brilliance of my observations and incisiveness of my insights, the way a bottle of fine Napoleon matures to golden mellowness as it ages in a darkened chateau cellar. It has fallen to you, mysterious reader, to uncork the bottle and drain it to the lees. I give you fair warning: This brandy was not made for the faint of heart. I advise you to sip it a little at a time to prevent yourself from being overwhelmed. If you do that, I promise the experience will prove satisfactory.

You have me at a disadvantage.

You will soon know a very great deal about me, while I can only imagine you holding these pages, eighty years into the future, eighty years after my death, puzzling over my account of so many strange and troubling events. Such is the unequal nature of the intercourse between a writer and his reader, communing across the centuries.

Since I cannot know your identity, I will think of you as I would like you to be—a lovely young lady, certainly far better company for an aged roué than a barrister with an overdeveloped sense of his own importance and a perfectly tied cravat.

I imagine myself sitting beside you now, breathing in the perfume lingering about your neck and hair. I see the intelligence in your eyes, and evidence of a sparkling wit and lively spirit. I watch the gentle rise and fall of your breast as you read. Your lips are slightly pursed, an expression of indulgence belying your genuine curiosity about the secrets I have to tell. And oh, dear girl, what secrets I have to tell!

You experience a twinge of guilty pleasure.

There is something delicious about a secret, is there not? Anything concealed invariably has the scent of scandal about it. Illicit, dishonest, disgraceful, immoral behavior— they are always so delicious to hear about. And yet that is not the ultimate purpose of this memoir. You will indeed find herein gossip from the loquacious companion of princes and kings, but my deeper intent is to leave behind a history of something terrible to serve as a kind of warning to future generations—and to *you* personally, my dear!

When you start to feel afraid, try to remember it is better to understand the way things really are, even if it means being frightened, than it is to remain ignorant of the danger while maintaining a naive sense of safety.

But do read on, dear reader. Certainly, it is already too late for you to stop!

Your obedient servant,
Posthumous Blackley

PART II

✦

The Physician

3

✧

Die Fledermaus

I REMEMBER THE first time I heard the word *vampire,* though the term's meaning was not immediately obvious to your devoted narrator.

It was in the Royal Opera House, where I had repaired with friends to hear a production of *Die Fledermaus.* I have a vivid recollection of the exact moment I got my first inkling of the hidden world about to open up under my feet, dropping me into an abyss of darkness and uncertainty. Lady Gray leaned toward the Prince of Wales during the intermission, put her tiny white hand over his and whispered: "Surely you have heard the stories going around about the *vampire*?"

Her free hand was thrown across her bosom in an intimate gesture of protectiveness, and when she whispered the strange word—*vampire*—she gave herself a little squeeze. As a physician who has seen countless breasts of every size, shape, age, and quality of perfection, you must acknowledge that I know of what I speak when I say Lady Gray's breasts were extraordinary. Seeing her goose herself like that in public is what made me remember the moment—and the word.

Vampire: I remember thinking it had a Slavic sound to it. I confirmed my suspicion the next day when I looked it up in the dictionary. Yet a "vampire" was not, as I initially suspected, an exotic sex toy imported from Eastern Europe.

13

There were eight in our party. Bertie* was with Lady Gray, his favorite mistress at the time. I was with Mrs. Stensvad, whose husband, a Swedish diplomat, was diplomatic enough to pretend not to know that his wife and I were carrying on an affair. Ashley Duncan, the noted artist, had brought his wife. It might strike you as strange that Mrs. Duncan was in our little party, considering the mischief Bertie and I had got up to, but she could have cared less. Maude Duncan was a free-thinking American girl who did not give a whit for the usual conventions. A Guardsman with a Webley revolver in the pocket of his evening clothes, which he wore with obvious discomfort, sat bolt upright behind Bertie. It was his job to look after the Prince. Captain Lucian, the Prince's equerry, rounded out our little group. Lucian was mad for any sort of music. He had the annoying habit of stopping in the street to listen to Gypsy violinists or beggars making merry with a squeeze-box or penny whistle. I like music as much as the next person, but Lucian's appreciation for it bordered on a mania.

The opera was good enough, if you like Strauss. I found my mind wandering midway into the first act. People interest me more than music, and I often divert myself at the opera by studying the audience. I spotted that infamous fop, Oscar Wilde, seated on the main floor. He was wearing preposterous velvet breaches and patent leather shoes with little bows. Seated beside him was Lillie Langtry, who in 1880 was on the verge of becoming a famous actress. It was obvious to me that Miss Langtry would become the darling of millions. And it was equally obvious to me that Wilde was destined for disgrace. If there were a way to make money by judging casual acquaintances, I would be even wealthier than I already am!

Lord and Lady Shaftbury were there, seated nearby. Boxes in a horseshoe-shaped theatre radiate away from the royal enclosure, reflecting one's status accordingly. The closer

---

*As this is a personal memoir, I will speak of friends in familiar terms. No disrespect is intended.

one's seat is to the royal box, the higher the status. Lord Shaftbury glanced our way frequently, but not because the Prince of Wales was present. It was Lady Gray's eye he hoped to catch. She had been Shaftbury's mistress before Bertie stole her away. I was disinclined to feel charitable toward Shaftbury, the snappish prig, but I did feel a bit sorry for him that night. I could only imagine how I would feel if I had ceded my welcome in Lady Gray's bedchamber to Bertie. Poor Shaftbury. How could a lord compete with a prince for her tender affections?

Franz Liszt sat beside a ravishing young woman in a box on the other side of Shaftbury's. The brilliant pianist was as famous for his amorous exploits as for attacking the keyboard like a man possessed. Liszt was said to have bedded more women than any other man in Europe. Old and thin as a scarecrow, his long wild hair turned to gray, he continued to draw beauty like moths to his flickering old candle. How I envied the ancient devil!

"Who is that creature with Liszt?" I asked Lady Gray during the intermission.

She raised her opera glasses and looked nonchalantly past Lord Shaftbury, causing elation and then defeat to flicker across his face in quick succession. Captain Lucian leaned forward to learn the answer. The young woman had not escaped the Captain's sharp eye.

"That is the tragic Lady Olivia Moore," Lady Gray said. "You know the story?"

"Sir Brendan was a friend," I replied. "A very sad story indeed." As sad as his surviving daughter, Olivia, was lovely.

We stood as Bertie returned to the box, squinting down at the program through his pince-nez. *"Die Fledermaus,"* he said, then translated the opera's title, "The Bat."

A little shudder went through Lady Gray. "The mere thought of bats terrifies me."

"Nonsense," Bertie said, giving her the look men give women when they think they're being foolish. "They're harmless enough creatures."

"Bats eat their weight in mosquitoes every night, I'm told," Mrs. Duncan said. "Think of all the pests they destroy."

Lady Gray looked down at the stage, shaking her head, unconvinced.

Bertie handed his program over his shoulder for the Guardsman to take. The houselights went down, and conversation in the theatre abruptly fell to an expectant hush. That was when Lady Gray turned toward Bertie, put one hand over his and the other over her breasts, and said in an excited whisper: "Surely you have heard the stories going around about the *vampire*?"

Music swelled to fill the darkened room.

"Hush, my dear," Bertie said, and pressed a finger to the bearded royal lips. "We do not want to be rude."

4

✧

The Hellfire Club

LUCIAN TOOK AN early leave of us after *Die Fleder-maus*. The young captain's duties as the Prince of Wales's equerry required him to rise from his bed—or whomever's bed he happened to be occupying—at a relatively decent hour of the morning. Having previously assigned Dr. Enfield, my resident, to act in my stead at the office the next day, I was free to accompany the others to a late supper at Rouchard's. The ladies were sent home after that under the protective wing of our dour Guardsman. Bertie, Duncan, and I then proceeded unescorted to our favorite midnight haunt, the Hellfire Club, for a nightcap and perhaps a bit of whoring.

What good are wealth and social standing to a man unless he is free to abuse them? Dreary virtue is the chilly province of the middle classes. I have always said that an aristocrat is bred for debauchery. And in my day there was no better place than the Hellfire Club for a gentleman who wished to comport himself in a discreetly wanton fashion.

Dear old Hellfire—how I miss the place! It was without parallel in the world: the loveliest courtesans, the finest paintings, the truest billiard table, the loosest roulette wheel, the best wine, the most exotic "entertainments." I have visited the best men's establishments throughout the Continent and India and none were more than a desultory campfire next to Hellfire's perpetually blazing bacchanal. Perhaps in Turkey, Ethiopia, or some other ancient sunburnt country, where passion was elevated to the highest pinnacle of art thousands of years ago, there exists a brothel to best the Hellfire Club—yet I doubt it.

The retiring rooms of Hellfire's upper floors were scrupulously clean, the girls scrupulously healthy. This latter circumstance was due to the ministrations of a handsome young doctor who shall remain nameless. This able physician was recompensed for his duties in various unorthodox fashions, but I can assure you the payments were entirely to his liking!

To gain admission to Hellfire you had to be well-born or wealthy, preferably both. The doorman did admit the odd tycoon or rich foreign industrialist, but the vast majority of the club's patrons were at the very least knights or baronets, many were dukes, marquises, viscounts, earls, princes, and kings.

Though never mentioned in polite company, Hellfire was known to everybody who mattered—and to some who didn't. The existence of so much delicious excess in the heart of London could not but help draw the attention of the self-appointed watchdogs of public morality. Though most professional do-gooders understood well enough which side of their bread was buttered, there were a few who labored vainly to douse Hellfire. Once or twice a year one of London's scandalmongers would attempt to publish a condemnation of the club in one of the city's lesser newspapers, scribbling a tedious polemic declaring the Hellfire Club to be a chancre on the rose of the Empire. These sanctimonious eructations were easily suppressed. We knew how to keep a tight rein on the press in my day, and the world was a better place for it.

The Contessa Saint-Simon met us in the foyer and conducted us through the casino to the banquette reserved for His Majesty's use when he visited Hellfire. A round of champagne cocktails was served, and we began to critique the Strauss performance for the Contessa, who, like Captain Lucian, was an enthusiastic patron of the city's concert halls.

"I am surprised you did not enjoy *Die Fledermaus,* Monsieur Duncan. The reviews have been most positive."

"It was, oh, I don't know," Duncan said, rummaging his untidy artist's mind for the right words. "I suppose it was all somehow a bit unsubstantial. I kept expecting the actors to begin waltzing about the stage."

"You raise an interesting point," the Contessa mused in her French-accented English. "Can popular music be serious? Or can serious music be popular?"

Bertie sipped his cocktail with a bored expression, but I felt my enthusiasm for the discussion—and the delectable Contessa—rise.

"Duncan is quite right," I said. "The opera was a sugary confection that takes away your appetite but leaves you quickly hungry for something of substance. Mozart and Beethoven are my meat in the concert hall, and Bach, of course, in church." In music, politics, and religion, my tastes have always been soundly conservative.

"I thought you were smitten with Wagner," the Contessa said and slowly blinked her heavily lidded eyes. Her teeth, white as fine porcelain, were almost straight across the front of her upper jaw instead of following the usual convex line. Strange how a slight physical anomaly, which might even be considered a mild imperfection, can serve to make a beautiful woman even more bewitching!

"I was mad about Wagner for a time," I confessed, remembering how I had gone on at great length to her about *Der Ring des Nibelungen* earlier in the season. "My love proved to be nothing but a passing infatuation. With Wagner everything is too loud and too long."

"Hear hear!" Bertie said. He abhorred operas that went on for very long. "I have had enough music for tonight."

"But not of the theatre, I hope, Your Majesty. We have a special entertainment planned for tonight."

"What is it going to be?" Duncan asked the Contessa. "I heard the Swedish milk maids are in town."

"That is next week, monsieur. Tonight we have something new for you. It is something unusual, something daring and different. I dare say that you may even find it shocking."

"We can always hope!" I said.

"Certainly you have heard the stories about the London vampire?"

I exchanged a look with Bertie.

"What the deuce is a vampire?" Duncan asked. "Lady Gray was saying something about a vampire earlier this evening."

"She's always rattling on about some thing or the other," Bertie said with a roll of the eyes. He was growing tired of Lady Gray; Lord Shaftbury might get her back in his bed yet, I thought.

"If you have not heard about the vampire, you are all in for a surprise," the Contessa said. "You do like surprises, don't you?"

"Oh, Blackley lives for them," Bertie said. "Tell the Contessa about that night at Lord Allyn's country house in Wales."

"The rooster story?"

"That's the one."

"Do amuse us, old boy," Duncan said. "We have time."

I paused for a sip of champagne cocktail before I began.

"As we all know, country houses can be the stage for elaborate dramas of clandestine romance. For the sake of this story, let us imagine that a certain rakish young doctor wanted to arrange an assignation with the beautiful wife of a certain member of Parliament, who was himself at the time off at another country house, with one of his several mistresses. Let us assume he found an obliging hostess and arranged for her to invite him and the lady to her country house on the same weekend. In the evening, after dinner, music, conversation, a few hands of cards, and all the other social niceties, the guests retired to their bedchambers. Following a suitable interval to preserve decency and discretion, our amorous hero tiptoed down the darkened hall to open both the unlocked bedroom door and the charms of his awaiting paramour."

"It sounds as if this is a routine you have practiced once or twice yourself, Dr. Blackley."

"With distinction, I dare say, Contessa. Yet on this particular night my overly gracious host compelled me to drink one too many glasses of port before retiring. As the clock approached midnight, I made my way to the darkened west wing, carefully counting the knobs on the bedroom doors.

"One . . . Two . . . Three . . . Four . . . Five . . . Seven."

This was Bertie's favorite part of the story. I paused while he laughed, then repeated the pregnant line without any special inflection, which is how the story is properly told.

"One . . . Two . . . Three . . . Four . . . Five . . . Seven.

"I silently opened the door. My thoughtful hostess had instructed her servants to keep the door hinges well oiled. I whispered my lady's name, but no response came back. Either she had dozed off while awaiting her beau or else she was playing a game of opossum in order to tantalize me.

"The door was expertly closed without making the slightest sound. A little moonlight spilled in through the window, enough light for me to easily make my way to the bed without barking my shin, tripping over the rug, or falling victim to any of the other pitfalls that embarrass and humiliate less accomplished seducers. I stood there a moment, holding my breath. And then I leaped into the bed and cried out, 'Cock-a-doodle-do!' "

I paused to let the image sink into my listeners' minds. Life may not be a comedy, but it is usually best to think it so.

"The Bishop of York and his prune-faced wife both sat bolt upright and began shrieking, as if the Devil himself had jumped into their bed."

"Maybe they thought you were the vampire," the Contessa said, laughing merrily but less raucously than Bertie and Duncan, who seemed on the verge of apoplexy at the thought of me leaping into bed with the pious old bishop and his wife. I did not respond to the Contessa's remark about the vampire except to nod. I still had no idea what the blazes a vampire was, though I was about to find out.

"But—the end," Bertie said. "That's not—the end."

"Unfortunately not," I said. "A strange smell assaulted my nose. I say strange, and yet the aroma was entirely familiar. I felt a warm dampness wetting my hands and knees. One, maybe both, of the frightened old fools had wet themselves."

"Mon Dieu!" the Contessa said, clapping her hands with delight at the concert of embarrassments in my tale.

At that moment a Russian giant dressed as a jinni rang the brass gong that signaled the entertainment was about to begin. As we joined the others moving down the hall, the Contessa put her arm through mine and pulled my head toward hers.

"Tell me, Dr. Blackley: Did you ever find door number seven?"

"Are you joking? After all that trouble, not even the Archbishop of Canterbury himself would have been able to keep me from completing my assignation."

"And it was worth the trouble?"

"She wasn't as delightful as you, my dear, but, yes, it was well worth it. It always is."

Hellfire's theatre was made over to suit whatever fashion imagination demanded for the productions: a dungeon in the Spanish Inquisition, a hospital room, a women's prison, a barn, a Roman bath, a crofter's shack, a nunnery. On the night we went to Hellfire after *Die Fledermaus,* the theatre had been done up as the bedchamber of a fashionable London house. I was a little disappointed, though ordinary settings were sometimes the scenes of the club's more depraved entertainments. The theatre quickly filled to capacity, late arrivals lining up along the back wall. A Polynesian girl in a grass skirt came onto the stage carrying a placard above her head. I lifted my eyes from the brown nipples of her small but well-shaped breasts to read the play's title—*The Vampire*—lettered in bloodred ink. The house lights went down and a lone pianist began to play in the orchestra pit—the music Debussy, I think, judging from the bizarre melody.

A woman strode onto the stage. She was an impressive specimen—tall and striking, with magnificent breasts, a wasp waist, and brick-red hair piled high upon her head. She came to the edge of the stage and turned in profile with a sweep of the skirt, looking out over the audience as if we were the ones on display. I was undressing the bold hussy with my eyes when I noticed a mist swirling onto the stage from the wing. Miss Red reacted to this with alarm, as if the fog harbored a menace within its impenetrable folds. Her hands flew to the high collar of her dress in a gesture of distress as she took several halting steps backward. The mist began to recede, leaving in its wake the lone figure of a man. He was turned away from us at first, the collar of his cape pulled high, his face concealed. He seemed to have floated in upon the fog, a rather disconcerting impression.

The figure extended his arm and pointed a long index finger at the woman. She stopped backing away and stood frozen in place, as if impaled upon an invisible shaft of energy flowing from the tip of the man's bony finger.

He walked to a side table and removed his top hat and cape, his back still to us. The woman continued to stand where she had been, her eyes wide and unblinking, apparently mesmerized. When he turned toward us, I saw he was an ordinary sort of fellow, with a face most women would regard as handsome, though there was something cold, even cruel, about his expression. His eyes were his most pronounced feature: They were dark and mesmeric. The man who had floated onto the stage on a puff of fog had put the redhead into a hypnotic trance.

"A chair," the mesmerist commanded. He was Hungarian, judging from his voice.

The redhead dragged a cane-bottom chair before the man and stood there, staring blankly ahead, as he sat.

"Take off all your clothing," he commanded.

The woman began to undress, her stare straight ahead, her fingers blindly working the buttons and hooks of her garments. By degrees her lovely body was revealed to us—neck, shoulders, arms, legs. Her breasts were full and milky white, with large pink areoles. Her delta of Venus was thatched in brick-red hair.

The mesmerist stood then and indicated with a gesture of his hand that the woman should take his place in the chair. He was grinning now, a crooked half sneer that gave his face a distinctly lupine appearance. It took me a moment to notice the unusually prominent canines. Indeed, his teeth were like the fangs on a wolf. Small details reveal much: Those two incisors, simple stagecraft, implied the inner beast within the man. It was at this point that I began to understand. A vampire was a demon disguised as a man, an incubus imbued with mesmeric powers to prey upon women.

He snapped his fingers and the woman's sinews became unstrung. She slumped backward in the chair, her arms hanging limp, her legs spread wide, her eyes staring blankly at the ceiling. The vampire made himself free with the redhead, his hands roaming her body, caressing and exploring its most intimate places. His tongue, which was unusually long and pointed, flicked the woman's ear. She did not show even the smallest reaction to these assaults, so completely had she been taken into the vampire's spell. The vampire kissed her full on the lips, forcing her mouth open, his tongue disappearing inside like a serpent slithering down a dark damp hole. He kissed her cheek, then nibbled it, then began to lick, the eel of a tongue moving slowly to her jaw and down her neck, pausing when he reached the soft skin in the hollow between her neck and shoulder.

The woman's muscles contracted suddenly as if from a powerful jolt of electricity, the sudden motion startling the audience. She would have flung herself out of the chair if the vampire hadn't held her body firmly in place, like a specimen pinned to a dissecting table. A trickle of scarlet ran down her neck and between the perfect whiteness of her breasts.

The vampire had sunk his teeth into her jugular!

"Doctor," the Contessa whispered, her hand gripping mine the moment I started to stand. I saw her smile and relaxed. I had been gulled. The action on stage was, after all, mere action on a stage. This was not *real*.

Down toward the front of the theatre a man got up and hurried up the aisle. The entertainment, so unexpectedly violent, was more than he could take.

"Mr. Raphael," the Contessa whispered. "You would not know him. He is a wealthy American and not very sophisticated, it seems."

On stage, the dramatics were about to rise to a new level of sophistication. The vampire carried the naked redhead's limp body toward the bed. Her neck, like his mouth, was smeared with blood. She pretended to be dead. But the vampire, judging from his trousers, was very much alive.

"This is based on accounts of the London vampire," the Contessa whispered.

"Do you mean there really is such a fiend at large in the city?" I asked in amazement.

"Shhh!" Bertie commanded. He did not like being distracted from the action on stage, which was building toward a predictable sort of climax.

5

✦

A Summons to
Downing Street

AFORTNIGHT AFTER our trip to the Hellfire Club, Algernon Turnor, the least fun of Dizzy's three secretaries (none of whom were particularly fun), came to collect me at my Harley Street office, insisting I accompany him to the Prime Minister's residence without delay.

"Whatever is the rush, Algae? The Prime Minister's asthma acting up again?"

"No, sir."

"A touch of dropsy?"

He shook his head.

"Now listen here, Algae," I said, "I just left Lord Salisbury sitting in my examining room in his knickers, mad as blazes. I trust this is more than some piffling trifle."

"The matter is of the utmost urgency, sir, but I am not at liberty to say more. The Chief will take care of that himself."

"The Chief," I puffed, not particularly caring for the nickname Dizzy's political underlings used to denote the Prime Minister. I grabbed my coat and medical bag, assuming the problem was medical, perhaps something uncomfortable, embarrassing, and potentially scandalous. Like most men who achieve old age, the old lion was paying for the ex-

cesses of a colorful life. Disraeli's asthma made him suscep-
tible to bronchitis. I had recommended to him a half hour of
brisk walking daily, but the P.M. was steadfastly opposed to
exercise. If he took a constitutional, it was only because he
had a beautiful young woman or an interesting conversationalist to accompany him.

Algae said something about the weather as we went out of
doors—some complaint about the wind, if memory serves,
that caused him to be even more of an irritant than usual to
me. I make it a practice to ignore the weather, and in recompense it ignores me. I sat with my bag on my lap and listened to the clip-clop of the horse pulling us along the busy
street, wondering if the malady at hand was of a nonmedical
nature, as was sometimes the case.

The Aylesford Affair was fresh in my mind as we trotted toward No. 10 Downing Street. I had helped Dizzy untie that
particular Gordian knot, though it had been no easy task. Lord
Randolph Churchill had gone so far as to threaten to expose
Lady Aylesford's love letters to Lord Blandford, unless the
Prince of Wales intervened to prevent Lord Aylesford from di-
vorcing his wife. A few years earlier and such a thing would
have ended in a duel and one of the antagonists dead. As it
was, the contretemps resulted instead in a complicated and
vexing row that tore London society in two. Dragging poor
Bertie into the mess had been particularly unconscionable,
but matters of the heart have a way of disregarding the rules,
and the consequences be damned. Dizzy had rather enjoyed
playing peacemaker, with my assistance as go-between
among the warring factions. I have provided this sort of service on more than a few such occasions. My family's ancient
name has always made me welcome in the best places, while
the fact that I am a physician makes most people willing to
discuss with me the most personal sort of problems.

When we arrived at the Prime Minister's residence, Algae
bustled me into the Green Drawing Room, leaving me in
eclectic and not altogether respectable company. The first
person I clapped eyes on was Charles Darwin, the notorious

bald-headed crank who believes us all descended from monkeys. Even if we *are*, I am sure it is part of God's plan. Keeping company with the Lord of the Apes was a strapping man who exuded an air of health and rawboned physical strength. He had the erect posture of a cavalry officer and the bronzed face of a common crofter. He wore his trousers tucked into the top of high riding boots, an eccentric sort of thing to do, I thought. In the journal I kept during this period, I wrote that I was convinced the fellow was a plantation owner just in from Africa—which turned out to be completely wrong.

Chief Inspector Palmer, Dizzy's pet policeman, nodded to me when I glanced his way. He seemed to be keeping an eye on a rumpled little man whose hair and beard were badly in need of grooming, and who had sallow, jaundiced skin. Liver trouble, I guessed, probably the result of an excess of drink or narcotics, perhaps both. The possibilities were equally likely. London was a gurgling cesspool of sin—which is what gave the city its charm.

Lord Shaftbury stood before the fire, holding a match to his cigar. The game was afoot if Shaftbury was involved. He was an ambitious fellow, drawn to power the way a drunkard is to cheap gin. Dizzy employed Shaftbury as his political cat's paw, using him to catch and dispatch insubordinate mice at the master's bidding. Shaftbury fancied himself Dizzy's political heir. In those early days of 1880 few would have doubted he would be the next Tory prime minister.

Captain Lucian, the young equerry to the Prince of Wales, lounged against the mantle near Shaftbury, smoking a cigarette with typical insouciance. He lifted his chin at me, an inquiring expression in his eyes. I made a small, almost imperceptible shrug in reply to the unspoken question. Neither of us had the slightest idea why we'd been summoned to Downing Street. We had been together at Skittles a few days previous. I seemed to recall something about Lucian, Bertie, and I throwing empty champagne bottles off the roof. I hoped we hadn't hit someone on the head. I cast a glance at the policeman, but he continued to be preoccupied with the disreputable man in the abominable suit.

The doors opened and the dyspeptic C. A. Cross entered, followed by a priest. To be honest, I would have been less surprised to see the Home Secretary lead a nanny goat through the door. Dizzy was not known for excessive piety. In all the times I had visited him at Downing Street and Beaconsfield, I do not recall there ever having been a member of the clergy among the party.

Cross and I were friendly but not friends. He was an able Home Secretary but a tremendous bore. Dizzy called him the Lancashire Swami for his otherworldly knowledge of the mechanics of administration—which translated to an almost supernatural ability to manipulate important votes with parliamentary hocus pocus. Cross obviously knew what was up. He caught my eye and gave me an arch look, as if to say, "You're not going to believe this!"

I stifled the impulse to let out a deep sigh. Whatever Dizzy's problem was, I knew then that it was going to require substantial jiggery-pokery to set it right. Another Aylesford Affair was in the making, I feared.

The priest struggled to keep his eyeballs from falling out of their sockets. I'd seen the look before on the faces of ordinary men summoned into the halls of greatness. He was pale, rather like an unhealthy plant that has seen insufficient light. An Oxford bookworm, I guessed—this time correctly.

Dizzy made his entrance, dressed in his usual foppish manner. He dressed the part of a literary dandy—bottle-green breeches and, beneath his coat, a richly embroidered canary-yellow waistcoat. He walked with the aid of a golden-headed cane, wheezing a bit as he came into the room. He had applied rouge to his sallow cheeks for a bit of color, and his hair was an unnatural shade of black, dyed to conceal the gray. It appeared that his bronchitis had mostly cleared up. I had convinced the Prime Minister to augment his medication with generous doses of the finest Chateau Lafite. Regular doses of this tonic had plainly done him good. Dr. Kidd, the old butcher who had treated him for years, had him on a mild course of arsenic to clear the bronchial tubes. I did not approve of the regimen, but I did not think the arsenic would hurt him much in such minute doses.

Cross began his introductions with what seemed a bit of sarcasm. I was presented as "the eminent physician," which was, of course, completely accurate. But Palmer was "the distinguished detective," which I thought was painting it on a bit thick. The man with his britches tucked into his riding boots was Professor James Cotswold, the noted American anthropologist.

Dizzy, smiling, interrupted Cross to confess he was unfamiliar with the field of anthropology.

"I study dinosaur fossils at Harvard," Cotswold said. "Think of me as a professor of old bones at Harvard."

Cross added that Cotswold had been invited to London to address the Royal Society on his research. The papers had written it up, although I had missed his speech and do not think I read more than a few paragraphs about it in the *Times*. The subject was of very little interest to me.

So much for my theory that Cotswold was fresh off a plantation near Nairobi.

The priest was the Reverend Christopher Clarkson from Christ College, Oxford. "Reverend Clarkson is a theologian," Cross said. "He should be able to assist us in the event—in the unlikely event—that this affair touches on aspects of the demonic."

I felt the hair stand up on the back of my neck. The beady eyes of Wellington's beastly portrait stared down at me. They seemed to follow me as I shifted in my seat. I somehow knew where we were going by that point, but I tried to put it out of my mind, as I had since that day in Hyde Park when the policemen roughed up the absurd Indian boy who yelped about his "rights" as they beat him.

The only intercourse I want to have with the Great Beyond is in church on Sundays and, inevitably, when the time comes for me to pass from this world into the next. At Black

Friars, the ancestral Blackley home, I learned to dread the spirit world. Black Friars is haunted by the specters of monks put to the sword when Henry VIII confiscated the ecclesiastical property. My boyhood was peppered with ghastly encounters with ghosts. I would come around a corner and glimpse a malevolent presence—a suggestion of rough brown cloth and mournful countenance—which invariably disappeared the moment I looked in its direction. I cannot begin to count the nights my sleep has been disturbed by strange footsteps, disembodied moans, and phantom tappings. Late on nights when the winds howl around the battlements, you can hear faint strains of ghostly chanting. Little wonder I am seldom in residence at Black Friars!

Cross's introductions got to the most disreputable one of our company. "And this," he said, indicating the rumpled little man, "is Dr. Van Helsing, the professional vampire hunter from Budapest."

I looked at Dr. Van Helsing with new respect.

"As some of you know and the rest of you have no doubt guessed, I have invited you here to discuss the widening plague of vampire attacks in London," the Prime Minister said. "Among the fiend's victims is a friend of the Prince of Wales, indeed, an intimate friend. His Royal Highness must be protected from any hint of scandal."

"If you will permit me to be so bold," Dr. Van Helsing interjected in his heavy Hungarian accent, "it would be far better for you gentlemen to concern yourselves instead with protecting Prince Edward Albert from the vampire. The monster must be hunted down in his lair and destroyed."

The Prime Minister's chin jerked up, as it often did when he was about to pounce. I had a sinking feeling, already knowing what he was about to say.

"That is precisely why I have asked you all here today," Dizzy said.

I entertained a brief hope of slipping discreetly out of the parlor, but Darwin and the dour Scotland Yard inspector blocked any chance of a quiet escape. I was trapped.

6

✧

Inspector Palmer's
Macabre Catalogue

PERHAPS WE COULD begin by you giving us a précis of the vampire's depredations to date, Chief Inspector Palmer," Dizzy said. The P.M., never one to sit back and watch events unfold, was impatient as ever to take matters by the shank.

The policeman withdrew a notebook with a black leather cover from his waistcoat pocket and paged deliberately through his notes as if preparing to give evidence at the Old Bailey. Policemen tend to be cautious and methodical, I have noticed, two traits lacking from my own mercurial humors.

"The first victim was Annie Howard. She was a fifteen-year-old serving girl at Moore House in Mayfair."

The poor benighted Moore family, I thought. The Moores had seen more than their share of tragedy. I recollected how, through one of those strange peregrinations of fate, I had happened to see Sir Brendan's daughter, Lady Olivia, at the opera several weeks earlier, in the company of that old satyr, Franz Liszt.

"Miss Annie was found dead in the kitchen there at approximately 10:00 P.M., November first. There were two puncture wounds in her neck, just here."

C.I. Palmer indicated on his own neck where Miss

Howard had been injured, pressing the skin over his jugular vein with his fore and middle fingers.

"She was pale as milk when discovered. There was a distinct puckering of the skin in the lips and fingertips. The wee lass had been almost completely drained of blood. But even more unusual than that was the matter of the wounds." Palmer glanced up to meet Dizzy's steady gaze. "By the time the body got to the morgue, the wounds in her neck had completely disappeared."

"That is impossible."

We all looked around. The words had come from Professor Cotswold.

"No wound can heal that quickly," Cotswold said in a tone of stark disbelief. "And if the girl was dead, they would not heal at all."

Alas, the cheeky American was dead on right.

"If I'd not seen it with me own eyes, I would find it difficult to believe myself, Professor," Palmer replied. "A total of three residents of Moore House witnessed the oddly disappearing wounds, along with the surgeon summoned to the house, and six policemen. I was one of the aforementioned policemen, Professor. I can attest personally to the fact that the punctures in the girl's neck disappeared in a little over an hour."

"The vampire is capable of many subtle and sinister tricks," Dr. Van Helsing intoned in a grim voice thick with his Hungarian accent.

Cotswold looked hard at Van Helsing for a moment, then shook his head and turned toward his friend, Darwin. "It is preposterous," he pronounced.

"Perhaps not." Darwin's retort seemed to catch Cotswold off balance. "It could be that some hitherto unrecorded enzymatic action was responsible for what I will be the first to agree is an altogether unprecedented phenomenon."

"I'm afraid I don't really understand what is being proposed here," Cotswold railed. "You think a series of murders is the result of a monster that sucks out people's blood without leaving a wound? I don't know these other people, but you, Charles—how could you fall for such a wagonload of claptrap?"

"An open mind is the first requisite of scientific inquiry," Darwin said to his young American counterpart. "Certainly this is difficult for us to accept, but people once found it impossible to believe that the earth was not the center of the universe, with the sun and stars revolving around its stationary position in the cosmos."

"It is fortunate for you, Professor Cotswold, that you have had little experience with the *nosferatu* in America," Dr. Van Helsing said. "The creature is indigenous to Transylvania, or, according to one theory—to which I do not happen to subscribe—the Russian steppes. It is the ultimate embodiment of evil and must be destroyed at all costs."

"You talk as if it is some kind of devil or hobgoblin."

"But that is precisely what it is, Professor Cotswold. A vampire is a living corpse. By day the *nosferatu* must lie in a coffin containing at least one handful of the soil of its native land. It cannot bear the sunlight. If touched by the sun's rays, the vampire bursts into flame and is destroyed. The vampire's only other weaknesses are garlic and the sight of the cross. The monster can abide neither. The *nosferatu* rises at sunset to drink the blood of the living. Every person it kills becomes a vampire, and in doing so loses its immortal soul to become a member of the undead. This is why we must be zealous about finding this monster and killing it by driving a wooden stake through its lifeless heart."

I expected Cotswold to scoff, but instead he stared at Dr. Van Helsing with his jaw fallen open. His level of incredulity was such that he could not even respond.

"There are elements of truth in most folk beliefs," Darwin said, talking mainly to the American. "For the moment, let us consider that Dr. Van Helsing is at least partly correct in his assertions. Something we don't understand happens to people, giving them the need and means to drink the blood of living human beings. The condition changes them in other significant ways. Given what we know, it appears their saliva contains an agent that promotes rapid healing. I suppose that means that if they do not drink too much blood, their host survives—and the vampire escapes detection because he hasn't left behind any evidence of his activity. It is therefore possible that the population of vampires is much greater than we suspect, that there is not a single vampire preying on London, but hundreds, or even thousands."

The room had become very still as Darwin spoke, his scientific perspective somehow even more chilling than what Dr. Van Helsing had said.

"And what if the vampire is not a supernatural creature, not the embodiment of ultimate evil, but a genetic adaptation, a mutant in the continued natural selection of our species?" Darwin went on. "If so, these beings could threaten the existence of the human race. A superior species preying upon us like cattle presents a frightening picture, gentlemen. *Homo vampirus* could be in the process of replacing *Homo sapiens,* the same way Cro-Magnon man overtook and wiped out the more poorly adapted Neanderthal."

The room lapsed into nervous silence as we considered the prospect of bands of vampires playing the hounds to us as foxes. None of us would sleep very soundly after hearing such a thing. It was the vampire hunter who spoke next, bringing us back to the matter at hand.

"Moore House was the site where the vampire first claimed a victim in England?"

"I would not go so far as to say tha', Dr. Van Helsing," the policeman said. "Annie is the first victim we know about. There might be others."

"There might indeed," Dr. Van Helsing agreed. "But I am most interested in Moore House. What does anyone know about the family?"

Dizzy's eyes settled on me, so I felt compelled to offer the first testimony to the vampire hunter. "I was off in India with Sir Brendan," I said. "We were once quite close, but that was many years ago."

"Sir Brendan Moore was one of the finest diplomats to have ever served Her Majesty," Dizzy said. "Unfortunately, he met with a tragic end. He was on station in Budapest when he was blown up by anarchists. His young wife was killed in the blast, along with a Hungarian cavalry officer. It was a cowardly crime and a great loss to the Foreign Service. Surely you read about it in the Budapest papers this past autumn."

"For the past year I have been engaged wiping out a band of *nosferatu* deep in the Carpathian Mountains, without recourse to newspapers or other civilized amenities," Van Helsing replied. "Still, the fact that Sir Brendan was stationed in Budapest is significant. Hungary is infested with vampires. And the other members of the Moore family? There were children with them in Budapest? A niece or nephew perhaps?"

"There are two children in the household," C.I. Palmer said, glancing down at his notebook. "A daughter, Lady Olivia Moore, age eighteen, Sir Brendan's child by his late first wife. And there is an infant boy named Andrew. They reside at Moore House."

"Were they with their father and mother in Budapest?"

"They were, Dr. Van Helsing," Dizzy said, giving him a curious look.

"Surely you don't think they are mixed up in this," I said, remembering how delicious Lady Moore looked that night at the opera.

"Of course not," Dr. Van Helsing said. "But there could be a tangential connection, since they are just returned from Budapest. Did they bring any Hungarian servants with them?"

"Lady Olivia and the boy, Andrew, returned in the company of Andrew's Hungarian nurse," Dizzy said. "I called on them when they returned to London to express my condolences. Lady Moore was bearing up well, like a proper English girl."

"A nurse?" Van Helsing said, perking up. "Then the child is ill?"

"In Britain, a 'nurse' is a governess for a young child."

"Just so, I must speak with the Magyar woman," Dr. Van Helsing said in a voice somewhat commanding for such an unprepossessing creature. He used the stub of a pencil to scribble in a cheap notebook.

"As you wish, Doctor," Dizzy said. "And after Annie Howard, Chief Inspector?"

"The second victim was one Fannie Turner."

I felt as if I'd just been hit in the stomach, but I must have done a good job of concealing it since nobody acknowledged my discomfiture.

"She was a cook's helper at Sir Richard Graham's house. Not long in his employ, but reported to be an obedient and capable girl of nineteen. Sir Richard's residence is adjacent to Moore House. Miss Turner was not attacked at Sir Richard's residence, however. A constable found her body early on the morning of November fifteenth in Hyde Park."

"She was ensanguined?"

"Begging your pardon, Mr. Darwin?"

"Had she, too, been drained of blood, Detective?"

"Yes, sir. But the pathologist at the morgue was unable to find any sign of injury whatsoever. Right mystified by that, he was. Perhaps Dr. Blackley has a remark or two to add on Fannie Turner's case. He examined her body in the park."

I cleared my throat and drew myself up in the attempt to conceal the fact that my bowels were about to let go with fear. The vampire had already brushed my life, and I had not even known it! It was enough to make me forget all about the beastly way the police treated the Indian boy they suspected of having been involved in the crime.

"I briefly examined the body before it was taken away from Hyde Park. I remember being particularly puzzled. The girl appeared to be extremely anemic. Her lips and fingertips were blue, there was a slight puckering, and the skin was fallen in against her face, as if she'd lost a great deal of blood. I could find no evidence of a wound, however. It never occurred to me the girl had been killed by a . . ." I listened to my voice trail off. "To be perfectly honest, gentlemen, until only recently I had never heard that there was such a creature as a . . ."

"Vampire," Dr. Van Helsing said, finishing the sentence for me when my voice again trailed off. "Fannie Turner was killed by a vampire."

"Yes, I suppose she may have been," I said, feeling the perfect ass. Out of the corner of my eye I saw Cotswold make an impatient gesture. To blazes with him, I thought. I knew what I had seen—at least I did *now.*

"It was a month before the killer struck again," Palmer said. "His third victim was Lady Margaret Burke, whose residence is on the other side of Grosvenor Square from Moore House and Sir Richard's residence."

"Good God, man!" Lucian exclaimed. His outburst was the only thing that prevented me from expressing my own bitter shock.

"Steady on now, Captain," Mr. Disraeli said. "She was an acquaintance of mine, too, but it is important we hear the facts. Out with the grim details, Chief Inspector," the Prime Minister ordered, glancing from Lucian to the policeman and back. "Spare us nothing."

I took a sideways step toward Lucian and put my hand on his shoulder. We had all felt the blow when Margaret died, but to learn she had been murdered by the vampire—we were both devastated. I wondered if Bertie knew the real cause of her death, which had been attributed to stroke. Probably not, I thought, or he would have reacted differently to the references to vampires the night we went to the Hellfire Club after the opera. My eyes and Dizzy's met, and I knew in that brief electric moment this was the P.M.'s ultimate concern in the matter. Lady Margaret Burke had been, at the time of her death, the Prince of Wales's mistress.

"Lady Burke was thirty-two, older than the first two victims," Palmer said. "She was found dead in her bed when a maid came to wake her the morning of December fifteenth. There was no sign she had been . . ." The policeman glanced at the priest's collar but pressed on. "There was no sign Lady Burke had been molested in any way. The other particulars were similar to the way it was with Annie Howard. The maid who found her thought Miss Burke had two punctures on the neck, but there was no sign of them by the time the doctor arrived. Her skin had the same white, bloodless appearance. When they opened her up at the morgue—"

"They found no blood," the Prime Minister interrupted with a wave of the hand, looking a bit bloodless himself as he indicated to Palmer that he need furnish no additional details concerning the postmortem.

"Correct, sir," Palmer said, and obligingly proceeded to the next victim. "The killer did not strike again until New Year's Day. This time he went on a spree, killing three women. Miriam Agar, seventeen, a servant in Lord Humphrey's household on Grosvenor Square, had been dispatched on an errand. Sir Robert Swan was taking his evening constitutional when he spotted her crumpled body in the mews. The killer had been unusually savage. She'd been drained of her blood like the others, but her throat had been torn to shreds."

"This time the wound failed to miraculously heal itself?" Cotswold asked, his tone arch.

"Yes, sir, it did not heal."

"There can be no healing once the damage to the flesh reaches a certain magnitude," Dr. Van Helsing advised us. "The abuse heaped on the unfortunate Miss Agar indicates the vampire has learned to enjoy killing. The vampire, you see, derives orgiastic pleasure from drinking the blood needed to keep his own lifeless corpse animated. He has abandoned himself to his perverse revels."

The old priest gasped, but Palmer paid him no mind and plunged on.

"A match girl, Eliza Cole, thirteen, was killed the same night near Charing Cross. A constable frightened off the monster before he could drain her as completely as the others, but the poor girl died on the way to hospital."

"Then he's striking out beyond Mayfair," Lucian said. "The vampire is enlarging his hunting territory."

"So it would seem," Palmer agreed. "The third victim that night was Mary O'Connor, age twenty, a seamstress and occasional prostitute. Begging your pardon, Reverend Clarkson, but in this case the woman was outraged by her killer."

The priest, face red and eyes bulging, seemed about to explode.

"How is it possible to draw such a conclusion, Detective?" Lord Shaftbury, who had been listening to the proceedings intently, asked. "Considering that it is her profession to have carnal relations with men, how can you tell she was raped?"

"She had been violated with an unmistakable savagery," Palmer replied. "She might have bled to death from the damage, had she had any blood left to lose. The pathologist believes some of the damage was done after she was already dead."

"The fiend," Lucian muttered.

The policeman snapped his notebook shut and slipped it back into his pocket. His testimony was finished.

"How much of this do people know?" Dizzy asked, turning to the Home Secretary.

"We have kept it out of the papers, but not without having to use a certain amount of influence. The editor of the *Pall Mall Gazette* will need something to help sell papers when the time comes. I had to threaten to shut down his newspaper if he published a story about Mary O'Connor."

"The common people are starting to talk," Lord Shaftbury said. "It is impossible to keep news about this sort of thing from spreading."

"We instruct the witnesses to keep quiet, but the temptation to tell a friend or neighbor what you know about something as sensational as a murder is too much for most to resist," Palmer said.

"If the loss of public order is considerable," Dizzy said, "there are those who would use the situation to advance their own political ends, to bring down the government, even to bring down the monarchy, if they could manage it. You have not been here long enough to know it, Professor Cotswold, but London is filled with communists, anarchists, levelers. We live in a social tinderbox waiting to catch fire. Why, consider the chaos in France earlier in this century."

"We have our eye on the usual troublemakers," Cross said with a scowl.

"There will be panic in the streets if this gets out of hand," Dizzy said. "Britain is the greatest empire on earth. I will not—" He rapped his cane on the floor for emphasis. "—allow it to happen on my watch."

"Hear hear," Lucian said low in his throat, moved by the Prime Minister's determination to stand fast.

"Which brings us back around to you gentlemen," Dizzy said. "I am empaneling a secret committee to investigate and bring this to a halt as quickly and quietly as is possible. Captain Lucian, I am sure that I can count on you."

"I am at your service, Mr. Prime Minister."

"Mr. Cross, your services are required elsewhere, and I gather your scientific skepticism, as you call it, has gotten the better of you."

"There is no such thing as a vampire," Cross said and made a sour face at Disraeli.

"Very well, then," Dizzy said, dismissing him. "Lord Shaftbury, I want you to serve as group chairman. You will be my personal eyes and ears on the committee."

"As you wish, Mr. Prime Minister," he said and bowed.

"Mr. Darwin?"

"I must plead age and infirmity, Mr. Disraeli. I am certain you understand."

"Only too well. The only thing worse than old age is the one thing that cures it. Would you be so good as to consult with the committee?"

"Night or day, whenever it needs me. Professor Cotswold is a far better man than I to look at the science side of this," Darwin said.

"Then can I count on your assistance, Professor Cotswold?

I realize you are not one of Her Majesty's subjects, but justice knows no borders."

"I am not sure you really want my participation," Cotswold answered. "I am completely with Mr. Cross. I do not believe in ghosts, bogeymen, or vampires."

"But you will help us?"

"Only to prove that vampires are bunkum."

"An end to the killings is all I require, Professor Cotswold. In this matter the truth is of secondary importance to me. I will be satisfied with whatever the committee determines is the cause of these grim crimes, be it a vampire or merely a human vermin.

"C.I. Palmer, you will continue to head up the official part of the investigation."

"Yes, sir."

"Dr. Van Helsing?"

"But I have already volunteered my services to you, Mr. Disraeli. I have devoted my life to exterminating these creatures. Wherever they go, I go. Granted the proper resources, I promise you I will find and destroy the creature terrorizing London."

"Reverend Clarkson, that brings us 'round to you."

The clergyman looked back at Disraeli with startled eyes.

"It is important to me personally, and to the Archbishop, to have the Church involved," Dizzy said. "If science can explain the vampire to us, then well enough, but the explanation needs to be tempered to take the Almighty into consideration. Messrs. Darwin and Cotswold might disagree, but it has always been my contention that the real purpose of science is to help us understand God and His creation, not pose false proofs that He does not exist."

Reverend Clarkson nodded agreement, and in the next moment realized he had been tricked into seeming to agree to become a member of a committee he didn't want to have anything more to do with than did I. It would be embarrassing indeed for him to extricate himself now, and Dizzy, the old fox, knew it.

"Dr. Blackley?"

The finger of fate was pointed at last in my direction.

"What benefit could I possibly add to so distinguished a panel, Mr. Prime Minister?" I dissembled. "I am a simple physician, not a distinguished expert like these other gentlemen."

"We'll have none of your false modesty, Doctor. The merits of having a physician close at hand are prima facie obvious. You also have the trust of people in the highest of places, Dr. Blackley," Dizzy said, by which we all knew he meant Buckingham Palace. "That makes you exactly the right person to help deal with a sensitive problem that has touched the highest level of British society."

"In that case, it would be an honor to serve on your committee, sir," I said, smiling as I lied.

"How do you plan to proceed?" Dizzy asked, turning to the Hungarian. "The tactical lead in this matter is yours at this point, Dr. Van Helsing."

"If we are to stop the epidemic from spreading, the graves of the victims must be opened and stakes driven through their hearts to ensure that they do not rise as vampires."

I found myself exchanging a look of shock with Clarkson in his dog's collar.

"The desecration of Christian women's graves is more than I can allow," Reverend Clarkson said.

"Is it not better to ensure that they do not rise up from their graves with the night to go forth as living corpses, claiming the lives of more innocents, condemning more souls to eternal damnation?"

The priest had no answer to that.

"Bear in mind that epidemics of vampirism spread exponentially, just as with smallpox," Dr. Van Helsing said. "One person infects two, the two infect four, the four infect sixteen, ad infinitum. The virulence literally explodes through the population if left unchecked."

"I'm in favor of doing as Van Helsing says," Cotswold said.

"You surprise me, Professor," the Prime Minister said. "I thought you had agreed to play the role of skeptic."

"I have, and I promise I will," the Yank said with a mirthless smile. "If we examine the corpses and find the tissue is intact and supple, if we discover no signs of decomposition, I'll admit there may be something to Van Helsing's outrageous claims. But if the bodies are fetid and rotting, then I will be able to say we have evidence that this vampire business is nothing more than hysteria."

"Reverend Clarkson, do we have your permission to proceed?" the Prime Minister said, turning the full force of his charm toward the clergyman, as if the decision were up to him instead of Disraeli.

"I hardly know what to make of this business," the priest stammered.

"Nor do I," Dizzy said. "Aristotle reminds us knowledge flows from experience and observation. But without faith to guide us, knowledge is a ship without a rudder. Do we have your leave to go forward with Dr. Van Helsing's direction? Will you agree to provide the rudder to Dr. Van Helsing's considerable knowledge in this dark matter?"

The priest swallowed dryly, then nodded.

"Tomorrow you will learn that my methods are correct as well as effective," Dr. Van Helsing said, walking to the window and looking out at the gathering darkness. "But for now night is falling. Soon the vampires will rise from their graves. Nightfall is the most dangerous time. The creatures are ravenous when they first wake. We must wait until the morrow, when the vampires will have returned to their coffins to sleep. That is when we begin our work."

7

$\diamondsuit$

Postmortem

I WAS DRESSING for dinner when Algae called on me a second time that day.

"There's been another murder," Algae said breathlessly before my servant Roberts had gotten halfway out of the room.

I shot Algae a furious look. One didn't involve one's servants in such matters. Roberts, for his part, did his usual job of pretending not to hear. Lord knows he'd turned a deaf ear on some frightfully private utterances during the time he'd been in my employ.

When Roberts had closed the door behind him, I asked Algae if the vampire had struck again.

Algae swallowed hard and nodded. "A young lady, sir. Her body was found just this afternoon in Mayfair. The body has been taken to St. Alban's. The Chief wants you to have a look at her posthaste."

I promised to attend to the matter directly and dismissed Algae.

Straightaway I dashed off a note to the lovely barrister's wife I had intended to take to the opera that night while her husband was away, arguing a case in Portsmouth. In my apology I promised to come to tea one day next week—she knew what *that* meant—and sealed it in an envelope with a kiss before asking John, my porter, to deliver it.

As a young doctor I had learned the wisdom of keeping victuals close at hand, for one never knew when it would be impossible to sit down to a decent meal. I told Roberts to have the carriage brought around and went into the kitchen to help myself to a sandwich of bread and salami. I uncorked a bottle of Madeira and threw back a quick glass as I chewed my supper, sticking an apple in my coat pocket to eat on the drive.

St. Alban's was north of Grosvenor Square on the far side of Tiburn Road. In 1880 it was London's newest and most fashionable hospital. My first thought was that the body had been taken there instead of the city morgue for proximity's sake. It later occurred to me that Dizzy, or perhaps Cross, had ordered it as a way of disguising the fact that the vampire had struck again.

My initial sense of dread had attenuated somewhat by the time I arrived at the hospital, giving way to the Madeira and a certain medical curiosity. I had been too naive during my first encounter with the victim of a vampire to pay sufficient attention to the strange nature of its handiwork. I wanted to observe the inexplicable rapidity with which the vampire's bites allegedly repaired themselves.

Cotswold was waiting in the hospital lobby. With him were Lucian, Palmer, and Dr. Van Helsing, whose experience and bravery as a vampire hunter we were all depending upon. Algae had already informed me that Lord Shaftbury was at a dinner at the Russian Embassy and unable to join us.

"The Reverend Clarkson left word he was going to evensong, but we were unable to find him. He must have stopped at a tavern for something to eat."

Which was lucky for him. I'd have wagered a crown that the parson would have been unable to have a late dinner afterward. Maybe not even breakfast the next day. Palmer would bear up well enough. Observing autopsies was a familiar part of his professional repertoire. Dr. Van Helsing was undoubtedly experienced in the arts of vivisection, but I suspected Lucian would have a hard time of it. As for Professor Cotswold, I was entirely prepared to see the cocksure Yank make an embarrassment of himself.

The morgue at St. Alban's was in the basement. Indeed, I have never been in a hospital where it wasn't. The examining room was walled in white tile and looked as if it had been washed down and made neat and tidy for our visit, the scales and instruments gleaming. Thomas, the attendant in charge, was an unusually diligent young man. He had worked previously at the city morgue—a mossy, fetid, crowded chamber of horrors. Perhaps that is why Thomas seemed especially intent on keeping the St. Alban's morgue a pristine contrast to the abhorrent municipal corpse locker.

Thomas rolled a single gurney in from the cold room.

My witnesses stood against the far wall, grouped shoulder-to-shoulder in a grim-faced queue, every bit of their attention focused on the draped figure on the cart. Palmer looked relaxed, perhaps even bored. The others might have been facing a firing squad.

Beneath the cotton sheet was the outline of a slight female figure. Thomas took the shoulders, I the heels, and we transferred the covered body onto the marble dissection table. I removed my coat and jacket and hung them in the wardrobe.

"How long has she been dead?"

"She was last seen alive yesterday evening. The body was not discovered until late today. She was thought to have gone out visiting. She was in her room in the attic all along."

Lucian shuffled his feet and looked up into a far corner. For an officer, the poor lad had little acquaintance with death, I thought, knowing his education was about to commence in earnest.

Thomas helped me into a surgical gown and gave me a pair of rubber gloves. I nodded that I was ready to begin, and he pulled the sheet off the body. I was peripherally aware of a tensing of posture among my colleagues. Lucian's hands came up to his mouth.

"If you are feeling light-headed, sit down and put your head between your knees," I said a bit curtly. Palmer was looking at Lucian with particular harshness, a comment on the young man's squeamishness, I thought.

On the table was a lovely young woman stretched out on her back, entirely naked, as helpless as only the dead can be. The vampire was obviously attracted to beauty, damn him, I thought. Her face was comely even in death, her full bluish lips parted slightly as if her last act had been a gentle sigh. To wipe out the pleasure those lips would have given and known was an act of wanton criminality that richly deserved to be repaid with a swift trip to the gallows, though Dr. Van Helsing had an even harsher punishment in mind. I recognized the slight puckering to the lips and fingertips I had seen before with the poor girl in Hyde Park, all indicative of blood loss.

Her cheekbones, her high, intelligent forehead, her perfect nose, her jawline—such divine artistry! Her breasts had achieved the perfect fullness of womanhood; children would make them larger, but never would they have been more firm or curve with such exquisite lines. If she was a domestic— at that point I knew neither her name nor her social position—she would have almost certainly become the mistress of some wealthy older man. Beauty seldom went to waste in London in those days.

I walked slowly around the body, giving it a cursory inspection.

"The subject is a female of perhaps sixteen or seventeen years, with no readily apparent outward sign of injury. The body is well-developed and outwardly healthy in appearance."

Thomas took down my words in shorthand. They would later be transcribed as my formal report.

"There is some outward evidence of ensanguination. This is noteworthy given the absence of any trauma to correspond with the apparent blood loss."

I probed the girl's neck on either side, looking for evidence of puncture wounds.

"There is no evidence of injury to the subject's neck. There is no sign of any kind of animal bite."

Thomas gave me a questioning look, but I did not stop to explain. If he did not know about the vampire already, he would have to learn as we went. He had good reason to wonder what sort of game was afoot. My cursory exam of the girl's neck, and my comments about the absence of dental cannulation, were entirely outside the usual autopsy sequence.

"The body shows a degree of rigor expected approximately twenty-four hours after death. Please help me turn her, Thomas. The back and posterior of the arms and legs show light signs of lividity, but not at all what one would find under typical circumstances."

I pushed the chestnut tresses up off the girl's neck. If the vampire had bitten the girl, the wounds had healed themselves. We turned her back over and Thomas handed me a scalpel. I positioned the blade and then hesitated, but not for myself or the job I was about to do. It was at that moment I realized that the American had come forward to have a closer look at the girl's neck.

"Have you ever witnessed an autopsy, Professor Cotswold?" I asked, balancing the scalpel in my hand.

"I've dissected cadavers in anatomy class."

It was scarcely the same thing, I thought, but did not say so aloud. If anatomy classes in the Colonies were taught the same way they were in Britain—and I suspected they were—over the course of weeks you took apart the body of some poor old pauper whose skin had turned leathery soaking in a huge vat of formaldehyde. Working a little at a time, with a partner or two, going slowly and being able to joke quietly about it, was an altogether different experience from cutting into the flesh of someone who had, until a few hours earlier, been a living, breathing human being.

Giving Cotswold no further thought, I paid a final silent compliment to the poor girl's beauty before I destroyed it with three deep incisions. The time had come for her body to surrender its secrets. Upon the autopsy table, the dead are sacrificed to serve the living.

I put the scalpel into the girl, the sharp blade penetrating layers of epidermis and muscle as I exerted a moderate downward pressure. I have never been a tentative cutter, though in an autopsy there is certainly little reason to be tentative. My incision was shaped like a Y, extending in classic fashion from either shoulder to the pit of the stomach, and down to the pelvis.

I folded back the flaps of skin and muscle.

Thomas handed Lucian a bucket in time to catch the remains of his lunch. The acrid stench of vomitus filled the air. The smell would get much worse before we finished.

A body on a marble slab loses its humanity the moment you cut into it during an autopsy. For me, from that point on, the flesh beneath my hands becomes a complex but inert object, a specimen to be dissected, weighed, tested, studied; it is no longer a person to be considered tenderly or pitied. I had Thomas saw through the ribs and lifted out the breastplate, revealing the organs for inspection.

"There is no evidence of internal bleeding," I said. "Indeed, there is a marked absence of blood."

"Aye," a mystified Thomas said. He finished wiping his hands and resumed his notations.

I glanced backward at the sound of a stool being dragged across the tile. Dr. Van Helsing, looking very pale, was sitting down. Lucian was on the floor, the bucket between his knees. Cotswold was pale but remained standing a few feet away from me, his curiosity stronger than his revulsion. I caught the policeman's eye and noted a hint of a smile in his eyes.

When it came time to examine the girl's sexual organs, Lucian excused himself to smoke a cigarette. Dr. Van Helsing lasted until Thomas began to saw through the cranium so I could examine the brain. That left Thomas, Palmer, and Cotswold, for whom I was beginning to have a certain grudging respect.

We learned two important things from the autopsy. The first was the cause of death. She had died from hypovolemic shock. That explained the absence of lividity markers, the liver-colored spots that appear where gravity pools the blood postmortem. There was little blood in her body to pool. All of this would have been a mystery, with neither external wounds nor internal injuries to account for the bleeding, if we hadn't known that a vampire was probably responsible for the death.

The second thing we learned during the postmortem was that the girl had had sexual congress shortly before dying. Judging from the degree of tearing, I surmised it was the first time she had been with a man. It did not appear to have been forcible rape, but it was impossible to know conclusively.

Dr. Van Helsing and Lucian, who for some minutes had been watching from the doorway without trying to actually see anything, came back into the room as I flipped the sheet over the girl's body and pulled off the rubber gloves. Thomas stood patiently by, pen poised over his copybook.

"This will be a new one for you, Thomas," I said with a grim smile. "List cause of death as—"

"Undetermined," Palmer interrupted.

"I was unaware that you are a physician as well as a policeman, Chief Inspector," I said, offended by his effrontery. For a policeman to overrule my conclusions in an autopsy—why, it was damned impertinent!

"I am acting on Prime Minister Disraeli's express instructions," Palmer said.

The look Thomas gave me! I owed him an explanation and a stiff drink, but it would have to wait until another time.

"You have trumped my hand, Chief Inspector," I said. "List the cause of death as undetermined, Thomas. I can always amend the report later, if need be."

"Do we know the girl's name, C.I. Palmer?" Thomas asked.

"Maude Johnston—that's Johnston spelled with a T. She was a member of Lucian's household. A maid."

"Good God, Lucian," I cried, "why did you put yourself through this?"

"She was my servant. I am responsible for her."

The wind had completely gone out of young Lucian's sails. Learning that Lady Margaret Burke had been one of the vampire's victims had been bad enough, but now the monster had claimed one of his own servants as prey.

"Do you know whether she had a beau, Captain Lucian?" Palmer asked, regarding him with unpleasant closeness. Indeed, I realized we were all staring at Lucian. We were all thinking the same thing: Had he been Maude's lover? I would have had her in bed in a pistol shot if she'd been in my household. Lucian's views, however, had been touched by the wretched rectitude that characterized the later decades of Queen Victoria's reign. For some strange reason, he thought seducing his servants was somehow beneath him, the poor deluded man.

"Not that I know of, although I suppose it's likely, considering how attractive she is—or was." Lucian began to look green again, but he drew in a deep breath and pulled himself together. "I confess that I pay little attention to my servants' private lives. It does not concern me."

"Miss Johnston had intercourse shortly before her death," Palmer said, his tone unforgivably blunt. "When a girl loses her virginity and then turns up dead shortly thereafter, the man she has been with usually knows something about the matter."

"I honestly have no idea who the girl was with. The vampire, I presume."

"Vampire?" Thomas said, looking at me with a combination of amazement and disbelief.

"The girl was killed by a vampire," Dr. Van Helsing said.

"I would appreciate it if you refrain from public speculation," Palmer said in a warning voice.

"It is not speculation, Chief Inspector," the rumpled little Hungarian said. "She was killed by a vampire."

"Not officially," Palmer said, squaring his shoulders as if for a fight.

"What is this all about, Dr. Blackley?" Thomas asked, momentarily forgetting his place.

"I am afraid none of us are at liberty to discuss the matter further," Palmer said.

"I will discuss what I want, when I want, with whom I want," Professor Cotswold said, standing up to the policeman. I would not have wanted to tangle with Palmer, but in a fair fight I would have been inclined to give the gangling American odds.

"Van Helsing claims a vampire killed this girl and several others," Cotswold said. "It's complete hogwash. There is no such thing as a vampire. There's a rational explanation. Given time, we'll find it."

"A vampire, Dr. Blackley?" Thomas whispered to me, though in the tiled room everybody heard. "Is that even remotely possible?"

"Good God, man, you've just seen the evidence with your own eyes!" Lucian cried. "We all have."

"There is one last duty to perform before we leave," Dr. Van Helsing said, getting down on one knee to rummage in a carpetbag that had seen better days. He stood up with a wooden stake in one hand and a maul in the other. "We must ensure she does not rise from the dead."

"You can't be serious," I said. "We put things back in the general vicinity of where they belong and stitched her back together, but her chest and abdomen are a bag of loose guts and organs. This woman has for all practical purposes been internally dismembered."

"Even so, we must not take the chance. I have seen entire provinces laid waste by the vampire."

"The Prime Minister has given Dr. Van Helsing total authority in these matters," Palmer said in a barking voice.

Dr. Van Helsing drew back the sheet. The girl's bare breasts were crossed with ugly stitches running like a railroad track toward each shoulder. He positioned the spike above where her heart would have been and began to raise the maul. The wooden stake shook a little in his left hand as he held it against the breast. I could smell brandy on his breath. Under the circumstances, I could hardly blame him. I could have used a stiff drink myself.

When the double-hinged door began to swing, I did not have to look to know Lucian was fleeing this final outrage against his poor servant. I kept my eyes on Maude Johnston's face, watching for evidence of supernatural life the instant Dr. Van Helsing hammered the crude wooden spike into this newborn child of the *nosferatu*.

8

✧

The Exhumations

WE ASSEMBLED THE next day in a private dining room at Bartley's Hotel. Lord Shaftbury stood us all to bracing glasses of whiskey, except Cotswold, who expressed the absurd opinion that it was unhealthy to drink alcohol at so early an hour. Americans, I have learned, are filled with all kinds of foolish notions.

With the help of C.I. Palmer, Dr. Van Helsing had outlined our campaign. He had drawn up a list of cemeteries where the bodies of the vampires were interred. Palmer had already sent notice to the sextons, instructing them to keep everybody out of the way as we conducted our secret inquiries. A squad of four young bobbies with thick arms and strong backs stood by to do the actual labor.

Cotswold was in ill humor that morning—all the more reason he should have knocked back a stiff drink to buck himself up for the work ahead. He sat staring morosely into his coffee cup, saying nothing until Dr. Van Helsing began to brief us on the operation.

"We must inspect the bodies for evidence of vampiric activity," Dr. Van Helsing said, "and take the steps that are necessary to ensure that the undead do not rise from the grave, going forth into the night to claim more victims."

"And if we find no evidence of so-called vampiric activity in the corpses," Professor Cotswold said, "then can we stop chasing chimera and get down to the serious work of learning what it was that really killed these women?"

"We have already gotten down to serious work," Lord Shaftbury said brusquely over the top of his glass. "The facts speak for themselves, Professor Cotswold."

Cotswold caught my attention and gave me a look. For some reason, he seemed to regard me as the only other sane person in our party. No doubt this was because I was a physician. People think doctors are wiser and saner than other people, which is utter bilge. We're no smarter than other people and often we're a good deal crazier. I have yet to meet a banker or shopkeeper who thinks he is God, a delusion that is all too common among us physicians.

We left Bartley's in separate carriages to avoid attracting attention. We began with Mary O'Connor, the seamstress and part-time whore killed during the vampire's New Year's spree. She was buried in the Catholic cemetery on Whitechapel Road, where mainly Irish from the East End are laid to rest. The cemetery was small and poorly kept. Many of the headstones had been imperfectly set and leaned in one direction or the other, Celtic crosses stuck in the ground at odd angles as if they'd been as drunk as their owners when they were put in the ground. Life can be small and harsh, but to end up in such a shabby spot seemed especially unfortunate to me. There should be some dignity in death, if nowhere else.

The four policemen set to work at the dirt with pickaxes. It did not seem possible they could work the frozen earth, but it was still unsettled enough from the burial a week earlier to turn. The dirt came out of the ground in frozen clumps the men heaped up like a pile of coal. The rest of us stood around the hole, stamping our feet and slapping our shoulders to keep warm. I had a silver flask filled with cognac in my pocket, but I wanted to save it until I really needed it.

Mary O'Connor wasn't buried deep. The men were only down four feet when they started scraping the coffin. I made a mental note to report the sexton to the civil authorities. It was difficult enough keeping disease in check in over-crowded London without burying the poor in shallow graves. It hadn't been so many years since an outbreak of ty-phus was traced to a similar cemetery that had been so monstrously overused that decaying limbs would jut up out of the soil after a heavy rain, pools of the most foul kind of corruption collecting in the low spots.

The coffin was a cheap pine box in the usual shape, broad in the shoulder, pinched at the head and feet. The policemen worked the foot end loose and hoisted the coffin out of the ground with a grunt, dropping it unceremoniously on the frozen turf.

"You can see the coffin remains sealed, Dr. Van Helsing," Cotswold said with evident satisfaction. "Unless vampires are magicians, Miss O'Connor remains within her coffin, as one would expect of a dead person."

"There is an incubation period, Professor. Once that period has eclipsed, she will rise from the grave and go in search of the people to satisfy her unnatural cravings for the blood of a living human being."

"Open her up, boys," Palmer ordered.

The policemen glanced nervously at one another but set about it, probably more terrified of the Chief Inspector than they were of any vampire. One of the men took a pry bar out of a burlap sack of tools they'd brought. He inserted the bar between the walls and roof of the coffin, tapping it in with the heel of his gloved hand. This was accomplished easily, for the coffin was very poorly joined. I jumped a little as a shriek split the air, thinking it the vampire crying out in horror of the sunlight, dim as it was on that overcast day. However, it was only the sound of nails protesting being dragged from their seats.

The body had suffered little deterioration during the short time it had been in the ground. I knew the temperature made it likely that the more recent victims we examined would be relatively well-preserved. This would frustrate Cotswold, who wanted nothing more than to see rotting corpses, yet I said a silent prayer of thanks for it. Anyone who has ever had to examine a decomposing body knows it is one of the more singularly unpleasant tasks imaginable.

Mary O'Connor's face was lifeless gray and a bit puffy, as if the wake had been in an overheated room. While she was not an especially attractive woman, one could imagine how, with the artful application of rouge, she would have been rather fetching, especially in an alley dimly lit with flickering gaslights. Her glory was her hair. Mary O'Connor had a thick head of hair of the sort that would have driven a man mad with desire to see falling down about her naked shoulders. She wore a green velvet dress, no doubt her finest, the "working" dress she wore out whoring. I tried to remember if I had ever seen her in my visits to the sporting houses, but I could summon no recollection of her. She wouldn't have been in any of the nicer houses, of course, but I did not always go to the nicer houses. I have always had a taste for the common trade, but that is a subject left for another time.

Whore or not, Mary had gone to her grave as a Catholic. Her hands were folded over her abdomen, in them a crucifix and chain. I wondered how a vampire would deal with *that* upon awakening. I imagined the monster wouldn't be able to get out of the ground fast enough.

Dr. Van Helsing came forward with a wooden stake and his mallet, the chief weapons of his arsenal in the battle against the undead.

"If what you say about vampires is true, how can she stand lying there in what passes for sunlight on a January day, a crucifix in her dead hands?" Professor Cotswold asked.

"As I said before, the transformation is not always instantaneous," Dr. Van Helsing replied crossly. "The cold weather slows the process. Even as snakes and reptiles become sluggish when the chill winds blow."

"A reptile? I thought she was a vampire," Cotswold said.

"Please!" Reverend Clarkson said, squeezing the bridge of his nose between thumb and forefinger. "This is trying enough without your insufferable sniping."

Cotswold kept his mouth shut for once and stared at the ground, chastened.

"Let's get this finished," Lord Shaftbury said. "We have five more to go and do not need to see how long a job we can make of it. We will all catch our own deaths in this cold."

The old priest turned away as the vampire hunter positioned the stake over Mary O'Connor's breast. I moved a step closer to watch the face for some sign of reaction that would prove a spark of supernatural life existed in the corpse. Cotswold moved silently forward with me, intent upon the same purpose.

Dr. Van Helsing brought down the maul with a swift, powerful stroke that took me by surprise. The breast seemed to repeal the stake, but then I realized the woman was frozen solid as a clod. He brought the maul down a second time and made a start of it. It was hard going, like trying to force a knife into frozen beefsteak. When the stake was halfway into Mary O'Connor's breast, the vampire hunter had to stop to remove his overcoat and wipe the sweat off of his brow. He glanced around at us, but no one offered to help with the job.

"That will do it," Dr. Van Helsing puffed when the job was finally finished, throwing the hammer aside and leaning forward, hands on his knees to recover. "She'll do no harm now." He gulped several deep breaths. "We've saved her soul, Reverend Clarkson."

The expression on the priest's face had nothing to do with relief.

"All right, men, let's wrap this up," Palmer said, in a hurry to move on.

One man shut the coffin lid. He had to force it down against the stake, which stuck up too high, finally succeeding in closing the box by forcing the corpse onto its side. He held the coffin closed while another copper pounded the nails back in. They wrestled the box back into the ground, dropping it with an unceremonious thud, and took up their shovels.

"One moment, please," Reverend Clarkson said. He had a

red Book of Common Prayer in his hands, a gloved finger marking a place in the pages. "We cannot put this poor girl back into the ground without prayer."

"She has had the funeral rites read once, Reverend," Lord Shaftbury said, stamping his frozen feet.

"And she has been exhumed, and violated, and now she is about to be buried a second time."

"She was a *Catholic*," Shaftbury said, as if that would make a difference to the Church of England priest. I have never objected to Catholics myself, but Shaftbury was a bit of a snob.

"We are all children of God," Reverend Clarkson said, opening the prayer book, "even this poor woman."

"Then perhaps it would be wise for some of us to go ahead and begin the next exhumation while you finish up here, Reverend."

"You and you," Palmer said, pointing to two of the policemen. "You two stay and handle the spade work. When you're finished, bring Reverend Clarkson along to our next stop."

I turned away as Reverend Clarkson began to read the funeral rite, anxious to get under a rug in my carriage and warm up a little.

"I am the Resurrection and I am the Life, says the Lord. Whoever has faith in me shall have life, even though he die . . ."

Clarkson barely caught up with us by the time we left Eliza Cole. The girl—child, in fact—had not yet been buried. We found her stacked in a shed with two score of other dead, awaiting a thaw so they could be buried communally in a pauper's grave.

This time even I could not bear to watch as Dr. Van Helsing went about his grim work. I presumed little Eliza would not snarl and claw at the rumpled Hungarian as he pounded the stake into her frozen heart. I had seen evidence of the vampire's subtle violence on the autopsy table, but I had yet to witness anything to support the proposition that a person killed by a vampire could rise from the grave and sally forth like a succubus to suckle on the blood of the living. Perhaps Professor Cotswold's skepticism was not as ill-placed as the rest of us seemed to think.

Reverend Clarkson said a hasty blessing over the girl and the other departed souls awaiting interment, and accompanied us to Miriam Agar's grave.

As a brief aside, the next day I sent my porter to the cemetery with the money to see Eliza Cole's body decently and quickly put into the ground. I plead guilty to an unfortunate streak of sentimentality: I could not bear to think of the match girl stacked up like cordwood, only to be dumped into a common pit wearing nothing but a winding sheet.

Miriam Agar was buried in a smallish Presbyterian cemetery. The autopsy on Miss Agar had been performed by a man named Glyndwr, an alcoholic Welshman. I know this because I later made my own inquiry to learn the pathologist's identity, and used my influence to have the butcher dismissed from his position. Glyndwr's handiwork was crude indeed. He had made no effort to clean up after himself. The interior of the wound, opened even farther than its original extent during the autopsy, was a gaping black cavern in the neck. She had been laid to rest in a hospital sheet, Glyndwr's incisions hastily sewn with coarse black thread in irregular stitches.

On the ride to Highgate Cemetery, I availed myself quite liberally of the comforts of my flask, finishing off most of the pint. Lady Margaret Burke had been a good friend, and I was not keen to violate her grave or watch Dr. Van Helsing drive a shaft of splintering wood into the heart that once resonated with the Prince of Wales's affection. I did not allow myself to wonder what Bertie would think if he knew of our visitation to his lover's grave. A prince, one day a king, is not someone one wishes to have as an enemy.

Margaret had been put to her final rest in the Burke family mausoleum. The sexton unlocked the doors. A marble plaque inscribed with the dates of her birth and death barred the way to the wall crypt in which her coffin was entombed.

The sexton instructed the policemen on how to remove the bolts holding the slab in place without damaging it.

"Mind you don't drop it," he warned. "It is monstrous heavy and will shatter if it falls."

Palmer pushed the man to the door so we could begin.

Two of the policemen braced the stone in place while the others removed the bolts. It nearly fell when it came free, but with Lucian's and my help we managed to get it on the floor in one piece. I thought of how Margaret's eyes used to dance with wicked delight and had to turn away. I could not force myself to stay and witness the deed.

Annie Howard's final resting place was but a short walk away. Lady Olivia Moore had paid to have her servant buried in good style in a section of Highgate, where she would be surrounded for all eternity by her betters. Half drunk and more than half frozen, I numbly followed the others, leaning against a marble statue of a grievous angel as the others gathered silently around the grave. The strain of knowing what they'd done to Margaret, the exhaustion of being out in the cold all day, the cognac—all of these things slowed my mind to the point that it was nearly a minute before I realized that the earth heaped up around the grave was not the handiwork of the four stout policemen. Someone or something else was responsible for opening Annie Howard's grave. I walked stiffly forward and peered into the gaping hole in the frozen earth. The coffin was open. It was also empty. Annie Howard's body was inexplicably gone.

"We are too late," Dr. Van Helsing said. "She has made the change. Annie Howard has become a vampire."

I looked at Cotswold, who seemed to be very surprised and very angry, all at the same time.

"What now?" Lord Shaftbury asked. "Should we wait for her to return and destroy her then?"

"There is no reason for us to remain here," the vampire hunter said. "She has abandoned this grave for another, taking a handful of dirt to put in whatever coffin she crawled into when the sun came up today. She has made a nest for herself somewhere in London. Perhaps she is with the vampire who transformed her into one of the undead. If she is alone, she will not remain so for long. Vampires beget vampires. That is why we must redouble our efforts and wipe them out before they gain more of a foothold in London."

"But how can we find her?" Lucian asked.

"That will be easy," Van Helsing said, looking at the young man as if he pitied his naiveté. "We need only wait for the killing to continue."

9

✧

Moore House

THE SITTING ROOM at Moore House was a place where two worlds collided. Atop a British background of heavy furniture, wainscoting, and draperies was a layer of Indian culture, tropical and exotic. The room was as filled with ferns as a jungle clearing, their drooping green arms partly concealing ancient statues of Krishna and the Buddha. Above the fireplace were displayed crossed elephant tusks, the ivory intricately carved with scenes from the Veda. An ornately carved teak chest with brass hinges served as a table in front of the sofa. The glass doors of a curio cabinet enclosed enough miniature bronze gods and goddesses to populate a Hindu heaven, all manner of lotus blossoms, knives, and skulls waving in their supernumerary arms.

These were the relics of Sir Brendan's years in India. His first wife, Delia, had gotten him started collecting native statues. She died of fever, leaving her young husband with an infant daughter to care for, a baby who had grown into the lovely Lady Olivia Moore. In the parlor corner was a magnificent new grand piano. In my mind I saw Lady Moore at the opera, seated next to Franz Liszt. The grand piano was most likely hers. I wondered if Liszt had been to Moore House to play it—to play her. The possibility filled me with irrational jealousy.

Our committee had repaired to Moore House to continue

its infernal inquiries. There were concerns the vampire Annie Howard, so notoriously missing from her Highgate grave, might return to the house, seeking shelter or, in the service of some less benign motive, putting Lady Olivia and the household in jeopardy. Dr. Van Helsing also wanted to question the Magyar who served the family as nurse to Sir Brendan's son, Andrew.

Though Cotswold remained immovably stubborn on the subject, I felt foolish for having doubted Dr. Van Helsing. His dark predictions had been proven true. At least two vampires—Annie and her "parent"—and maybe more, were roaming London, turning the city into a monstrous hunting ground for creatures possessed with an unholy thirst for blood.

After a hot supper—and many cups of black coffee for me—we went to call on Lady Olivia, there being no time to waste. The butler admitted us to the sitting room. The committee was present that evening in full force: Lord Shaftbury, our leader; Captain Lucian; the Reverend Clarkson; C.I. Palmer; Professor Cotswold; Dr. Van Helsing; and myself.

Sir Brendan and I had known one another when I was a young physician and he was still Brendan without the *sir*. He had been a subaltern in the Foreign Service in those days, starting his career in Bombay. As for me, I had gone to India for my health. The husband of a woman I'd seduced wished to kill me with a dueling pistol. Since the cuckold was a crack shot, I decided my continued well-being was contingent upon a prolonged tour of the Subcontinent. I repaired to India to hunt tigers and visit its exotic brothels, meeting Brendan and the sadly virtuous Delia on my travels. By the time I returned to London, the offended party had moved his bride and his dueling weapons to Canada, never again to return, thank God.

When Lady Olivia came into the room to greet the committee that night, it was as if the sun itself had been awakened to dispel the cold winter night. She floated into the center of the room as elegantly as any princess, and yet her eyes were modestly lowered, as if aware of the effect her body had—as perfectly proportioned as an idealized Greek statue—on the men attending her. She had the kind of radiance that would lead artists to forego commissions for the honor of painting her face. She had an aristocratic forehead, large eyes, delicious cherry lips, and translucent skin. Her long auburn tresses were swept up on her head. By gad, she was a stunner! Though she was still mourning her father and stepmother, black only made her appear even more elegant.

The butler, Ballantine, was dispatched for the sherry decanter and glasses.

"My condolences on the deaths of your father and his wife, Lady Moore," I said.

"May we all say how shocked and sorry we were," Lord Shaftbury said. "It was a terrible crime and a distressing loss."

"They are in a better place now," she said with a sad smile. "Do you have news of the people responsible?"

"I am afraid we are here on other business," Shaftbury said.

Olivia nodded, a little disappointed, then turned her attention on me.

"You were a friend of my father's, Dr. Blackley."

"I am honored he thought enough of me to tell you about our friendship. We were out in India together many years ago." I nearly told her about holding her when she was just a baby, but thought better of emphasizing to her the difference in our ages.

"Father told me about the tiger you shot."

"Oh, that," I said, remembering the beastly episode. "I assure you it was hardly as grand as it sounds."

"You were very brave, he said."

"To be perfectly honest, I was terrified." Which was the perfect truth. I *had* been terrified. "A tiger isn't afraid of a man with a powerful rifle, even if he's perched atop an elephant. A Bengal will go straight up the elephant to get at the man, if he puts his mind to it."

"My father and Dr. Blackley volunteered to track down a man-eater that had been terrorizing the village near an estate where they had gone bird shooting," Lady Moore said, telling my story to the others, which was just as well, for I would never have told it. "The tiger had killed—how many natives was it, Dr. Blackley?"

"Six," I said, remembering how my fear had grown each of the six times the beast crept into the village to drag away another screaming victim. Brendan and I were safe enough in our bedrooms at the local Maharaja's place, though I slept with a revolver under my pillow. It was a miracle I managed not to shoot myself while asleep—or one of the servants. Every time I heard some unidentified night sound, I was convinced it was the tiger, coming for me. I pointed the revolver at my houseboy so many times that he was terrified to come into my room and help me dress.

"The villagers were in a state of complete terror," Lady Moore said. "No one was brave enough to kill the beast."

"Oh, they were brave enough," I said, "they just didn't have the firepower. As for volunteering to do the deed, your father and I didn't have a choice but to kill the blighter. Everybody looked up to great white bwana to save them. Besides, it was either that or lie in bed every night, wondering if it would be our turn next to die."

"Dr. Blackley shot the tiger between the eyes as the creature leapt at them."

Pleasant as it was to have the others looking at me with admiration—which was due as much to Lady Olivia's clear admiration for me as the trumped-up story about my exploits—it was anything but enjoyable to remember the episode. When the tiger jumped out of the bamboo thicket, the muscles in my right hand reflexively contracted, firing the fatal shot. Hitting the beast was the dumbest kind of luck.

"It was a lucky shot," I said with complete and utterly uncharacteristic honesty.

Lady Olivia turned back toward Lord Shaftbury. "But if

you are not here about my father, you must be here on account of Annie Howard."

"You are as intelligent as you are lovely," Lord Shaftbury
replied.

"You believe her death is connected with the vampire
murders."

Cotswold looked at me and raised an eyebrow, though I
had no idea what was going through his head.

"And what do you know about *that,* Lady Olivia?" Palmer
asked.

"Only what I have overheard the servants whisper. The
vampire is almost the only thing the servants in Mayfair are
talking about these days. I doubt I could find a maid in this
part of London brave enough to attend to a simple errand after dark. Perhaps that is for the best, with a killer loose."

I found myself nodding.

"But a *vampire*—who except the uneducated could believe in such nonsense, gentlemen?" she said with a smile.

"Then you do not believe a vampire is responsible for Annie Howard's death?" Cotswold asked, triumphant to have
found another skeptic.

Olivia started to laugh, but quickly covered her lovely
mouth with a dainty hand. "I do apologize, Professor
Cotswold. This is no laughing matter. But do I think a vampire killed poor Annie and the others? Stuff and nonsense.
Surely you do not believe such creatures exist."

"No, ma'am, I don't. But you saw the puncture wounds in
Annie Howard's neck."

Lady Moore's grief came to the surface for a moment.
She looked down at the floor and took in an uneven breath,
as women sometimes do just before they begin to cry. Lucian took a step toward her as if in comfort. By the look of
him he was as taken by her as the rest of us. But Olivia did
not lose her composure. When she looked up at us again,
she had gathered together the formidable powers of her
breeding.

"I do not have an explanation for what happened to the

poor girl. Still, it seems to me believing a vampire was responsible for her death is hardly the most likely explanation. Certainly creatures of the imagination—dragons and unicorns and other such fancies—have no real influence on the world in which we live."

"The vampire is not a mythical creature, Your Ladyship," Dr. Van Helsing said. "I have seen evidence of his evil work in my homeland."

"I have no doubt of it," Lady Moore said with surprising equanimity. "Myth and superstition have undeniable power over the minds of believers. Highland shepherds believe in banshees and faeries, but that is hardly proof of their existence, even if the country folk do take to their beds from time to time, sick with belief the wee people bear them animus. But certainly there are limits. Can superstition kill? I doubt it. And does ignorant credulity in legendary monsters make them real? I hardly think so."

"Well said," Cotswold chimed in, like a back-bencher in Parliament.

"We have seen proof," Van Helsing said. "I neither can nor would go into the details with a young lady, but I have seen proof with my own eyes."

Lady Moore returned the vampire hunter's earnestness with an indulgent smile.

"Do not dismiss Dr. Van Helsing so quickly," Shaftbury said. "Today we visited the graves of the women we think were killed by the vampire. Annie Howard's body is not where it was buried."

"Her body has been stolen?"

"You miss Lord Shaftbury's point entirely," Dr. Van Helsing said. "Annie Howard has risen from the grave to join the undead."

"I do not believe it," Lady Moore said, to nobody's satisfaction but her own and Professor Cotswold's.

"We need to speak with your servant, Karol Janos," Palmer said.

"What does Janos have to do with any of this?"

"She recently came here from Budapest, did she not?" Lord Shaftbury said.

"Janos came with us when my brother and I returned to London to bury our parents. I was unaware it was a crime to be from Budapest."

"Certain regions of Hungary have been subject to vampire infestations since the twelfth century," Dr. Van Helsing said.

"Which has led you to conclude Andrew's governess may be a vampire?" She looked from Van Helsing to Cotswold and smiled. He was her one ally in the room. "But Dr. Van Helsing, you are from Hungary, are you not?"

Van Helsing looked a little uncomfortable as he nodded.

"Then perhaps you are a vampire."

Dr. Van Helsing made an elaborate show of pulling a gold crucifix from beneath his shirt and kissing it. "Better to be dead than to take unholy communion with the *nosferatu*," he said, scandalized.

"We need to speak with Karol Janos," C.I. Palmer said doggedly.

"I have no objection," Olivia said, "although she will be able to tell you nothing to satisfy your appetite for the fantastic. You would be well-advised to pay more attention to Professor Cotswold, who does not appear to believe in vampires any more than I."

The look Lucian gave the Yank! He was completely smitten by Lady Olivia. I was surprised Lucian didn't proclaim his own disbelief in vampires to put himself in the lady's good graces.

Lady Moore rang the bell and sent Ballantine to fetch Janos. Karol Janos was a severe-looking woman of about forty. She came from sturdy peasant stock and had a serious expression that verged on anger. Like her mistress, she was not a woman who could be easily intimidated.

"They are here about Annie," Lady Moore said. "They think she was killed by a vampire."

Janos nodded, seeming a little more furious.

"You are from Budapest, Miss Janos?" Dr. Van Helsing began, taking over the interrogation.

"I am from a village a day's travel from there."

"Then you know about the *nosferatu*."

"I know the *stories*. There is a difference between what is a story and what is real."

"Then you have never known of someone who had an encounter with a vampire?"

She spat the answer: *"Never."*

"And you never had an encounter with a vampire yourself?"

"You and Andrew should return with me to Budapest," she said to Lady Moore, ignoring Van Helsing. "The men in London are lunatics."

"For the record, Miss Janos, what do you know about the death of Annie Howard?" Palmer asked, his pencil and policeman's notebook ready.

"I told you before."

"Tell me again, if you please."

"I found her body in the kitchen. She was dead."

"Do you know what killed her?"

"No."

"Do you believe it was a vampire?"

"No."

"Do you think it is possible that it was a vampire?"

"No. Do not be so foolish. Perhaps she had a stroke. I do not know. I am not a doctor. She was young and healthy."

"In your experience, Miss Janos, do healthy young women drop dead for no reason?" Dr. Van Helsing asked.

"People die," she said and nodded.

"What would you tell me if I told you Annie Howard had been completely drained of blood?"

"I would not tell you anything."

"There must be an explanation," Lady Moore said, appealing to me.

"A vampire seems as likely an explanation as any."

"I have my doubts, ma'am," Cotswold said.

"Yes," Lady Moore said, favoring him with a brilliant smile.

"Do you have more questions?" Janos asked. "I must attend to my duties."

"Do you own a crucifix?" Dr. Van Helsing said, thrusting a cross in Janos's face.

She snatched it from his hand, examined it closely front and back, and returned it. "Mine is gold. If you paid for gold when you bought yours, you were cheated."

The interrogation was interrupted then when a pink-cheeked cherub with a halo of golden hair materialized in the door. He smiled the instant his eyes found Olivia. He ran toward her in the comical fashion of toddlers, flinging himself into her arms as she bent to pick him up. A harried middle-aged woman appeared at the doorway, looking for her fugitive charge.

"Begging your pardon, ma'am, but the tyke is too swift for me," she apologized in an Irish brogue.

"The tyke is too swift for us all," Olivia said. "If you have no further questions for Janos, it is time for her to put young Andrew here to bed."

Shaftbury and Palmer looked to Van Helsing, who after a brief hesitation nodded. Lady Olivia passed the squirming child to his nurse.

"I realize you put little stock in the premise that Annie was killed by a vampire," Lord Shaftbury said when the door had closed.

"That is true enough, Lord Shaftbury."

"Nevertheless, I am concerned for the well-being of your household. If Dr. Van Helsing is correct, there is a chance Annie Howard might return here."

"We are perfectly safe. We lock the doors and windows at night."

"Still, I would like to have C.I. Palmer assign a policeman to watch over Moore House at night until the danger has passed."

"That is extremely kind of you, Lord Shaftbury, but it is hardly necessary."

"Think of little Andrew," Lucian said. "Please be reasonable, Lady Olivia."

Olivia gave Lucian a surprised look, softening visibly. The effect her look had on Lucian—oh, he *was* smitten!

"Then for Andrew's sake, yes," she said with a sigh.

"I'll have him keep to the kitchen when he's not rattling doorknobs to make sure everything is secure, ma'am," Palmer said. "You won't even know he's here."

"I'm sure he will be no problem," Lady Moore said with a frown.

"I must ask that you say nothing about our inquiry," Shaftbury said. "The situation is explosive."

"What makes you think I would say anything? Do you think I want people to believe me mad?"

"And would you be so good as to ask Janos to keep the matter confidential?"

"If that is all, gentlemen, I must beg your indulgence. I am accustomed to retiring to bed early."

Olivia had scarcely reached for the bell pull when Ballantine opened the door to usher us out. He had been listening, I realized. Our visit would not remain a secret long among Mayfair's downstairs set. Disraeli's Special Committee was doing its own part to sow the seeds of the London Vampire Panic.

I went out, leaving Lucian behind. He had contrived a thing or two to say to the delicious Olivia, damn him. London could have stood to have fewer handsome, well-born bachelors, and more beautiful, available young women the likes of Olivia Moore.

PART III

First
Interregnum

10

More British Than
the British

The following correspondence, presented here in English translation, is from the business archive of Srinivasan & Sons Trading Co., Bombay, India.

November 18, 1880

My dear elder brother Pradheep,

I pray this letter finds you in healthy and happy circumstances. I am very well. Our business in London is also very well, as you will see from the accompanying receipts. The attached latest contracts will give you much delight, I think! If our good fortune continues, you may be obliged to give Prakash enough rupees to expand our docks.

I was very happy indeed to read in your letter that Ramesh is coming to work beside me. It will be helpful to have another person in our London office speaking Hindi. There are certain language difficulties with the English clerks, and these sometimes cause unfortunate misunderstandings.

Tell your son he will find London similar to Bombay in many ways. It is a bustling, crowded city, the streets lined with prosperous shops conducting many types of commercial enterprise. There are not nearly so many beggars here, and the slums do not approach the unimaginable, as they do in Dharvai. The climate is somewhat inhospitable, but Ramesh will get used to the weather. The sunny disposition of the Srinivasan family fortunes due, in part, to Ramesh's position at our London trading house, will make it easy to forget about the cold and rain!

I am certain Ramesh will prove to be a more able assistant than Wajidali Kalyanaraman, who just spent a night in jail as a result of his foolishness. I fear this young man stayed out too long in the midday heat playing Maidan cricket and suffered permanent damage to his good senses. I have come to greatly regret agreeing to serve as sponsor to our cousin Gopesh's imprudent youngest son.

You would not believe the change that has overcome Wajidali. He has gone from hating the British to loving them in the few short months he has been in London. To Wajidali if a thing is not British, it is not anything. He dresses British and affects to speak British. He reads only the London newspapers, caring nothing for Bombay and wishing only to think about things that concern the British. He has taken a flat outside the quarter where most Indians live, furnishing it with uncomfortable foreign furniture. He balks at eating anything but British food—bland, boiled dishes that are no doubt perfectly suited to natives of this damp, cold climate, but hardly make a healthy diet for a Bombay boy. Wajidali has even Anglicized his name. This is his latest conceit. He insists everybody call him "Wallace," though I steadfastly refuse. Perhaps this is not so surprising, since *Wajidali* means *obsessed*.

Wajidali's dream of becoming more British than the British is leading him to disaster. There are places a young Indian man is simply not welcome, but Wajidali refuses to acknowledge this simple fact. As a result he was arrested and spent the night in jail, bringing disgrace upon himself, our family, and our business.

It started with a terrible crime—of which I hasten to report Wajidali was completely blameless, unless it is a crime to be a fool. It seems an unfortunate young woman was murdered in Hyde Park. She was British, not Indian, a servant in the house of a respected gentleman residing in Mayfair, a neighborhood where many members of the aristocracy live, adjacent to the park.

It goes without saying Wajidali had no business being in *that* part of town. However, possessed by an inexplicable folly, Wajidali had decided to embark on a walking excursion of Mayfair. He proceeded into the park, where by most unhappy circumstances he happened upon the poor woman's body. That would have been bad enough, but Wajidali decided to stick his nose farther into the business. He covered the woman with his new coat, which he now can never wear again, and went to summon the police. It wasn't very long before the police got it into their heads that Wajidali was somehow involved in the crime. They asked what business he had in Hyde Park. Finding his explanation insufficient, they accused him of visiting the park in the hope of arranging an assignation with a white woman. They insinuated the unfortunate woman had rejected Wajidali's unwanted advances, and that he had attacked her in a fit of anger over her rejection.

One of the policemen put his hands on Wajidali in an unfriendly manner to search his person for a double-pronged weapon that could have caused the mortal wound in the woman's neck. Since Wajidali carried no weapon and was entirely innocent of any wrongdoing, the wisest course would have been for him to submit to a search. Instead, Wajidali attempted to pull himself free, which only provoked the policeman to strike him. Wajidali was called all manner of filthy names and given quite a beating. It might have turned out very badly for him indeed had not a doctor intervened on the foolish boy's account.

Today I paid a call on the doctor, to thank him on behalf of the family. His response was most curious, and in its way completely British. Dr. Blackley said he had no objection to the police thrashing a criminal, but that his service with the army in India had left him "bloody tired" of the high-handed way authorities treated people because of their skin color. In other words, had Wajidali been British, as Wajidali secretly wishes, the doctor would have stood by while the policemen kicked in his ribs!

After a year of living in London, these people remain inscrutable to me.

The police took Wajidali to jail to punish him for his impudence and remind him of his place. He remained there overnight, though there were no more beatings, thank heavens! The police had already lost interest in Wajidali. He overheard them talking about a strange demon who is killing women in Mayfair and drinking the blood! He didn't believe the story, but I am not so sure myself, for what sane person would do such a wicked thing? If it was not a demon, then it is certainly a man possessed by one. It makes me shiver to think of some icy-fingered British equivalent of Kali stalking the city, looking for blood to drink. This is all the more reason to be home in the evening, the door safely barred, instead of out carousing like Wajidali.

After collecting Gopesh's misguided boy from the police, I sat him down and gave him a stern rebuke. Instead of crying tears of shame, as any proper young man would have done, he went on at some length about "his rights as a British subject"! Truly, his foolishness is without measure. No wonder Gopesh wanted him out of Bombay. Consorting with the troublemakers who want to start an Indian national congress would have landed Wajidali into trouble sooner or later. I would be rid of the British as quickly as the next man, but they are as useful to us as we are to them. You cannot feed an empty belly with idealism.

I look forward to Ramesh's arrival. Perhaps when he has learned the ropes I can come home for a visit. (I would never trust Wajidali to look after affairs.) It would be pleasant to be in Bombay in August, when it is dry and not too hot, for the Ganesh Chaturthi festival. I miss sitting in the shade of the mango trees in the courtyard of our home on Malabar Hill, discussing such matters face-to-face, over tea.

Kindly present my regards to the family, and tell Ramesh to have a safe journey.

Your devoted younger brother,
Bhaskar Srinivasan

11

A Murder in Drury Lane

The following account, written for the *Pall Mall Gazette*, was suppressed at the order of the Home Secretary.

Murder in Drury Lane
Actress Attacked Before Horrified Theatre Audience
Is Madeline Salisbury the Latest Victim
of the "London Vampire"?
Police seek popular actor, the suspected vampire killer

A popular actress was murdered Saturday night during a performance of the comic opera *HMS Pinafore* at the Theatre Royal.

Authorities are seeking a well-known actor suspected to be the "London Vampire," the dreaded murderer who has preyed on young women in Mayfair and elsewhere since late last year. The suspect is said to drain his victims of their blood, which he is reputed to need to maintain supernatural powers.

Madeline Salisbury, who played the leading role in Gilbert & Sullivan's *Pinafore,* was killed on stage at the opening of Act II, in front of a sold-out performance.

According to several people who were present in the theatre to witness the crime, the murder occurred as the orchestra was playing the overture to Act II. As the curtain parted, Miss Salisbury and Edmund Castle, the actor who played the lead opposite her, were seen in an intimate embrace at center stage. A murmur passed through the theatre as those familiar with the production realized something was amiss. When members of the orchestra noticed that the action on stage was not following W. S. Gilbert's libretto, the overture's performance wavered noticeably.

Miss Salisbury and Mr. Castle seemed unaware that the curtain had parted, revealing them, witnesses said. They continued to embrace for nearly a minute, their arms tightly around one another. Mr. Castle's face was buried in the declivity between Miss Salisbury's neck and shoulder, and Miss Salisbury was described as standing "with her pretty head thrown back, her eyes closed and her lips parted, as if in rapture."

Then Mr. Castle seemed to become aware that he and Miss Salisbury had been exposed to the crowd in an indelicate moment. He released her and stepped back. Miss Salisbury collapsed to the stage in a heap.

This signaled something was seriously amiss. The overture sputtered to a ragged stop.

Mr. Castle, his mouth smeared with blood, took several steps backward.

"I will never forget the look on his face," a theatregoer said. "It was a look of pure horror, as if the audience he was regarding was responsible for the monstrous crime instead of he."

Several women began to scream. A few of the musicians scrambled up from the pit to assist Miss Salisbury. Mr. Castle turned and disappeared into the wings. He vanished in the ensuing bedlam and remains at large as this edition of the *Gazette* goes to press.

Sir Posthumous Blackley, the eminent Harley Street physician, was in the audience and observed the incident. He made his way to the stage, but Miss Salisbury was already dead from blood loss.

Interviewed briefly at his surgery, Sir Posthumous discounted the notion that Mr. Castle was a vampire. He attributed the attack to a "strange fit of mania" in the actor. He said vampires exist only in Eastern European fairy tales, and that there are "other explanations" that better describe what was responsible for the deaths of the women generally believed to be among the vampire's victims.

Edward Apple, stage manager at the Theatre Royal, disagreed.

"Miss Salisbury was definitely killed by a vampire," Mr. Apple said. "I saw the two holes in her neck and the blood on Castle's face as he ran past me. I saw it with my own eyes."

Mr. Apple said several men tried to detain Mr. Castle backstage.

"He threw them off like nothing. He had the strength of ten men," Mr. Apple said.

The murder and its bizarre circumstances have shaken the tight-knit London theatre community. The authorities have closed the Theatre Royal, popularly known as "Drury Lane." The theatre's management was uncertain when, if ever, *HMS Pinafore* would resume production. There is talk of closing other London theatres. The Home Office refused comment on that and all other aspects of the crimes that have left London on the verge of panic.

Isaac Lohmuller, the impresario who has worked closely with Mr. Castle, said he had no indication anything was amiss with the actor.

"I find any of this very difficult to understand or believe," Mr. Lohmuller said. "I had supper with Edmund two nights ago. Other than complaining he had been running a slight fever, he seemed right as rain to me."

Mr. Castle is best known for his portrayal of the evil king in *Richard III*.

"The irony is that Castle has achieved the greatest recognition for his Richard, Shakespeare's consummate murderous villain," said theatre critic Thomas Nelson.

Mr. Nelson decried the decision to close the Theatre Royal, and the talk of closing other theatres.

"Whenever there is a panic over disease or witchcraft or some other public hysteria, the authorities have historically looked to blame the usual scapegoats: actors, foreigners, Jews, whomever are the most convenient people to blame at the moment. People need to keep their heads. Miss Salisbury's death is a terrible thing, but a vampire, if there is such a thing, and it is responsible, is no reason for London to panic."

But Mr. Nelson's opinion did not seem to be shared by the groups of rough men who combed the streets and alleys around Drury Lane, armed with barrel staves, axe handles, and hammers as they searched for the vampire.

12

The Burning

Captain Charles Fagan, Queen's Guards, wrote to Captain Lucian after an encounter with a vampire on the heath. Fagan had been on an errand for Lucian, inspecting a horse Lucian was thinking of buying for the Prince of Wales's stables.

January 10, 1880

Lucian,

Hearing some mention of your work with the Special Committee, I knew you would want to know straightaway about the violent encounter I had tonight with the vampire.

I was returning from having a look at the Irish cob you sent me to examine. About that matter I need say nothing but that the dealer is either deranged or dishonest to believe the animal is worth anywhere near what he is asking.

It was dark and cold, but thinking of softer things than a bed at an inn, I determined to ride back to London. I was galloping Sultan across the heath when I came upon a crowd of ruffians gathered around a tumbledown cottage that looked as if a strong wind could have knocked it down.

What's the game, then? I asked, pulling up at the edge of the crowd.

It's the vampire, one of the rustics said, claiming to have him trapped inside the house.

Sultan reared up, pawing the air with his front legs, twisting his neck, snorting. I pulled hard on the reins and made him settle.

I asked who was in charge.

The men looked around at one another. As suspected, nobody was in charge of the unruly mob, which had whipped itself into a frenzy of fear bent on violence. I wished I had a saber or my pistols. As it was, I had only the advantage of being on horseback.

A vampire? I asked. What makes you think there is a vampire in this hovel?

We chased him here after he killed Long Liz, the man said.

By this time the crowd had quieted enough to listen to our dialogue.

After several more questions, I learned Long Liz was a prostitute who worked in a tavern at the edge of the heath, in a village about half a mile from the cottage. She had been found in a room a few minutes after the vampire came out. She was dead, drained of her blood, a pair of bite marks in her neck. The men pursued the vampire to the cottage, which had stood empty since the death of the old peat cutter who had been its last tenant.

By now I was slightly more convinced there might be something to the mob's claim, having heard the stories going around London about the vampire. I suggested they bring him out and bind him up for the authorities. The crowd grumbled. They were brave enough as long as they were part of a mob, but there was precious little individual courage among them.

Come on then, I shouted. Which of you lads is brave enough to go inside with me and bring him out? The men mostly looked down at their shuffling feet, but four stepped forward as volunteers. I climbed down from Sultan and gave the reins to my interlocutor.

I gathered my squad together and told them that, when the enemy is outnumbered, a frontal assault is the best attack. We'll burst in through the door and overpower him, I said, then bind him with rope or strips of cloth, whatever we can find, and hold him until the authorities arrive.

I kicked the door open and we dashed in. The vampire was standing in the middle of the cottage's single room, as if waiting for us. We threw ourselves on him, only to have him toss us back like a mighty stag using his antlers to fling yelping beagles into the air. He managed to grab one of the fellows and sink his teeth into the poor man's neck. I have never seen teeth like that on a man—long, curving, cruel, like the teeth of a tiger yet narrower in gauge, like a viper's.

With the vampire thus engaged, the others in my squad lost their courage and fled through the open door. I looked around for a weapon. A spade was the only thing handy, so I picked it up and swung it down hard on the vampire's shoulder and neck, snapping the wooden handle. The vampire seemed to hardly notice. He looked up at me with eyes that glowed red in the torchlight coming through the door. It was then that I realized I had done everything I could do but make a strategic retreat. I backed slowly out and pulled the door shut behind me.

The mob made it unnecessary to decide on an alternate campaign. Torches had already been thrown onto the thatch roof, which began to burn like tinder. Armloads of wood from a ruined shed were piled against the door, the only way out of the cottage, and set afire. Within a minute the small house was transformed into a conflagration.

I climbed back on Sultan, who was doing his best to terrify the man who was holding his reins. I had a choice to make if the vampire escaped the blaze, impossible though that seemed. I could ride hard for armed reinforcement, or pursue him on horseback. Before I could come to a conclusion, a weird animal howl rose above the roar and crackle of the fire. Next came two loud thumps as the vampire threw himself against the door. The wood cracked a bit, I think, but the burning boards and timbers made escape impossible.

The howl began again, a terrible banshee wail that made Sultan stamp and rear.

And then, to the complete astonishment of all, the vampire shot like a signal rocket up through the burning roof. He must have jumped thirty or forty feet in the air, like a circus performer shot out of a cannon. His clothing and hair were on fire, so that he trailed flame and smoke as he rose into the cold, black night. He seemed to hang there for a moment against the starless sky, his face and hands upstretched, as if to beg God for help or forgiveness. And then, slowly at first but then with fast-gathering speed, the monster plunged back toward the earth. He had risen up straight, as if standing, then he became horizontal as he fell, his arms outstretched almost in the shape of the cross at the moment he crashed into the burning thatch roof in an explosion of spark and flame.

The burning cottage collapsed on the vampire.

After that, there was no sound or movement but that of the fire. Not even the witnesses spoke or moved until after it was certain the vampire's immolation was complete.

I stopped at the Cock & Ball Tavern on my way back into London, to look over the few personal belongings the vampire left behind when he fled. There were papers that identified him as Edmund Castle, the actor who killed the actress in Drury Lane last week. I suspect that if the authorities inspect Madeline Salisbury's body closely, they will discover two puncture wounds in her neck, as were found in Long Liz. Though Liz's body was gone by the time I got to the Cock & Ball, the innkeeper confirmed the details I had heard from the mob about the neck wounds.

We can discuss this in more detail if you wish. As for me, it is nearly dawn and I must go exhausted to my bed.

At your service,
Captain Charles Fagan,
Queen's Guards

PART IV

The Paleontologist

13

The Jabberwock

From the field journal of James Cotswold, Ph.D., Harvard University, kept during his visit to London, 1879–80.

January 11, 1880. Blackley dragged me to a ball. It was a full-blown formal affair, as insufferable as a Harvard faculty meeting. The men were dressed up like monkeys in boiled shirts and tails, and the women in ridiculous plumage of gowns and jewels. They paired up like prairie chickens to prance about the floor in a courtship ritual while the orchestra played waltzes.

The soiree was at Lord Shaftbury's residence, which is more of a palace than a proper house. A king—one of the Henrys, I think, though not the bloody one who had his wives' heads chopped off—built the place for one of his mistresses. It's a sprawling marble pile that makes it easier to understand the men who get up on soapboxes in Hyde Park to rave about reform.

Blackley said I needed to attend the ball because "all of society" would be there, including Mayfair's luminaries, several of whom are entangled in the so-called "vampire epidemic." I think Blackley's real motive in wrangling me an invitation was that he simply wanted to show me a good time, which I ended up having in spite of myself.

What little objectivity the committee could have claimed

went out the window after Blackley had the ill fortune to be in the theatre when an actor named Edmund Castle killed an actress on stage, supposedly by drinking her blood. Madeline Salisbury *did* die of blood loss, and there *were* puncture wounds in her neck that apparently healed postmortem. Still, I remain correctly skeptical, although I am the only one on the committee making the least pretense of doubting the existence of vampires in London. Castle appeared to bite Miss Salisbury's throat, but there was nobody close enough to actually see it. It would have been useful to question Castle, but that was made impossible when a mob burned him to death in a house outside London. I have read the account of a witness, one of Captain Lucian's friends. I was shocked to learn that even an army officer could become caught up in the hysteria to imagine the poor man "jumped" some forty feet into the air, *through* the burning roof, to escape the flames.

As there has been little hope of achieving any science in the course of this dubious investigation, I intended to inform Shaftbury at the ball I was resigning from the committee and returning to America to get ready to dig tyrannosaurus bones in Wyoming in spring when the ground thaws. But I changed my mind, and for entirely personal reasons—more on that in a bit.

The ball was in honor of Sir William Petersen, the Viceroy of India, congratulating him, I presumed, for his role in the ongoing plunder of the colony. I discovered, to my surprise, that Sir William was an altogether agreeable man. He is a tall, barrel-shaped fellow who must weigh three hundred pounds, with unruly hair and a full brown beard shot through with streaks of gray. His hand swallowed mine, his fingers nearly as big around as an infant's arm. Viking stock, I guessed, an expression of robust Nordic physical characteristics in the watered-down English gene pool.

"I heard your talk to the Royal Society last week, Professor Cotswold. Absolutely smashing."

We agreed to get together at another time to talk about dinosaurs, which have the power to intrigue the most unlikely people, I've found. I made my way to a quiet corner. A servant offered me a glass of champagne, which I accepted. I have never cared for it but the prospect of getting a glass of beer or a whiskey at Shaftbury's shindig seemed remote.

"Why the glum face?" Blackley asked as he joined me. "Don't tell me you're disappointed I forgot to arrange an invitation for Professor Van Helsing."

"I can understand why a boy like Lucian would fall for this tripe, but the rest of you are old enough to know better."

"There are more things under heaven and earth, Horatio, than are dreamt of in your philosophy."

"Quoting Shakespeare is especially appropriate, if you mean to infer the committee's scientific horizons extend no farther than an Elizabethan's. That does appear to be the case."

"I know what I saw at the Theatre Royal."

"You know what you *think* you saw," I said in retort. "As for Van Helsing, I have no doubt the man is a fraud."

"How do you explain Annie Howard's empty grave?"

"If an empty coffin proves Annie Howard is a vampire, does an empty pocket prove I am a pauper?"

"I could lend you a few bob if you are hard up, Professor."

"As a matter of fact, my pocket isn't empty, but thank you anyway. My point is that appearances are superficial. They stand for something, but they are hardly a substitute for hard data. Inferring Annie Howard's transformation into a vampire on the evidence of her empty coffin is the least likely of several explanations that come to mind. Someone could have taken the body. Or maybe the body was never in the coffin in the first place. Did you attend the funeral? Did you see the body placed in the coffin, and the coffin placed in the ground and covered with dirt? Maybe the body was stolen. Or maybe it was dumped in a common grave to defraud Lady Moore."

"Why would anybody steal a corpse?"

"What a question for a physician to ask, Blackley. You went to medical school. You dissected cadavers."

"You may be forced to rob graves to supply anatomy classes in the United States, Professor, but I assure you there is no shortage of paupers to supply the universities in Britain."

It was at that point Lord Shaftbury whirled across the floor with the most beautiful woman in his arms that I had ever seen. Her hair was so blond it was nearly white, topped by an emerald tiara, and her neck and delicate ears were covered with a matching emerald necklace and earrings. The gown was cut dangerously low over her bosom. As they waltzed, she looked at Shaftbury with an arch expression, as if whatever he was saying amused her on several levels.

"The Contessa Saint-Simon," Blackley told. "A real stunner. I hear she's Shaftbury's mistress."

"I've met Lady Shaftbury," I said. "If she were my wife, I doubt I'd have much interest in a mistress, even one as lovely as the Contessa."

"You betray your provincial origins, old boy. In British society it is almost in bad taste to be in love with one's wife. Besides, Shaftbury is most euphoniously named. He is quite intent on burying his shaft wherever he can."

I asked if it was common then for English men to keep women on the side.

"Of course, but most of the women aren't 'kept' in the way you mean. It is far more convenient to carry on with someone who is safely married. Why my dear Cotswold, you look positively scandalized. Do you find us decadent?"

I said nothing to dissuade him of the idea.

"We are, in our way, extremely moral. One must strictly obey the rules of the game or face disgrace. Discretion must be observed above all else. Scandal is anathema. Liaisons can be overlooked as long as one is discreet."

There was a commotion at the entry. A visible thrill shot

through the crowd, as if the doors had been opened to admit a refreshing breeze into an airless room.

Someone cried: "His Royal Highness, Prince Edward Albert."

The dancing stopped as the men and women in the room turned as one toward the figure in the entryway. The Prince of Wales was not at all what I expected. He was short and stout, with a round, bearded face and thinning hair. He looked more like a prosperous banker than a prince. The crowd parted as the Prince made his way toward the dance floor. The orchestra started again, and there was the Prince, waltzing with Contessa Saint-Simon.

"Poor Shaftbury," Blackley said. "I think Bertie has just stolen his mistress."

Shaftbury stood at the edge of the crowd, watching his Prince dance with his mistress with a look of seemingly authentic joy on his face. In some ways England is like an Oriental satrapy, where everything and everyone is subject to the monarch's whim.

"Professor Cotswold, may I present Charles Dodgson?"

I stuck out my hand and said hello to the fellow Blackley was introducing.

"P-P-P-Pleased to meet you," Dodgson stammered.

"Dodgson lectures in mathematics at Christ College, Oxford. How's the work coming on the treatise?"

Dodgson looked flustered and nodded.

"He's writing a book about symbolic logic," Blackley explained. "It's all beyond me, I'm afraid."

"A dive into the lake of pure reason," I said helpfully.

"That's the g-g-g-general idea," Dodgson replied. He had an unfortunate way of opening his eyes wide and gulping when he became stuck on a word, as if a fish bone were caught in his throat. "I'm a-f-f-f-f . . ." He looked around with bug-eyed horror, as if in fear he might prove unable to finish the thought. But he started over and got it out. "I'm afraid it isn't g-g-g-going well."

"Mr. Cotswold is a paleontologist. He was invited to address the Royal Society."

Dodgson nodded, duly impressed.

"Any luck with the v-v-v—" He took a gulp of air. "—v-vampire, Blackley?"

"One woman he killed has risen from the grave. We presume she has become a vampire."

"Personally, I presume nothing of the sort," I said shortly. "Is it really a good idea to discuss committee business publicly, Blackley?"

"You needn't worry about Dodgson. He's proven himself enormously helpful to the government. Codes, you know. He says they're all a matter of mathematics. He has the Prime Minister's confidence."

"You're too k-k-kind. I've always been good at p-p-puzzles. You do not b-b-b-believe in the vampire, Professor?"

"Not by what I've seen."

"Then wh-wh-wh-what is the explanation? Is it a h-hoax?"

"I don't know. The murders are real enough. There may be something unusual going on here, but it is too early to say what. The growing atmosphere of hysteria isn't making it any easier to sort out the facts."

"You have attended two autopsies," Blackley said. "You saw how the women bled to death without the slightest evidence of a wound."

"You are trying to use a conclusion to explain the evidence, when you would do better to use the evidence to arrive at a conclusion," I countered. "We are no closer to a scientific explanation than when we started. Perhaps the agent responsible for these deaths is not a vampire, but infection by an unknown tropical virus, some heretofore unidentified pathology that causes the blood to be absorbed by the tissues."

"You saw how pale their organs were," Blackley said. "There was no blood in the tissue."

"Then perhaps the virus itself consumed the blood. We're like the proverbial blind men trying to describe an elephant.

We're grabbing at parts of the creature and mistaking them for the beast in its entirety."

"It is rather like your Jabberwock, Dodgson," Blackley said.

I had to ask what a Jabberwock was, since I apparently was the only one of the three of us in the dark on the subject.

"Dodgson's hobby is writing children's books. Maybe you've read the Alice books. They're very popular. He publishes under his pen name, Lewis Carroll, since it would hardly do for a lecturer at Oxford to write children's stories."

I said that as a bachelor, I didn't read a great many children's books.

"Oh, but Dodgson's books are quite marvelous combinations of fantasy, reality, satire, and pure nonsense, and as enjoyable for adults as they are for children," Blackley said. "One of his creatures is a monster called a Jabberwock, which one can't get a picture of no matter how hard one tries. Be a good chap, Dodgson, and recite a bit of it."

Dodgson swallowed dryly and squeezed his eyes shut. I doubted he had it in him, but from within his private world he began to recite, his voice deeper and more assured than the one he used in ordinary speech, and without the stammering.

> " 'Beware the Jabberwock, my son!
>   The Jaws that bite, the claws that catch!
> Beware the Jubjub bird, and shun
>   The frumious Bandersnatch!'
>
> He took his vorpal sword in hand
>   Long time the maxome foe he sought—
> So rested he by the Tumtum tree,
>   And stood awhile in thought.
>
> And, as in uffish thought he stood,
>   The Jabberwock, with eyes of flame,
> Came wiffling through the tulgey wood,
>   And burbled as it came!

One, two! One, two! And through and through
The vorpal blade went snicker-snack!
He left it dead, and with its head
He went galumphing back."

Dodgson opened his eyes, quite pleased with himself. Blackley was inexplicably beaming, as if Dodgson's nonsense had rendered some abstruse and difficult theorem simple and understandable. The British are completely mad, I thought, as Dodgson tottered off in triumph.

"I wonder what it is like to sit through one of his lectures," I muttered.

"I understand they are an ordeal. Dodgson is an ordained canon, but so far as I know, he has never preached a sermon."

"Proof there is a God," I said.

The music ended and we found ourselves facing Lady Olivia Moore, who had been waltzing with Captain Lucian. She was not dressed to the teeth, like the Contessa Saint-Simon, but in a restrained and elegant manner. Her blue silk gown modestly covered her bosom and arms. Her hair was held up with lacquered combs. The only other adornment she wore was a pearl choker. She was younger and more visibly innocent than most of the others at the ball, a young Diane surrounded by jades, roués, and sodomites—or as they are collectively known, the British aristocracy.

Blackley asked Lady Olivia for the honor of a dance.

"If I'm not mistaken, you promised Lady Jones you'd dance with her," I said, lightly touching Blackley's shoulder. It was a lie—though innocent enough. The aristocracy was beginning to rub off on me.

"I had forgotten," Blackley said, smiling at me.

"If you'll allow me the honor," I said as I interposed myself between Blackley and Lady Olivia as the music began.

I felt an inexplicable weightlessness as she placed her hand upon my shoulder, as if I were a nimble sailboat setting up to a rising breeze. *Lady Jones*—I wished I'd thought of something better, but for all I knew there actually was a Lady Jones at Lord Shaftbury's ball. We joined the pairs of dancers swirling across the floor.

By the end of that dance, I still didn't believe in vampires. I had, however, forgotten about my intention to resign from the committee and return to America.

14

Specimens

JANUARY 12, 1880. Today I went to study the vampire bats at the Zoological Society of London in Regent's Park.

The bat is a fascinating subject. The only mammals that truly fly, an evolutionary left turn, a weird melding of the mammalian and avian. Their ability to navigate in the dark is noteworthy, listening to their cries echoing against their surroundings—a method of aural "seeing" that is as unique as their capability for flight. The adaptation suits them for habitation in caves, where they sleep unmolested by predators during the day. Of course, bats fulfill an important housekeeping function in nature, eating prodigious numbers of mosquitoes and other insects.

Of the many species, only one—the vampire bat—is a parasite. And yet it is so wonderfully adapted that I cannot help but admire how well-suited it is to its niche in the natural world.

The specimen I studied at the Zoological Society was a common vampire bat—the *Desmodus rotundus,* family Phyllostomidae, order Chiropetra, class Mammalia. Vampire bats are small. This specimen, collected in the tropical lowlands of Central America, was reddish-brown in color, the tips of its wings white. It weighed in at only 1.8 ounces and measured 3.2 inches, but it needed to drink half its weight in blood each night to power its metabolism. The bat had keen eyesight and was as agile on the ground as in the air, able to run and jump with its well-developed rear legs.

Dr. Poynter, the Society's bat expert, said they had tried to feed the creature beef blood in a bowl, but that the vampire required fresh blood to thrive. I shall have to go back to the Society some night to observe the feeding ritual. A pig is kept in the bat's cage at night. The bat lands or creeps unnoticed onto the sleeping animal. It gently trims away the pig's hair, then licks the skin to soften it before opening a wound with its razor-sharp teeth. The bat doesn't suck blood from its prey but rather laps it as it flows from the wound. An anticoagulant agent in the bat's saliva, as yet unidentified, keeps the blood flowing until the bat has become gorged.

I cradled the bat in my gloved hands. Its face was amazingly human, until it opened its mouth and hissed at me. Its teeth were tiny porcelain needles.

Do vampire bats hunt in packs? Poynter said it had never been reported. They roost in groups of a dozen or fewer, one male, the rest females. However, colonies with as many as two thousand bats have been reported, but that seems to be the exception.

I asked if the vampire bats were known to have attacked humans.

Poynter said he had heard accounts of natives sleeping out of doors getting bit on the toe or finger, but the main danger was not the bat itself but infection in the wound and rabies. The vampire bat is tropical, Poynter reminded me, as if I suspected his little pet might be responsible for the crimes the committee was investigating; it wouldn't last long if it escaped the Society's hothouse.

I said I expected not.

Poynter got around to the subject I knew he was thinking about. "You don't believe any of this nonsense about a vampire killing women in London, do you?"

"Of course not," I replied.

7:00 P.M. Blackley is in my sitting room, agitated nearly to the point of dementia. There's been another murder. And a vampire has been captured. With any luck this will help bring this foolishness to an end. Fortunately, my belated package from New York has arrived. Better late than never, although I do not know if conditions will allow its use.

Later. At last we start to make some progress in this disturbing matter, though the truth remains as elusive as ever.

Blackley gave me the details as we hurried down the stairs. A young girl in the slums had just been dragged off the street and drained of her blood. The driver stared at us with wide eyes as we clamored into the hackney. He whipped the horse and it started off at a brisk trot. When Blackley informed me we were on our way to Scotland Yard to interview the vampire, I demanded that the driver stop. The driver looked back at me as if I were mad, clapping one hand on his bowler hat, which the sudden stop had jarred to an odd angle. People in the street were staring at us, pointing, as if they knew our business—and no doubt they did.

"Take us to Whitechapel," I ordered. The driver looked helplessly at Blackley for confirmation.

"The vampire isn't going anywhere," I said, "but the physical evidence will quickly degrade. As men of science, our first duty is to ensure that specimens are properly collected and catalogued. There isn't a moment to lose. If what I have been told is true, the wound is disappearing even as we sit here debating the proposition."

I expected an argument from Blackley, knowing how much he wanted to see the "vampire" with his own eyes, but he surprised me by agreeing.

The driver turned the hack around in the street, and with a crack of his whip we headed in the opposite direction at a fast clip. The well-mannered streets of London changed, block after block, into as vile a slum as can be found anywhere in the western world. The murder had occurred on

Fulson Street, a place of almost unimaginable squalor. Raw sewage ran in the gutters. The big houses overawing the narrow street on either side probably had been built for wealthy traders. The original buildings had been divided and divided again into smaller and cheaper residences, and added onto wherever possible to create more usable space, the air dense with the smoke of coal fires. These were the rookeries, as the worst slums were known, for the individual apartments were little more than squalid nests. Here, the poor were packed like rabbits in an overpopulated warren, living one on top of the next in the most unhygienic of conditions, subject to extremes of crime and disease.

We approached a widening in the street, a square with a public spigot. A group of women were gathered there, filling water jugs. They stood closely, like cattle when wolves are near. The stone basin was worn low in the center where countless feet had been propped. The runoff feeding the gutters had carved a little depression in the street.

The authorities were gathered in the next block, their lanterns lighting up the dim street, which was otherwise illuminated only by the flicker of irregularly spaced gaslights. There was a police ambulance, its rear door standing open, awaiting the body. One policeman sat on the stoop, his arm in a sling, talking to Chief Inspector Palmer, who was scribbling in his notebook.

As we alighted, a police van pulled up behind us, deploying another dozen constables who took up positions in front of the house, each armed with a club. The crowd of onlookers restricted to the opposite side of the street had a distinctly angry character.

I nodded at Palmer and went past him up the stairs, Blackley following.

The body of a young girl lay on the floor, covered with a white sheet. A quick glance took in the scene in its entirety. The one-room flat provided the minimum creature comforts, the furnishings consisting of a bed, a dresser, and a single chair. A small stove was vented through the wall. There was no fire in the grate and no coal in the battered scuttle. The light came from a kerosene lamp on the dresser, the ceiling above it blackened with soot. On the floor by the bed was a broken china teacup. It did not seem to belong, a lost bit of finery clashing with the surrounding poverty.

I got down on one knee and drew back the sheet from the girl's face. It was unnaturally pale even in death. She had been drained of her blood, it seemed. The set of wounds were over the jugular. I opened my valise and removed the ruler. There was an inch and a quarter separation between the wounds. The wounds themselves were barely a sixteenth of an inch in diameter, with a pronounced red swelling around their circumference.

"They're almost what one would expect to see from a hypodermic needle," I said to Blackley.

"That's because they are quickly healing, Cotswold," Blackley said, his breath puffing clouds in the frigid room.

He was right. The twin cavities were knitting themselves together almost visibly. I examined them with my magnifying glass.

"I've never witnessed anything like this."

"Let me have a look," Blackley said, taking the glass from my hand.

There were footsteps behind us.

"How long has she been here, Palmer?" I asked, guessing it was the Chief Inspector who had joined us.

"Nearly two hours."

"I am going to take a small specimen." I glanced over my shoulder at the detective, who shrugged his approval. I pulled a scalpel and glass vial from the valise and carefully removed a half-inch strip of tissue surrounding and including the anterior of the two wounds. I put the specimen into the vial and sealed it with a rubber stopper. I asked Palmer to collect as many police lanterns as he could to illuminate the wound.

Blackley and Palmer looked on with evident curiosity as I took my device out of its shipping box.

"This is the prototype of a new invention a friend, George Eastman, is working on. It's called a 'Detective' camera, appropriately enough. Since it's handheld, you can use it unobtrusively, without setting up a tripod and all the usual apparatus."

"You could use a camera like that to document crime scenes," C.I. Palmer said.

"That's what I plan to do. It's not available to the general public yet, but I have little doubt these cameras will become quite popular once Eastman perfects the design. I've suggested he call his new company 'Kodiak,' after the Kodiak bear. *Ursus arctos middenfoii* is a noble beast, and less illtempered than *Ursus arctos horribilis*."

I pulled the string to open the shutter on the lens.

"Is there sufficient light?" Palmer asked.

I confessed that I knew little about photography beyond the basic principles. The result of my efforts wouldn't be known until I exhausted the film in the "Detective" and shipped it back to Eastman for my photographs to be processed.

As I moved the lights closer to make a second photograph, I asked the policeman to tell me what he knew about the murder.

"The girl's name is Mary Katharine McGuinn. She had gotten hold of that teacup that's there by the bed, broken. Odds are she stole it. She was working her way up the street, trying to sell it, when she had the misfortune to happen into Kate Woolf. Kate is known to us—a prostitute and a petty thief. It seems Kate offered to buy the teacup but said she needed to get money from her room. She attacked the girl before they were even in the room. The girl cried out for help as she was bitten in the neck. When Constable Gordon arrived, he found Kate with her teeth still fastened onto the girl's neck. The door was wide open. He tried to apprehend her, but she picked him up and bodily threw him out of her way. Kate's a small woman. You saw Gordon on your way in, seated on the stoop with his arm in a sling."

"The vampire has supernatural strength," Blackley said.

"It would seem so," Palmer agreed.

"How many men did it take to subdue her?"

"Actually, Dr. Blackley, it was three women from the neighborhood that brought her to bay. They had heard the commotion and followed Gordon to the room. They stood at the door holding the crosses they wear about their necks. It's an Irish Catholic neighborhood. Kate hid on the other side of the bed, as terrified of those crosses as the women were of her. We clapped Kate into irons and hauled her away. I can attest to her strength myself. The only way I got her into the wagon was to threaten to put holy water on her unless she behaved herself."

"All as Van Helsing said," Blackley muttered, his faith in the Hungarian quack growing by the day.

"Was there any evidence the crosses actually caused Kate Woolf any physical distress?"

"All I know is she was afraid, Professor Cotswold."

"Then all we know is that she fears these objects, not that they actually have supernatural power over her."

"Oh, do let up on it, old boy."

"I'm afraid I can't, Blackley. Don't you see how much of this is based on conjecture and circumstance? She could have heard the same stories about vampires that Van Helsing has been telling us."

"The streets *are* thick with talk about vampires," C.I. Palmer said with emphasis. "I'm a little curious, gentlemen. Why did you two come here instead of the jail? I would have thought you'd want to examine the vampire."

"The same reason you did," I answered. "I wanted to see the evidence as soon as possible, before it could degrade or become contaminated."

Palmer gave me a small smile of appreciation. "That accomplished, we should join the others at the prison where they are holding the fiend," Palmer said. "Perhaps you gentlemen could be good enough to give me a ride."

"Chief Inspector! Chief Inspector!"

"Why the bloody racket, Grimes?"

"It's the vampire, sir," the young policeman said, out of breath from running. "She's escaped."

15

The Vicarage

JANUARY 13, 1880. At breakfast with the Special Committee, Palmer and Blackley related the details of the latest murder, including the autopsy (at least I'm getting used to seeing these), and the still-unexplained postmortem healing of the victim's neck wounds. I suggested we resume our efforts at the jail, to see what we could learn about the so-called vampire and her escape. After another round of coffee we were off.

Following her capture the night before, Kate Woolf had been taken to a secret prison near the Admiralty called the Vicarage, in honor of its first tenant, a priest accused of conspiring to overthrow the government and reinstate Catholicism as the state religion. The prison was originally part of an ancient fortification, now the basement of an innocuous government building where "clarks," as they are called here, pore over their ledgers. Access to the Vicarage was through a barred door at the end of a narrow, sunless alley behind the building. A flight of steep stone stairs led down into an almost medieval dungeon. The prison office occupied an antechamber at the bottom of the stairs. Just past the office was a heavily barred door, through which I could see a long, dim corridor lit with flickering gas jets extending into the distance. Metal rings where prisoners were once shackled by their wrists still hung from the walls.

The prison warden invited us to be seated and sent for the jailer who had been in charge at the time of Woolf's escape. After a brief wait, punctuated with the sound of metal doors being unlocked, opened, then closed and secured again, the guard stood before us. His name was Dennis Hammer—pronounced with a long vowel. The time he'd spent working in the unhealthy dungeon had been as hard on him as it no doubt was on the prisoners. Hammer was perhaps forty, though he looked a good deal older. His complexion was pasty from the lack of sun, and his big body had gone soft through lack of exercise, although I do not doubt he had the strength requisite for the job. His nerves were evidently raw from the previous night's experience: I detected the hint of whiskey on him.

No one had ever escaped the Vicarage, the warden observed.

Hammer stood with his head bowed, looking at the floor. He sagged visibly as his humiliation deepened.

"Let's have it then," the warden said. "Tell them how it happened."

The story Hammer told us was, from a purely objective standpoint, too fantastic to be believed, though he obviously was convinced he spoke the truth. In simple, straightforward language, absent the melodramatic embellishment Van Helsing would have given the tale, Hammer reported that Kate Woolf had been brought to the Vicarage in chains at eight the previous evening and had been duly registered—no doubt in the secret prison's secret registry. Woolf was taken to Cell 27 in Corridor B, shackled to the wall, and locked neatly in. There was nothing in the room besides a cot, a slops jar, and a pitcher of water.

About an hour later, Hammer said, he started to hear "something uncommon strange" coming from the cells—the sound of a woman singing. At first he ignored it and continued his game of solitaire. The guests at the Vicarage were subject to all manner of unusual behavior, which Hammer said he had trained himself to mostly ignore. However, after a time the "weird singing" began to have an effect on him.

"I can't rightly explain it, but it was as if I was dreaming. I swear on my soul I did not fall asleep, and yet it was like I was dreaming. The music somehow done it to me. Most uncommon strange, it was."

The next thing Hammer knew, he was standing in Corridor B outside Cell 27. The door was open. The shackles that had chained Kate Woolf to the wall were empty. She was gone.

"You let her bloody go?" Lord Shaftbury almost shouted.

"I can't say, sir," Hammer answered, hanging his head even lower, which was hardly possible.

"You must not hold this guard responsible," Van Helsing said.

"I bloody well can!" the warden exploded.

"You must not. The responsibility is not his. The vampire is to blame. They have mesmeric powers. It is part of what makes them so dangerous. She put him in a hypnotic trance with her singing."

"The guard was hypnotized?" Reverend Clarkson asked Blackley. He seemed to grow more befuddled by the instant. "Is that possible?"

"I suppose it is, Reverend," the physician answered.

Blackley shot me a private look, as if expecting me to attempt to debunk the latest claims. All I could do was shrug. I had nothing to say. I had no alternate explanation. For all I knew, the guard *had* been hypnotized by Kate Woolf's strange singing. Although I have refused to attribute these phenomenon to supernatural agencies, I'll be damned if I can explain what's going on.

We dutifully trooped through a series of locked gates and filed down the dark, dank corridor to inspect Cell 27. The padlock on the shackles and the door lock were closely examined and tested. Each worked as intended. It was difficult to imagine how anyone could escape from this inhumane and depressing prison, cruelly designed to defeat the spirit as well as the body.

As we returned to the prison office, a policeman burst in and announced that the body of a charwoman had been discovered nearby, drained of her blood like the others. Most likely that, too, was the work of the vampire Kate Woolf.

Blast it all, I've done it myself: I've described Woolf as a "vampire," and without experiencing the usual inner sneer that comes with condescending to the preposterous, the superstitious, the absurd.

It seems the hysteria has claimed its latest victim—me.

16

$\diamond$

A Game of Chess

JANUARY 14, 1880 (2:00 A.M.). The eyes, the hands, the mind—what have they seen? What have they done? What does it mean?

This question I must resolve to answer above all else, dear God: What does it *mean*?

I can scarcely believe what I have witnessed tonight. And yet I must. Confronted with the horrible, the impossible, the incredible, the unbelievable, I must coldly and calmly *believe*.

But dispassionate logic seems beyond me at the moment. The full weight of this awful truth only hit me after I had returned here to my hotel room, a stiff glass of whiskey in front of me. I picked up my pen to write this entry and my hand began to shake. *My hand began to shake!* I've ridden into a hail of Rebel bullets and cannonballs. I've been chased by Indians, attacked by grizzly bears, and tossed and torn by a hurricane off the Dry Tortugas. But never before now have I been so unnerved as to see my hand shake.

Thank God I did not panic earlier, or I would be dead.

At this moment I feel closer to madness than I could have imagined possible. I must draw from my deepest reserves and confront the matter squarely and honestly. I am not the first man to make a discovery that sets his universe on its head. Science must be based on objectivity. Expectations, experiences, and preconceived notions must never be allowed to pollute one's observations—or the dreaded conclusion to which they inevitably lead.

I must write this down, one step at a time, exactly as it unfolded, in careful detail, while the events are as fresh as a new wound.

The Special Committee reconvened at Downing Street late in the afternoon, as the winter darkness began to gather the light from the corners and alleys in the old city. Shaftbury opened the session with a report on the vampire who had been captured and escaped, but Disraeli cut him short. He already knew the details from his informants—probably one of them was Blackley, who had said one or two things to indicate he and Disraeli were thick as thieves.

The Prime Minister was not pleased with the committee's lack of progress.

"This simply will not do," Disraeli said. "London grows more agitated by the day. There would be an angry mob outside at this moment, if fear of the monster did not keep people off the streets. The anarchists and other misguided utopians will take this grim situation as an opportunity. The time has come for us to do something right. We cannot fail Her Majesty."

He gave us a look, as if wondering if *we* were going to fail *him*.

"I am open to your suggestions. I pray to God you have some."

"We should search for Kate Woolf," I said. "She is our one solid lead. I suggest concentrating on the East End. She's familiar with the territory and the people. It'll be easiest for her to blend in."

"Vampires tend to be creatures of habit," Van Helsing said. "I agree with Professor Cotswold."

"We could deploy a force of policemen in civilian clothing throughout the neighborhood, armed with whistles to signal for help at the first sign of trouble," young Captain Lucian said.

"My men are already spreading out through the neighborhood," C.I. Palmer said. "But I do like the Captain's way of thinking."

"Then make it happen," Disraeli said a bit crossly.

"The men must be well-armed with revolvers, stakes, hammers—whatever it takes to kill the monster," Shaftbury said. "We cannot take any chances. Any vampire we apprehend must be summarily executed."

"No!"

The explosiveness of my disagreement startled the others.

"We must make our best assessment of what agents are at play here. Is there really such a thing as a vampire? I can see from your expressions that I am the only one still harboring doubts. But let us assume for the moment that a vampire, or a band of vampires, is responsible for these crimes. We must make sure we understand their strengths and weaknesses, and the nature of so strange a condition. We must learn exactly what a vampire is, how the contagion is spread, how it is best battled. With all due respect to Dr. Van Helsing, do you really want to entrust the future of London—indeed, the future of the entire human species—to a Hungarian folk tale, Mr. Prime Minister? We must exercise scrupulous due diligence. I appeal to you, Mr. Disraeli. The fate of your country, the fate of the world, may well rest in your hands."

Disraeli looked to Van Helsing. The rumpled little man was slumped in a chair, his hands pressed together as if in meditation, index fingers pressed against mouth and chin. Fear was among the emotions reflected in his dark little eyes. The fearless vampire hunter was not, it turned out, beyond being afraid.

"I would advise you in the strongest of terms to allow us to destroy the fiends as we find them."

Disraeli was silent for a moment, brooding over the options.

"You may be right, Dr. Van Helsing," he said at last, "but

we must keep the broader picture in mind. I would remind you all of the question Charles Darwin put forth, simple and yet chilling in implication. Is the vampire an aberration, a lethal but confinable disease, or a threat to the existence of humanity?"

"Or is it the judgment of God?" Reverend Clarkson interjected.

"We can only find out through scientific inquiry," I said, still ensnarled in my own way of looking at the world. "We must recapture Woolf and examine her to learn what we can."

"But how will that be possible?" Shaftbury asked. "We already know a vampire can't be held in prison."

"I believe she can be held, even if she does possess the power to hypnotize her captors," I said. "From what I have been able to learn on the fly about autosuggestion, in order to be hypnotized, a subject must be either willing or at the very least unsuspecting."

"I can assure you Hammer was *not* willing," Palmer said.

"No, but he was unsuspecting. Whatever trick Kate Woolf used to get him to unlock the prison door, I doubt she could do it to him again. Therefore, when we apprehend her, I suggest assigning two or even four guards to stand duty. They must remain together as a group at all times, and, when not otherwise engaged in their duties, they should be instructed to play cards."

"Did you say—what?" Shaftbury sputtered.

But the Prime Minister was already at my defense. "I follow your reasoning perfectly, Professor Cotswold. If the men's minds are occupied, they will not be subject to any subtle, undue influence."

"I say, Cotswold, you are the sly one," Blackley said.

"Rotate the guards every few hours," I said. "The greater the mental fatigue, the greater the risk their minds will become subject to suggestion."

"Have you the men to accommodate this recommendation?" Disraeli asked the policeman. Palmer nodded. "Very well, then. We shall give Professor Cotswold's plan a try."

An East End map was unrolled on a table. Captain Lucian made several useful suggestions about conducting our search. I was gaining a little more appreciation for Lucian, even if he obviously had his eye on the lovely Lady Olivia Moore. That was a battle, I feared, he would lose to the more experienced tactician—me.

Blackley and I paired up, police whistles in our pockets to signal the others should we happen upon anything untoward.

The night was not bad for January, the air just above freezing and lacking the moisture that makes the cold penetrate the bones. The easy breeze was sufficient to keep the coal smoke of innumerable fires from hanging oppressively over the city, but too slight to penetrate my overcoat and scarf. The gaslights illuminated the deserted sidewalks. London had undergone a metamorphosis in the days since my address to the Royal Society. A pall of fear had descended over the city, driving the people indoors when darkness came.

"London will undoubtedly see less than the usual amount of crime tonight," Blackley said. "People who stay home fearing the vampire will avoid having their pockets picked or their empty houses burgled. They won't lose money gambling, contract syphilis from a prostitute, or get hit over the head by a gin-addled thug."

We paused for Blackley to light a cheroot. He squinted up at me through the smoke and flame of his match. "Since vampires have an undoubted moralizing effect upon society, perhaps you would like to import one or two to America when you return," he said.

I declined the offer.

We continued on our way, each consumed for a time by private thoughts. We walked briskly, our breath shooting out silver plumes in the cold air, our eyes alert and ever moving. As we traveled deeper into the East End, we gradually began to see a few more people. Though deserted by the city's overpopulated standard, people loitered here and there, going to and from the public houses, compelled by habit and addiction to engage in those practices that neither panic nor plague could discourage.

A woman stepped out of a doorway as if materializing from the shadows. Her face was garish with paint. She was aged beyond her years, the reward for hard living. The leer on her lips did not extend as far as her eyes, which even in the reflection of the gaslight were dark and hopeless, her existence but a simulacrum of life.

" 'Ello, gents," she said. "Care for a bit of flash?"

"Not tonight, love," Blackley said.

The whore returned to her station, where we could hear her talking to herself, questioning our manhood.

"She had better hope Lucian does not come this way. He would horsewhip her for such impudence."

"You're joking, of course," I said.

"Yes, but he does have quite a temper. I attribute it to his upbringing in Scotland's cold, Presbyterian climate. Do you know he once killed a man in a duel?"

"In London?"

"We are more civilized than that, if only just. It happened in Africa, when he was there with his regiment. Something to do with a girl, I believe."

"Usually is," I said, thinking of Lady Olivia Moore.

"A word to the wise for you, old man," Blackley said with a sidelong glance. He was thinking about Olivia, too, and the interest in her I shared with Captain Lucian.

"I can take care of myself," I said.

"I was rather thinking of young Lucian's continued well-being," Blackley said with a wink. "I'm rather fond of the lad. He is so very earnest."

We paused just then outside a building where a hackney was disgorging two upper-class Englishmen who were much the worse for drink. They stumbled up the stone stairs and pounded on the door framed by two gaslights. A window in the door opened. Whoever was inside evidently judged them suitable for admission, for the door opened and they disappeared inside.

"This is the last decent place to warm ourselves before the neighborhood turns for the worst," Blackley said. "Come in and I will buy you a whiskey."

I said I thought we should stay on the street.

"We won't be shirking our duty by paying a visit to the Hellfire Club. There is a chance, a rather small chance, we'll find Kate Woolf inside. It is the best brothel in London."

Blackley rapped on the door with his silver-headed cane, and the door was swung open wide by the doorman—a boxer, judging from his flattened nose and disfigured ears. It seemed the good doctor was not entirely unknown to the Hellfire's habitués. Indeed, an angelic figure separated herself from the crowd near the cloak room and flew to Blackley's arms, her jeweled wrists glittering brightly against his black silk cape.

"Mon cherie!" the Contessa Saint-Simon breathed into his ear.

She was even more ravishing than at Lord Shaftbury's ball. What she was doing in this lowly—if elegantly appointed—place was beyond me.

"Contessa, may I present Professor Dr. James Cotswold of Harvard University in the United States?"

"Enchanted," I said, bowing over the lady's hand.

"Lord Shaftbury has told me all about you, Professor," she said with a little laugh that could have come from a music box.

"I wish I could report the same, Contessa Saint-Simon. It is easy to understand why he keeps you a secret from other men."

"Flattery will get you everywhere, monsieur. Tell me *cherie,*" she said to Blackley, "did you come here looking for the vampire?"

I looked to Blackley, who, after glancing around to confirm that we were not being overheard, confessed as much.

"We are looking for a vampire who was, before her monstrous change, a flash girl named Kate Woolf. She was not of the caliber of your establishment, of course, but we thought it would be wise to be sure the premises are secure."

Your establishment? Contessa Saint-Simon was the Hellfire Club's proprietress? For a moment I was completely nonplussed. Hadn't I just seen her dancing with the Prince of Wales? And wasn't she Lord Shaftbury's mistress?

The Contessa caught me gaping at her and gave me a smile that made my knees weak.

I realized then that I had utterly failed to appreciate the extent to which decadence had eaten into British society, like worms drilling into fine old walnut paneling and oak posts, disfiguring and weakening a house until it is on the verge of collapse. And Shaftbury had built his reputation as a crusader against prostitution, yet openly consorted with London's leading madam. It was impossible to imagine a high political figure in the United States frolicking shamelessly with ladies of the night.

"Woolf is a flash girl off the streets?" the Contessa asked with a slight lifting of the lip. "You know I won't have trash working here, monsieur."

"But of course not."

"You are very welcome to inspect the premises and fully avail yourselves of our services. And if there is anything I can do for you *personally,* Professor Cotswold . . ."

"Perhaps some other evening," Blackley said. With a bow of the head, he grasped me firmly by the elbow and squired me into a salon off the main hall. I am embarrassed to admit it, but if Blackley hadn't been there, I would have been sorely tempted to take the French fox up on her offer.

We sat down on a divan in a salon. A liveried servant delivered us two whiskeys, either responding to some signal from the physician or out of habit.

"The look on your face," Blackley said with a shake of his head.

"Did the others know about the Contessa—at the ball, I mean?"

"You are green as the grass, old boy! Of course they knew. The proper women won't speak to the Contessa, of course, but the men all do. And she was hardly the only mistress or concubine at the party. I must say, Cotswold, you are the naive one."

"I guess I am."

"This is not Boston, you know. London is not full of bluenoses, though we put on a damn fair show of it to suit old Queen Vicky. I expect all that will change when Bertie is king."

A young woman opened a door across the salon, giving me a brief glimpse inside. Her customer, a portly man with gray hair and beard, swung naked from the ceiling, trussed up in some depraved contrivance of a leather harness. Beneath him was a second woman, dressed only in a pair of black stockings, spanking him with a bamboo cane.

Blackley poked me with his elbow. "Something for every taste," he said with a wicked grin.

"This isn't Boston," I said. "It isn't Cheyenne. It isn't even New Orleans."

"Then they are especially depraved in New Orleans?" he asked with enthusiasm.

"Especially."

"I shall have to visit New Orleans one day," Blackley said, and threw back his whiskey.

Not finding Kate Woolf at the Hellfire Club, and braced by our whiskeys, we made our way into the slums. The streets narrowed as we progressed into the older, medieval part of the city. The bricks and stonework on the buildings had long since turned black with soot. Years of neglect had denigrated the facades, though signs of former glory could be seen in certain architectural fancies that had managed to resist centuries of dereliction.

The gaslights were more distantly spaced in the East End.

At times the lamp behind us disappeared completely before the next flickering light came dimly into view, making it difficult to walk on the irregularly paved cobblestones. There was a certain lack of logic to scrimping on streetlights where crime was rampant. Blackley informed me there was no city government in London, at least not in the sense that there is in the United States. Important services are provided by parish councils, which tend to be no richer than the neighborhood they govern. Even when money is available for improvements, and corruption does not siphon it off into politicians' pockets, the difficulty of negotiating agreements and plans between parishes makes it all but impossible to coordinate municipal improvements on any scale.

When we turned down a particularly dark stretch of street—reeking with the smell of sewage and rotting garbage—my sense of danger, already in a state of alert, pricked up. There were scores of places on such a street where ruffians could hide to waylay the hapless passerby. Kate Woolf and other supposed vampires were less of a concern than the sort of thugs that make it unsafe to walk through bad neighborhoods at night. As if summoned from my thoughts, five silhouettes emerged from the shadows.

" 'Ello there, governor," said the middle figure, the largest of the band. "I wonder if either of you fine gents could spare a shilling or two?"

Without waiting for an answer, they stepped forward as one, their intent obvious in their postures.

Before I could take my hands from my coat pockets, I heard beside me a familiar enough sound, though I don't think I had heard it since I mustered out of the army: the sibilant hiss of a steel blade being unsheathed. In my peripheral vision—I did not want to take my eyes off the bandits—I saw Dr. Blackley draw a blade from where it had lain hidden within his cane. What small bit of light there was in the street reflected on the rapier blade. The shadows retreated several steps, turned, and broke into a run.

"That's a rather handy tool, Blackley," I said.

Blackley explained that he was frequently compelled to visit his patients at night, and that London, despite appearances, was rife with crime. The shriek of a police whistle interrupted Blackley's disquisition.

"Come on," I cried, and we began to run toward the sound. The signal became louder as we rounded the corner, insistent to the point of panic. Whoever it was needed help and needed it urgently. We hurried to the extent that we overshot our mark, now hearing the whistle *behind* us.

We turned around and found the place just as the whistle's frantic shriek stopped with abrupt suddenness.

Cloaked in darkness and ominous silence, we found ourselves peering into the dark recess between two one-story buildings. The building on the left was brick, its opposite stone. A third floor had been added between the two, linking them and creating a covered interior courtyard open to the street. A collection of handcarts—the sort merchants used to pedal their wares in the streets of London—were stored in the courtyard, pushed up on their ends, piled one against the other to conserve space. After a moment of looking, I found in the darkness the distinctive rectangle of deeper darkness that indicated a door to the building's interior. The irregular shape on the ground before the door looked as if it might be a body.

Blackley had his police whistle clamped in his teeth, and he blew several ear-splitting blasts to signal the forces to rally to our position.

"Come on," I said, and moved cautiously forward, scanning the shadows left and right for movement or an indication of an assailant.

The crumpled form was indeed a body—a man of perhaps sixty, bald, thin, with a walrus mustache above a mouth frozen open in the horror of his final moments. The cause of death was evident. His neck had been savagely torn open, as if by a grizzly bear's claw, his thin scarf torn to shreds. Dark liquid flowed freely from the wound. Unlike the others, this victim had not been drained of his blood.

The policeman! I thought with a start, looking up from this unfortunate man's body. It was easy enough to deduce what had happened. One of our policemen searching the neighborhood, either in uniform or plainclothes, had interrupted the killer and sounded the alarm, preventing the fiend from finishing the job of emptying the corpse of its blood. But the policeman was nowhere to be found—a bad sign.

"In there," I whispered, pointing inside. A door standing open in that part of London was in itself a cry of suspicion.

"Shouldn't we wait for the others?" Blackley whispered back.

"Whoever signaled us here with his whistle may need help," I said.

Blackley turned away from me and rushed toward the street. I confess my initial reaction was to think the worst of him, but after blowing three more blasts on his police whistle, he was back at my side.

Stepping over the body, we moved into the building, trying to make as little noise as possible. We found ourselves in a grocer's warehouse, the air a rich mixture of apples, spices, and dust. A light could be seen at the far end of the room, a dim, flickering glow coming from behind an impromptu wall of stacked flour barrels.

We found the policeman on his side, his head on his outstretched arm, as if he were reaching for the helmet lying a few inches from his hand.

Blackley picked up the candle and moved it back and forth in front of the policeman's staring eyes. His pupils did not respond to the light. He was dead.

Blackley rolled him onto his back, revealing, on the opposite side of his neck, a pair of ragged, gaping wounds an inch or more in diameter, each encircled with an angry ring of discolored flesh. Either the policeman had struggled against his assailant, or the killer had shaken him, the way a dog will shake a rabbit in its jaws. Like the victim outside, the policeman had been incompletely drained. A steady trickle of blood oozed from the fresh wounds, soaking into his woolen tunic.

"Where's his partner?" I whispered.

C.I. Palmer had been adamant that we search for Kate Woolf in pairs. The dead policeman must have a partner nearby, someone who was perhaps being killed as we crouched beside the corpse—an idea that gripped us both at the same moment. We stood and turned so quickly that the candle in Blackley's hand sputtered and nearly went out. It is fortunate the flame managed to stay alive—it is the only reason *I* am alive.

The instant we turned around, we saw the vampire—for there is no longer any doubt that there are *vampires,* even if we are far from understanding exactly what these creatures are.

She was standing just within the weak circle of light given off by the candle. Having never seen Kate Woolf, I had no way of knowing it was her. (It was, I later learned.) She was hardly larger than a child—not quite five feet tall, I should think, slight of build, narrow of shoulder, the product of generations of poor nutrition and breeding. Her face was smeared with blood that ran down her neck and soaked into the bodice of her dress. Her long red hair had fallen down around her face; several strands were heavy with blood. But the worst to behold were her eyes: They glittered with a cold, predatory malice I had seen once before—a look that would have been the death of me had I not fired a lucky shot that caught the charging grizzly bear right between the eyes.

I don't know about Blackley, but the vampire so captured my attention that it was only after taking in everything about her that I even noticed the man beside her. He was not a vampire—that much was evident from the way he tried to hold his body away from her, though she had one hand on his arm, the other being stretched up and around him, clamping his mouth so he could not cry out in fear or warning.

It was the Reverend Clarkson. The brass police whistle he had used to summon us dangled by its chain from his right hand.

I surmised that the priest and policeman had surprised the vampire in the act of killing the grocer just outside his warehouse. The policeman had bravely pursued her into the warehouse, only to come to a bad end. When he didn't return, Reverend Clarkson had even more bravely gone inside to try to help.

"Let him go," I said.

The vampire began to laugh.

"Pull yourself free," I urged.

The old priest struggled briefly, but he was as good as caught in a vise. The reports of the vampire's extraordinary strength were, it seemed, true.

"Why didn't she flee when she had the chance?" Blackley asked. The smile on her face answered the question: She had waited for *us*.

"Aye, lads, what you both are thinking is exactly what is going to happen," she said. "I smelled you coming down the street and didn't want you to miss the fun. I am going to drain you both bone-dry. But first you will watch Reverend Clarkson die."

I thought she started to choke the priest. His face contorted, and he grabbed at his collar with his free hand, as if unable to get his breath. At the same time, he seemed to fall against the vampire, his knees buckling, so that she had to let go of his mouth and hold his slackening body in her arms.

"Bloody hell!" she shrieked, letting go. The priest fell in a heap at her feet.

"He's having a fit or a stroke," Blackley said, sounding shaken, as he put the candle on a crate.

I half expected the physician to go to Clarkson's aid, but instead he drew the sword from his cane for the second time that evening—an altogether wiser course, given the situation. The vampire's eyes narrowed, and she drew back her lips in an awful leer that revealed a wickedly curving set of narrow fangs ideally adapted to puncturing the human jugular vein.

The vampire hissed as she flew at Blackley, her fingers tearing the air like the talons of an enraged eagle. Blackley took half a step forward to meet her and plunged his blade into her stomach, driving it forward until the point, wet with blood, came out her back and the silver handle stopped against her abdomen.

The vampire staggered backward, staring in horror at the darker, wetter stain radiating from where the blade was plunged in her already-blood-soaked dress. The expression on her face was one with which I was familiar from wartime. Somehow, the fact that you are going to die someday never really occurs to you until the moment arrives. It was no different for me. I went through many battles with soldiers dropping around me like flies, never believing it could happen to me.

"I've killed the vampire," Blackley said thickly.

She was still standing, but only just, leaning against a wooden post to keep on her feet. She grabbed the silver handle, which was shaped like a wolf's head, with both hands, and began to draw the blade slowly out of her belly. I could not imagine what kind of strength could enable her to withstand the excruciating pain. And yet, with a grimace distorting her face, she completed the extraction and dropped the slippery blade with a brittle clatter against the stone floor.

Now she will go down, I thought. I had seen men hemorrhage after a blade or shard of steel was pulled from the belly, releasing a torrent of blood.

But the vampire didn't go down.

She stood there almost doubled over against the post, slowly lifting her eyes until they met ours—and she was *smiling*.

For a moment, Blackley and I stood there in stunned fascination, like deer caught in the glare of a poacher's lantern.

She stood up straight, smoothing the wrinkles from her blood-sodden dress.

"I will give you a quick death, Professor Cotswold," she said. "You will get off easily, so that I might make Dr. Blackley suffer long and horribly."

How did she know our names? And how had she known Clarkson's? It was only then that I realized the strange incongruity of telling us that we were going to die, but only after watching her kill *Reverend Clarkson*. Did the vampire's powers include the ability to look into our minds and learn the secrets of our thoughts? The total horror of that possibility came flooding into me—we were facing a monster whose strength and infernal powers we had not begun to understand. Confronted, the creature seemed only to effortlessly metamorphose in startling, unexpected ways. The vampire was indeed very much like Dodgson's Jabberwock—its incomprehensible versatility and power seemed to defy logic and understanding.

> *Beware the Jabberwock, my son!*
> *The Jaws that bite, the claws that catch!*

The vampire's smile became an awful leer. The fangs, which had disappeared when Blackley stabbed her—probably retracted into cavities in the upper jaw—were again in evidence, superior and anterior to the canines.

She was moving toward Blackley as I pulled the revolver from within my coat and shot her in the chest—five times. Each bullet made her body jerk, but slowed her progress toward Blackley only slightly. I tried to put the last shot squarely between her eyes, but she unexpectedly changed course and lunged at me. The slug hit her in the upper skull over her left eye, blasting away part of her head.

I tried to twist away, but I could not escape. Her hands clutched at me, but there was no strength in her grasp. She slid toward the floor, smearing the left arm of my coat with blood and brain tissues. She lay with her face against my boot, motionless. I watched in mute fascination as the supernumerary fangs slowly retracted into her jaw.

"Good heavens, man, are you all right?"

By way of answering Blackley, I heard myself say: "You'd better see if there is anything you can do for Reverend Clarkson."

17

$\diamond$

Faust's Bargain

JANUARY 14, 1880 (7:00 A.M.) Resuming my narrative where I left off in the early morning hours, too exhausted to continue: As Blackley attended to the Reverend Clarkson, I knelt beside the vampire to see what a cursory examination would reveal about the creature and its superhuman abilities. What bizarre adaptations to the human physiology could account for its ability to withstand trauma that would have killed an ordinary member of our species?

I gingerly touched her upper lip. The skin was warm, even feverish. I pushed the lip back. The teeth had retracted completely into the jaw through slits in the gums. I was pressing my finger against the moist tissue, trying to feel for the underlying cavity, when I felt breath against my hand.

I gasped and reflexively pulled my hand away.

"She's alive!"

"Impossible," Blackley said. "You probably felt the natural relaxation of the muscles in the chest and diaphragm."

I nearly said something about needing to drive a wooden stake through the vampire's heart, but my good sense—or what I took for it—returned in time to stop me.

"How is Clarkson?"

Before Blackley could answer, we heard the scream of whistles from outside.

"It's all right," I cried out. "Come in. We need help."

A pair of wary-looking constables appeared in the doorway, breathing heavily.

"There's nothing to fear, men. Professor Cotswold has killed the vampire."

"And Reverend Clarkson?" I asked again.

"It's his heart, I'm afraid. Coronary thrombosis. Surely you noticed how bad his color has been."

"Is he going to . . ."

"I don't know. It depends on the damage to the heart. Time will tell."

I thought I saw something out of the corner of my eye—a faint movement, as if the vampire had taken a shallow breath. I stood up and took a step backward. Was it as Blackley had said, that the body was settling into the quietude of death? I stared down at the female body, unable to take my eyes off it—in truth, *afraid* to take my eyes off it. I was aware of others coming into the warehouse, of murmuring voices crowding around us. I blinked against the lanterns, my eyes not accustomed to the light. Reverend Clarkson was lifted onto a stretcher, covered with a blanket, and carried out.

"Blackley, come over here for a moment, if you please."

He came, but without much enthusiasm. His instinctive caution about coming near the vampire was, I thought, especially appropriate.

"See if she is really dead."

"Your imagination is running away with you," he said, and squatted beside the body. He placed his fingers on the woman's throat to feel for a pulse. His mouth opened as if to make some remark, but he said nothing.

"She's alive," I said. "Look!"

I used the toe of my boot to indicate the cranial wound, no longer raw but covered with a strange milky tissue that appeared to have the consistency of a spider's web. There was a scalpel in Blackley's hands. I suppose he carried it in his jacket, as I have known other physicians to do. He lifted the wet fabric of the dress between the thumb and forefinger of his left hand, carefully cutting it with the scalpel so he could pull back the material and examine the chest wound.

The hole was closed, as if it were an old wound in the process of mending.

"What in the name of the devil . . ." he said, his voice trailing off.

"Blackley!"

The physician looked up at Lord Shaftbury, who had come into the warehouse unnoticed. With him was Dr. Van Helsing. Apparently they had been together, a team, hunting for the vampire. Van Helsing had his filthy carpetbag of tools with him.

"She's alive," Blackley said, although he sounded as if he doubted his own words.

I felt a chill go up my spine. It wasn't the monster that put the scare into me so much as what it represented. I don't have any truck with the supernatural. Even at that sobering moment when we realized that almost nothing we could do to the vampire would kill her, I still did not think the supernatural played any role in explaining her powers. I didn't need thoughts of "the undead" to make my blood run cold. Whatever *science* explained the vampire was horrifying enough without involving ghosts and devils in the matter. Darwin had been almost presciently correct: A creature with superior powers of body and mind that preys upon the members of our species could be the real-life angel of the apocalypse. The body at our feet, I thought with an inward shudder, could be the harbinger of humankind's end.

"Is that Kate Woolf?" Shaftbury asked.

"That it is, sir," Palmer's voice boomed out, although I didn't see his face.

"Did you see her kill the man outside and the policeman?" Van Helsing asked. He gave me a curious look, as if something about the scene surprised him, as if the pieces of the night weren't fitting together to make a convincing whole.

"No, but she as much as admitted it," Blackley said. "She said she was going to kill Reverend Clarkson and then the two of us. I ran her through with the blade of my sword cane. She pulled it out and threw it away as if it hadn't bothered her any more than the bite of a gnat. And Cotswold here emptied a revolver into her. He had to blow half her head off to stop her. But she's not dead."

"Saints preserve us," a voice behind me said.

"Will she make it?" Shaftbury asked.

"It appears her body is beginning to heal," Blackley said. "Do you notice how the chest wound has already sealed itself? And this white tissue covering the cranial wound? I've never seen anything like it. It was fine as gossamer a few minutes ago. Now, it is almost as if someone has draped a cheesecloth over the exposed gray matter. I think she's going to survive."

"This is quite remarkable," Shaftbury said. "Monstrous, of course, yet remarkable."

Van Helsing threw down his carpetbag and began to frantically fumble with the clasp.

"What do you think you're doing?" Lord Shaftbury asked.

"I am going to drive a wooden stake through the vampire's heart while there is still time."

"You will do nothing of the sort," Shaftbury said. "The vampire will be taken to the Vicarage, where it will be put under special guard while it is examined and studied. The Prime Minister has already given the order, swayed by Professor Cotswold's eloquent argument."

An argument I almost wished I had never made! I think I would have preferred to throw science out the window to see whether a wooden stake would succeed where six lead bullets had failed. But I said nothing, frozen into inaction by the incalculable threat that rose up from the London night, its shadow darkening the entire world.

"We must do as Professor Cotswold suggested and study our patient to learn her strengths and vulnerabilities," Shaftbury said. "And her strengths—if only some of her strange, superhuman strengths could be transferred to our race, think of what it would mean for Britain!"

The slightly mad look in Shaftbury's eyes did not escape my attention—or Dr. Van Helsing's.

"Be careful what you wish for," Van Helsing warned. "You do not want to end up like Faust. One must never try to bargain with the Devil."

"That could never happen. Faust was *German*," Shaftbury said with a sharp laugh, amused at his own grim humor.

18

Experiments

JANUARY 15, 1880 (1:00 A.M.). What a bloody awful affair this has turned out to be! And God knows I had enough blood on my hands before this . . .

But enough self-pity, the most ignoble of emotions to commandeer one's intellect. The only escape for me is through work. And since there are no rocks for me to split open in search of fossils, I have no recourse but to pick up my pen and detail the most despicable of what has turned out to be a long series of despicable episodes.

I should never have let Darwin talk me into serving on the Special Committee.

I should never have come to London.

But here are the facts, the narrative, the accumulated detail of fear and violence that characterizes this enterprise. When our souls have grown sick with our clumsy, cruel, stumbling attempts to find the truth, we can take refuge in the easy harbor of *what happened*, recounting deeds that can, like the words of some poem, be taken to mean anything we want or nothing at all.

Feeling numb, the way I do when I haven't had enough sleep, and ragged and frayed, as if I had indulged in too much coffee, I went to join the others at the Vicarage the morning after our encounter with the vampire.

The remains of our committee gathered in the warden's office. Blackley looked more animated and alert than he had a right to, perhaps with the aid of some self-prescribed medication. Lord Shaftbury was impatient to gain access to the secrets behind the vampire's power to defy death and to read men's thoughts—indeed, to control them. Lucian and Palmer both looked grim.

Reverend Clarkson was, of course, absent. His condition was very grave, Blackley said.

Equally ominous was Dr. Van Helsing's mysterious absence. A policeman was sent around to Van Helsing's hotel, but there was no sign of the Hungarian. The policeman returned carrying Van Helsing's carpetbag, which Shaftbury accepted with distaste, as if he might contract a social disease from touching the portmanteau. We all regarded the carpetbag as a bad talisman. Van Helsing never went anywhere without it. Although no one said it out loud, we all feared the vampires had gotten hold of their nemesis. (I later overheard Palmer give orders to search the city for Van Helsing. No doubt his corpse will be found crumpled in some attic, his body drained of its blood. While I never overcame my instinctive suspicion of the Hungarian, I am sorry for the fate that most likely befell him.)

Shaftbury decreed that we would proceed with the examination.

We followed the warden down the dark, cramped passageway, the stone walls streaked with dampness. We passed through a series of doors, either steel-barred or solid oak ribbed in iron, each opened with one of the big metal keys on the warden's ring. Kate Woolf was incarcerated in a dungeon at the far end of the secret prison's deepest gallery. The room was roughly twenty feet by forty feet and divided almost in half with a wall of metal bars inset into the stone floor below and the masonry ceiling above. A dozen wooden chairs had been arranged for us on our side of the room. The only furnishings on the prisoner's side were a crude wooden cot in the middle of the space, with a bare mattress and a single blanket, and a battered bucket for a chamber pot.

The prisoner sat on the cot staring at the floor between her legs as we filed through the door. She wore the same clothing as when she was captured, the blouse and skirt stiff with dried and blackened blood. Even in the light of the flickering gas jets, it was evident her body had managed to heal most of the damage done to her skull. The slightly irregular arc to the cranium indicated the repair was either imperfect or as of yet incomplete. The skin over the head wound had a pinkish tinge, like the skin of a baby, and was covered with a downy growth of hair.

The warden said the vampire had been kept alone in her cell at the far end of an otherwise empty corridor. The jailers had not so much as looked in on her since we'd left her there the night before, mindful of Kate Woolf's previous escape. The guards had spent the night playing cards, as instructed, rotating at the prescribed interval, all without incident.

Woolf did not look up or give any indication she was aware of us.

Lord Shaftbury spoke first, calling out in his stentorian minister's voice, as if summoning her to the bar in court: "Kate Woolf."

She did not respond.

"Kate Woolf!"

She seemed about to speak, but instead a long strand of viscous drool spilled out of her mouth and fell toward the floor.

"I would hardly expect the brain to recover after such trauma," Blackley said.

"That will have little bearing on the tests Van Helsing outlined for us last night," Shaftbury said.

He held the carpetbag out to Palmer, who accepted it after the slightest hesitation.

"Open the cell."

One of the two guards who accompanied us—both hulking men who had the look of violence about them—inserted a heavy iron key into the door. They were to stand by with truncheons in case things got out of hand. Palmer went into the cell, followed at close hand by the guards. The rest of us trailed behind.

Up close, the vampire's head wound looked worse than it had from a distance. I could see her pulse beating against the pink skin. I wanted to press my fingers against the wound to see if the underlying structure was bone or the soft cartilagelike substance one finds in a baby's head. The physical examination, it seemed, would have to wait.

"The unholy undead are said to be unable to withstand the sight of a crucifix," Shaftbury said. "Let us begin there, Chief Inspector."

Palmer rooted around in Van Helsing's bag and came out with a crucifix. He held it by its chain and swung it back and forth in front of the vampire's eyes. She paid it no notice, not even when it was moved closer and closer until at last it rested against her forehead.

"She appears to be in a semicomatose state," Blackley said.

"Still, the crucifix should have some effect," Lucian added.

"Only if vampires are truly supernatural creatures," I said. "I have doubted that all along. Whatever it is that gives them their powers and their strange needs, I would wager it has more to do with science than superstition."

"Try the holy water," Shaftbury said, paying no heed to my words.

Palmer went into the bag and came out with a silver-clad flask of holy water Van Helsing had claimed came from a font in St. Peter's in Rome. The policeman unscrewed the cap and threw a splash in the vampire's face. She startled a little at this, but the reaction was no more than would be expected if you threw cold water in anybody's face. The caustic reaction Van Helsing had led us to expect—an agonizing searing, as if vitriol had been poured on naked flesh—didn't happen.

Palmer found a strand of garlic at the bottom of the carpetbag, which partly explained the bad odor it gave off. With the jailers standing at the ready with their truncheons, he draped it around Kate Woolf's shoulders. She continued to stare at the floor in front of her.

"This is extraordinary," Shaftbury said. "Could it be because she is unaware of what is happening to her?"

"If supernatural laws governing a vampire's existence make it unable to tolerate exposure to crosses, holy water, and garlic, why would mental awareness play any role?" I said. "If you are asleep and I hold a flaming torch against your hand, will it not burn you?"

"An excellent point," Blackley said.

"Then what of the things Van Helsing told us about these creatures?"

"Folk tales," I answered, "uneducated and inadequate attempts to explain the mysterious unknown, not through observation and experimentation, but through recourse to fear and superstition."

"And yet you yourself now admit the existence of vampires."

"Yes, although I still have very little idea what these creatures are, besides possessed with unnatural strengths and the compulsion to feed off human blood. I certainly have seen nothing to make me believe vampires are the risen dead, that they sleep in coffins containing a few handfuls of the dirt of their native soil. Kate Woolf doesn't seem to feel the need to crawl into a coffin."

"But she does possess extraordinary powers," Shaftbury said in a frankly admiring tone. "These vampires have superhuman strength and the ability to withstand being stabbed and shot. They even seem to be able to reach into men's minds to read and control their thoughts."

"True enough," I agreed.

"And what of the idea that vampires live forever, unless a stake is driven through their hearts?"

"That is difficult to imagine, yet the subject of immortality is an interesting one. I do not believe any living creature governed by nature could be truly immortal, and yet a being with a body possessing such unusual capabilities for regeneration could live to a great age. Growing old is nothing more than the slow and progressive wearing out of the body. The back goes, the knees, the organs. Good nutrition, exercise, proper medical care, and luck can make the aging process occur more slowly in some people than in others, but it still happens. My guess—and it is only a guess—is that vampires age much more slowly. So perhaps they do live longer than ordinary human beings."

"For how long? One hundred years?" Shaftbury asked.

"Possibly much longer, at least in theory."

"Unlocking such a secret would be like discovering the fountain of youth," Shaftbury said.

"I'm not sure the world would be a better place if people lived forever," Lucian said.

"It certainly would be more crowded," Blackley said.

At this, Kate Woolf looked up through her tangle of matted hair and smiled.

"I will live *forever*," she said triumphantly.

Only by grabbing the jailers' arms did Shaftbury manage to keep them from coming down on the vampire's head with their truncheons.

"This is most incredible," Blackley said. Then, to Woolf: "Can you hear and understand me?"

"Clear as a bell, governor, although I have a bit of a headache, courtesy of Professor Cotswold."

She gave me a look but continued to smile. I guessed my prospects would be dim if Kate Woolf succeeded in escaping from the Vicarage a second time. I had the most uncomfortable feeling she was inside my head with me, listening to my thoughts. At last I broke her stare and looked away to escape the sensation.

"I have a few questions to pose, Miss Woolf," Palmer said. "Things will go much better for you if you choose to answer properly and politely."

"You want to know all about how I became what I am."

"Exactly."

"It's a somewhat involved story. Perhaps you gentlemen should sit down."

We got our seats and sat down to hear Kate Woolf's extraordinary story. Since I have a transcript of her remarks, I won't bother repeating what she said here. I will only say that I had a very poor appreciation of the complexity and nuance of Miss Woolf's situation. It would not be entirely accurate to say I pitied her, for a large part of her fate was her own making—as it is for us all. Still, only the hardest of hearts would be able to escape feeling sympathy for the poor wretch's plight. No one is immune from misfortune, yet it is only when we come into contact with someone who has been dealt a truly bad hand that we realize the triviality and smallness of our own problems. None of this detracts from the danger she posed. A moment's delay on my part might have cost us all our lives.

It seemed Van Helsing had gotten only one detail about vampires right: They are burned by daylight and have to stay indoors as long as the sun is in the sky. During a brief consultation in the warden's office after she gave us her deposition, Shaftbury expressed the desire to find out for certain whether the vampire had been truthful on the point. To this end, he proposed an experiment.

Blackley objected, though not strenuously, on humanitarian grounds.

Shaftbury overruled him. Woolf was destined for execution regardless, due to the consequence of her crimes. Whether she was hanged or killed through exposure to sunlight mattered not at all. Furthermore, Shaftbury had been granted plenipotentiary powers in the matter. This was not the United States. The vampire's life was in Shaftbury's hands, and he had already made up his mind to conduct this final experiment.

I remained silent during the debate. Woolf's story had well apprised me of the danger vampires presented to humanity.

We had an obligation to mankind to learn the vampire's weaknesses so that they might be exploited in the defense of our own race.

We returned to Woolf's cell. She was standing with her back to the corner, regarding us warily through the bars. I have no doubt she knew exactly what we planned to do to her.

As I looked up, I saw for the first time the evidence of hinges and a trapdoor from the floor above, hidden among the shadows of the beamed ceiling. It seemed the cell in which the vampire was incarcerated served as the pit where the bodies of the hanged dropped upon execution in the room above. And unlike the dungeon, the gallows room was part of an old tower that remained open to the sky, though its top was heavily barred against possible escape.

"You condemn me to an unusually cruel death," the vampire cried out at the sound of a latch being undone above her.

"If so, it will be no more than you deserve," Shaftbury said coldly.

The halves to the trapdoor fell heavily open.

"Father, forgive them," she said under her breath in a horrified whisper.

The result was far from dramatic. It was late in the afternoon on a heavily overcast London day. There was not, it seemed, enough sun to cause much discomfort. The vampire stood in the center of the cell, her head thrown back, her upturned face a terrified mask.

The fear went out of her face, replaced with relief, and then defiance. The sun, it seemed, had no more power over her than the crucifixes the women brandished the first time she was captured (see deposition transcript).

The vampire began to laugh, quietly at first, then almost hysterically.

"Of course, you realize the only reason I am still in this prison is because I thought the sun would burn me. Now that I know it cannot hurt me, there is nothing to keep me from bending apart the bars and—"

She clapped her hands over her face as if in sudden horror. "It burns," she moaned lowly. "It *burns!*"

Her whimper transformed into an agonized howl at the increasing reaction. Although I don't have the evidence to confirm it, I believe some altered substance in the vampire's epidermal cells oxidizes rapidly when exposed to ultraviolet light. She began to shriek as her flesh spontaneously combusted, her entire body bursting into brilliant flame, as if she were a torch soaked in kerosene and touched with a match. She ran frantically back and forth across her cell, but there was no place to hide and no one to help her.

"For the love of God, shut the trapdoor!" Lucian shouted.

I believe it would have been more merciful to let her die, but Shaftbury did not have to decide. The vampire flung herself against the bars and began to pull them apart, bending them back as if they were thin strips of copper. I was raising my Colt when she came through the bars, but she collapsed after a single step. Her body was burned black, the flames having reduced it to a thin layer of charred muscle over a skeletal form. The sickly sweet smell of burnt flesh and hair was almost too much to bear.

"Behold, the vampire's Achilles heel is sunlight," Shaftbury said, as if speaking to himself.

Kate Woolf's right hand opened and closed.

"It is still alive!" Shaftbury exclaimed.

The hand, reduced to a burned claw, tiny in size but representing immense menace, extended an inch toward Shaftbury and grasped at the open air. It was at once a pathetic, useless gesture and yet it displayed an indomitable hostility. Any pity I felt disappeared as I realized the vampire's body could repair itself over time, left in darkness to regenerate, thirsting madly for the living human blood it craved to quench its inhuman thirst. Our species is no match for the vampire's superhuman resiliency. Its adaptive advantages were now beyond dispute. If there were many more like Kate Woolf, mankind could not help but become the cattle upon which the vampires fed, wiping us out—or, far worse, keeping us penned up like livestock, fattening us for slaughter.

"Shoot it!" Blackley exclaimed.

I shook my head. That had been tried. A bullet would slow the creature, not kill it.

As the vampire continued to grab at the air in front of Shaftbury's leg, I dashed out the door and down the claustrophobic hall toward the jailers' day room. There, I snatched a fire axe off the wall and retraced my steps, my footfalls echoing against the damp masonry.

The first thing I noticed when I came back through the door was that the guards and committee members were staring off into space, dazed expressions on their faces. Only Blackley had the power of mind to resist her. He was backing toward the door, his hands pressed over his ears, muttering, "No, no, no," as if to keep the vampire's suggestion from taking root in his mind.

Shaftbury knelt down before Kate Woolf and offered the inside of his wrist to the charred figure splayed on the floor before him.

The vampire drew back its lips, burned and cracked, revealing two incisors dropping down from the upper jaw. In contrast to the charred flesh, the fangs seemed very white indeed.

"Shaftbury, get back!"

He slowly turned his head, giving me a stupid, uncomprehending look.

I shoved him out of the way, but found myself quite unexpectedly standing over Lady Olivia Moore. She looked up at me piteously, silently begging me for help. She was so thankful I had come to save her, so grateful—if only I would hold out my hand, she would kiss it to show her gratitude. . . .

I knew I was looking down on an illusion, and yet Olivia was so helpless and lovely—how could I resist the sweetness of her desperate begging words?

On a deeper level, far down in my mind, in a place the

vampire could not reach, I somehow comprehended that my only chance of survival was to devise a way to block the vampire from my mind. It was at that moment the nonsense doggerel penned by Charles Dodgson—mathematics professor at Oxford, part-time cryptographer, part-time writer under the pen name Lewis Carroll—floated to the surface of my mind.

> *Beware the Jabberwock, my son!*
> *The Jaws that bite, the claws that catch!*
> *Beware the Jubjub bird, and shun*
> *The frumious Bandersnatch!*

What providence! Surely that bit of verse was the only thing that kept me from surrendering my life to the lovely mirage before me on the prison floor. The axe felt real enough in my hands—the curving ash handle against my fingers, heavier in my right hand than my left because of the steel blade.

> *He took his vorpal sword in hand*
> *Long time the maxome foe he sought—*
> *So rested he by the Tumtum tree,*
> *And stood awhile in thought.*

I had used an axe to cut down many trees when I was growing up, and I still prefer to chop my own firewood. It is an excellent tonic for the lethargy of winter, when men tend to spend too much time inactive indoors, breathing stale air.

> *And, as in uffish thought he stood,*
> *The Jabberwock, with eyes of flame,*
> *Came wiffling through the tulgey wood,*
> *And burbled as it came!*

The vampire begged and cajoled, whispered and sang, wiffled and burbled, trying to get inside my head. But I furiously concentrated on Dodgson's words, raising the axe high above my head, the simple tool infinitely more real than the power and immortality Kate Woolf was promising me.

> *One, two! One, two! And through and through*
> *The vorpal blade went snicker-snack!*
> *He left it dead, and with its head*
> *He went galumphing back.*

I brought the vorpal blade down with all my strength, snicker-snack, and stood panting and drenched in sweat, staring down at the thing I had done.

The Jabberwock was dead—and with it the vampire, the unfortunate young woman named Kate Woolf.

PART V

✦

The Vampire

19

The Meek

Kate Woolf deposition, dated January 14, 1880. The transcription was initialed A.T., for Algernon Turnor, Benjamin Disraeli's secretary.

"Make yourselves as comfortable as you can. I regret I am unable to offer you better hospitality, but no doubt you understand. You want to know—it is not necessary to ask—the story of how I came to be as you see me now. I will tell you and truly. You do not believe me? Bring a Bible, and I will swear an oath. And if you would leave it with me, I would read it and take comfort in its words. Does not the good book teach that the meek will inherit the earth?"

(Enigmatic smile.)

"If I am unable to tell you everything you want to know, it is only because there are parts I don't understand myself, but I will explain as best I can. I haven't the education to understand the science of my condition, as Professor Cotswold would like to know. And I do not know whether it is possible to divide the vampire's power from its terrible Hunger, Lord Shaftbury's secret question."

(S. asks how the vampire knows their names. Is it a demonic trick?)

"I know your names and more than that, sir. I can read

your innermost thoughts, if I try. That is how I came to see the bridled ambition that burns within you, my lord.

"I can also see what you think of me. One glance, and you all think you know me, as if people were simple things and easily categorized as hats or types of bird. You would despise me as a fallen woman. And for being a vampire, and the things I have done because of it. And yet you respect my powers. At least I *think* you do. Fear and respect smell an awfully lot alike. You admire my ability to withstand bullets and steel, my power to read your thoughts. Power is a wonderful thing, gentlemen. It has a curious transforming effect on people. One moment you're a Jezebel, a member of an invisible, untouchable caste. But then quick as you can say Bob's your uncle, you learn to have a sobering respect for me. You realize there are even things about the hated vampire you admire. Do not shake your heads, gentlemen. Like the eye of the Almighty, I see all.

"Am I ashamed to have sold my body? Of course I am, but I came to my way of life for my own reasons. It made me my own master. I am hardly the first poor woman to find herself in such circumstances. It could happen to anybody, even Lady Olivia, who is so precious to you both, Captain Lucian and Professor Cotswold."

(Lucian reacts with justified anger.)

"You men are such hypocrites," the vampire cried. "How do you know what life is like for someone like me? Men may do as they please. If your soul yearns for adventure, the entire world is your oyster. Lucian and Blackley, you went to India. Professor Cotswold has been around the world, looking for knowledge. Lord Shaftbury, nothing has stopped you from pursuing your unquenchable thirst for power. But what of a churchman's daughter, condemned to a life of genteel poverty in a deadly dull Midlands village parish? My father is rector of St. Thomas Church in—well, you can find that out easily enough for yourself, if you're interested. Ask Mr. Palmer if you are curious. I can see that he knows."

(Palmer does not acknowledge whether this is true.)

"I inherited my passionate nature from my mother. She died when I was a young girl. My mother wrote poetry, filling notebook after notebook in a neat feminine hand, I'm told. I was never able to read her literary creations. My father, you see, is the sort of man who finds any expression of emotion distasteful. He burned Mother's notebooks when she died. The great expressions of her heart and soul—her dreams, her secret desires, no doubt her disgust at finding herself trapped in the boring existence of a provincial vicar's wife—fed the coal fire in my father's parlor. Little wonder I grew up learning to take affection where I could find it.

"And you gentlemen would condemn me. We come into this world as a new bolt of cloth, leaving it to others to cut and stitch our lives to suit patterns known only in their own misshapen hearts. Why blame the dress when any fault in the tailoring lies with the maker? And what of the Creator's role? Is He not the ultimate tailor of our lives and days? Did He not shape me to suit His purpose? That is the question Reverend Clarkson would have wanted to ask today. Such a cold look, Dr. Blackley! You think me a modern-day Caligula, yet I did nothing to harm Clarkson. Indeed, I spared his life. Do you know what he was thinking when I snatched him up by the coat and made ready to sink my teeth into his neck? He was thinking about my soul! He wondered if the soul of the creature about to snuff out his life was beyond redemption. Think of it. There's a model Christian for you.

"But what of God? Am I so different from you? We all are sinners, the extent differing but in degree and detail. If you believe in God—as do I—then do you also believe becoming a vampire was part of God's will for me? I have prayed for God to lead me not into temptation, yet temptation is the only thing I find whichever way I turn. Is it possible I am somthing other than a monster? Could I be an agent of God's will? We are all in God's hands. I am no different. The things I have done repulse you, and they repulse me, but I did not come to them of my own free will.

"What am I? Why am I? I want to know the answers to these questions as much as you. We know you cannot kill me. If I am immortal, is it possible I am a messenger of God? Maybe I have become like the seraphim, an immortal burning one, burning with the twin flames of passion and Hunger. The choirs of angels listed in the Bible—the seraphim, cherubim, thrones, dominations, virtues, powers, principalities, archangels, angels—may be joined by a tenth: the choir of *vampires*. And if we are akin to archangels, cherubim, thrones, and powers, what message do we bring man? Or is our purpose to bring mankind to Judgment Day? Then I am a fallen angel of the Apocalypse, wandering the night drunk on the blood of saints, come to earth to inaugurate seven years of tribulation. I join you in hoping—in *praying*—this is not the case.

"Jesus came into the world to save sinners, not the righteous. I am a sinner in so many ways. Surely Reverend Clarkson is right in thinking there is still a chance for redemption for me."

20

✧

Bach's Prelude No. 1 in C Major

I MIGHT NOT be here today had I not been bringing flowers to church and stopped to listen to the new organist practice. I remember the experience very well. I was putting flowers on the altar and all at once I was standing there, looking at the light on the cut-glass vase, entirely intoxicated with the beauty pouring into the air.

"The music was Johann Sebastian Bach. I have always adored listening to Bach, which is like having God Himself whisper into your ear. But I did not merely listen to the music that day: I felt it deep inside in a way that was entirely new. In my fifteen years I had never experienced anything so intense and wonderful. It was an instant of perfect bliss that released the passions that had been welling up from my heart with increasing intensity.

"I thought Dietrich Morse was responsible for a long time, but I have decided that I was mistaken. Beauty flows through the brilliant artist, but he does not actually possess it. The essence of beauty belongs to the Almighty alone.

"But I have run ahead of myself. I need to introduce Dietrich Morse, the new music director at our parish. His predecessor, the consumptive Vincent Lytton, had gone away to Italy to recover his health and died there. He is no doubt buried in a sunny Umbrian cemetery. I have always loved music, but Mr. Lytton's playing never impressed me much. The light of his talent was dim indeed compared to his successor. Dietrich Morse was a consummate master of the organ, which I remain convinced is the mightiest and most expressive musical instrument ever invented. Seated at the keyboard, Dietrich would make it roar like Lucifer or sing as sweetly as the angels. His hands would fly across the manuals as swift as swallows plucking insects from the evening air. At the same time, his feet would dance across the pedals, so that he seemed to have not two hands but four, like some Hindu god. Every note, every passage, every flight of improvisational fugue was perfect. Even the dullards in our parish realized we had something special in Dietrich Morse. People would walk out of church, the postlude thundering behind them, and express amazement that we had been blessed with such genius in our humble parish. Certainly his talents suited him to a position at Westminster or Canterbury.

"Dietrich was no longer a young man when I heard him play for the first time. By the time he came to St. Thomas, his long black hair and beard had become shot through with gray. His eyes were an almost translucent shade of blue and typically had a faraway look, as if he was preoccupied with things beyond the dross of the ordinary world.

"I asked my father to arrange for Master Morse to instruct me in the piano. I was never better than an average musician, but I worshiped the air Dietrich breathed and yearned to bask in the reflected brilliance of his passionate genius. And so it came to pass that at four o'clock on a Tuesday in June, I presented myself to Master Morse for my first music lesson.

"I sat at the keyboard, Dietrich on a chair behind me to the right. He asked me to play something—anything I wished. I chose Bach's Prelude No. 1 in C Major, the first piece in 'The Well Tempered Clavier,' and the easiest. I managed to get through it without error, and I even managed to put a certain amount of emotion into my playing. Pleased with myself, I looked back at Master Morse for a sign of his approval. He was staring at me, a deep frown forcing his brow down over his eyes, so that he resembled the bust of Beethoven my father had sitting on the piano in the rectory parlor.

"I slid over to make room for him to sit beside me on the bench in order that he might illustrate a point or two about technique. The thrill I felt when his leg pressed against mine! Do not blush so, Captain Lucian. I promise not to be very explicit in my account.

"I noticed for the first time that Dietrich Morse's hands were amazingly delicate, his nails neatly trimmed and polished, like a gentleman's. In contrast to my own playing, depressing my fingers with somewhat mechanical deliberation, his hands danced across the keyboard as if each finger was animated by an intelligence and soul of its own. He played the same piece I had just presented, but there was little to compare between the two performances. Mine was crudely shaped from clay, his sharply cut and polished marble.

"When he finished, he looked down at me with burning blue eyes. He said something, but I cannot tell you what it was. My heart was pounding too loudly in my ears to hear. The prelude's aftertones seemed to hang in the air, shimmering around his face like a halo. In the next moment I was in his arms and he in mine, and together we made passionate music of an entirely different sort."

(P. protests there is no need for such scandalous detail.)

"But how can you understand what I have become if you do not understand what I was?"

(S. impatiently tells her to get on with it, no doubt anxious to hear about her experiences as a vampire. P. looks at S. and gives him a small shrug, as if to indicate it will be easier to let the madwoman tell the tale in her own fashion.)

"As I later learned, Dietrich Morse's willingness to work for small wages in our parish was not at all unconnected with his tendency to overwhelm girls and women with his passion. This was something of a cross for Dietrich to bear.

He did not wish to proceed from scandal to scandal, yet he seemed unable to escape trouble for long. Which was hardly surprising. You cannot escape your inner nature. Like me, Dietrich was a creature of his passion, and in many ways a slave to it.

"You can imagine how it ended for us. It was only a matter of time before we were found out. Dietrich lost his position, again, and left town in disgrace. As for me, I was packed off to live with an aunt and uncle in Colchester. My arrangements there proved unsatisfactory. Uncle Howell also had an eye for young girls, and found a niece of questionable character rather too much of a temptation to be resisted. While I found his attentions exceedingly distasteful, my only recourse to submitting would have been to bring the matter to my aunt Katharine's attention. I knew enough of human nature to guess she would likely blame me, already disgraced at a young age, rather than admit the harder truth about her husband.

"After an appropriate period of resistance, I gave in to my uncle. The business brought me little pleasure, I can assure you, but what was done was done. And worst of all, my uncle became totally besotted, his lust making him completely reckless. He would take me in the garden, in the carriage, or at night, in my room, while his wife sat downstairs sewing."

(L. interrupts the sluttish litany—and not a moment too soon!)

"Do not presume to tell *me* what is improper, Captain Lucian," the vampire said sharply. "Young women do not turn themselves into whores without help from men, who often escape any consequences. Perhaps one day men and women will be on somewhat more equal footing."

(Dr. B. urges her to continue. He has become transfixed with the story; his experiences as a physician have no doubt accustomed him to hearing the scandalous details of sybaritic lives.)

"My uncle made me pregnant."

(This proves too much for young Captain L.! He gasps

and jumps to his feet, looking helplessly around, seemingly unable to decide on the proper course. After a moment he re-takes his seat. The vampire patiently waits, as if knowing he has no recourse but to hear the rest of this sordid tale.)

"Despite my experience in certain matters, I was not the first to realize my condition. My aunt developed the odd habit of staring at my belly. At long last she took me into her parlor, sat me down, and demanded I make an accounting of myself. She summoned her husband, who of course denied everything. Neither my tears nor my aunt's rage could get him to admit the truth. He put my condition off on a soldier who had been staying in the neighborhood on leave from his regiment. The officer had, by then, decamped for Africa and was thus conveniently unavailable to deny the story.

"My belongings were put into trunks and I was put onto a train to London with a one-way ticket, a few bob in my purse, and instructions to never again show my face in Colchester. My aunt arranged for me to live in a home for girls in my particular sort of trouble. I didn't stay long. I lost the child and was put out on the street.

"Alone, friendless, nearly penniless—and I couldn't have been happier. London was the most wonderful place on earth to a girl from the provinces, a glittering, sophisticated city full of fancy ladies and handsome gentlemen on their way to balls and receptions. There was a hum to the place I could *feel*. I got the best lodging I could afford, in a barely re-spectable East End boardinghouse. I shared a single room with three other girls about my age, though none with as much finishing as I had, growing up in a rectory. We slept three of us in the single bed, the odd girl taking turns on the floor. It seemed like a grand adventure to me. I was young and filled with expectations, despite my disappointments. Such is the misguided glory of youth!

"I intended to find a position as a governess, but work was harder to come by than expected, especially for a girl with-out references. It wasn't long before my money was close to gone. I had heard other girls talk about the labor of last resort for desperate women in the city. While I had my own ideas about living the life of a glamorous courtesan, I was resolved to succeed in my original plan even if it meant resorting to subterfuge. With the help of a man I knew, I managed to obtain a supply of stationery belonging to a prominent family. The Osbournes had conveniently decamped to their plantation in Africa, and were, therefore, unavailable to consult concerning a certain young woman claiming to have worked for them. My forged letter of recommendation enabled me to get a position in a household in Mayfair."

(Vampire smiles.)

"This is hardly a reason for thinking 'Eureka!' My connection with Mayfair played a role in what I was to become, but it was only one piece in the puzzle. Causes are extremely difficult to assign. How are we to know that such-and-such is a result of *this,* when it might just as easily have been because of *that*? My position in Mayfair has as much to do with my status as a fallen woman as it does with my becoming a vampire.

"Some of you are no doubt acquainted with Nathan Brill, the Earl of Tesberry. I was hired to look after his son, Clifford. I am partial to children, as many women are, though I could take or leave young Clifford, a graceless, crude little lout who will no doubt fit in well with the other sons of lords at Eton or whatever prestigious school ends up saddled with him. I had even less affinity for his father, the Earl. He came into my room one night and raped me, tossing a gold sovereign on my bed by way of recompense.

"I can tell what you're thinking, Professor Cotswold: I *did* go to the authorities. I gave them the sovereign as evidence. For my trouble, I was threatened with prison for libeling the Earl of Tesberry. It goes without saying that I lost my position. I didn't even get the gold sovereign back. The police kept it.

"I couldn't agree with you more, Lord Shaftbury. I did only get what I deserved. After all, I had gotten the job through false pretenses, using stolen stationery to forge documents. That was when I began to think seriously about the merits of a life of ill fame. At least I would be paid for it. As it was, I was penniless and homeless in London, surrounded by people living in the most comfortable of circumstances. In my heart of hearts I did not see myself working at a modest and honest job until I could settle into a marriage with a clerk or minor bureaucrat. I wanted a grand house, beautiful gowns, rich jewelry, and a white carriage drawn by a matched team of horses, carrying me to the opera. London had done nothing but inflame the improvident passions I carried with me. And so I sought to make my fortune by the only means available.

"In brief, gentlemen, I surrendered to the obvious if not the inevitable fate, and became a whore. I had hoped to take a wealthy man as a lover, someone who would keep me in a town house and call on me for tea or when his wife was away visiting friends in the country. It did not occur to me I would end up taking a vampire as a lover. Is it not curious that my precipitous descent to ruination was the agency by which I have become so much more than merely mortal? The Bible is right: The meek *shall* inherit the earth. Look at me, lads. I am all the proof that any of you should require."

21

✧

The Music of the Spheres

I HAD MY sights set on the high life. I wanted to become the kept lady of a wealthy gentleman. I began working the streets, but I saved my money and bought a good dress, decent boots, and a cheap but acceptable necklace and earrings. Then, scrubbed clean, sprayed with perfume, my hair carefully done up, I presented myself to Madame Le Beau. She is not one of your first-rate madams—she is certainly no Contessa Saint-Simon—but it was a start. I met many fine gentlemen, and, unlike most of Le Beau's other girls, I could carry on a conversation without brutalizing the Queen's English or swearing like a sailor. Yes, I had great expectations at first.

"The work was almost a lark in the beginning. It was every bit as much fun as you are imagining, Dr. Blackley. But only at first. After a time, working in a brothel begins to wear on you physically as well as spiritually. The human soul can only take so much degradation, though perhaps my own debasement was what prepared me for the strange transformation that was to come.

"Madame Le Beau was an excellent businesswoman, and as such she realized the advantage of offering her customers something special. Her establishment specialized in the exotic and extreme. You could find the same sport at Contessa

162

Saint-Simon's house, but Madame Le Beau specialized in an altogether rougher sort of play. The name 'Hellfire Club' makes the Contessa's house sound like a fountainhead of damnation. Next to the brand of wickedness practiced at Le Beau's, the Hellfire Club's variety of sin seems almost innocently naughty.

"It was hard work. I would be up all night, whipping and being whipped, engaging in perversions even I could not speak of without blushing with shame. By the time I fell asleep in the weak early morning light, sore and exhausted, I would feel as faint as poor Captain Lucian looks at this moment. God designed the mind and body to withstand only so much. I had pushed myself to the extreme. I began smoking opium with a certain bishop who is a regular at Madame Le Beau's. Then Madame Le Beau introduced me to injections of tincture of cocaine as a means of waking myself up so I could start taking on another day's worth of customers. Before long I was injecting myself throughout the day and night, staying up sometimes for days on end. I used morphine to sleep.

"The hard use began to show in my face. That meant I would never work for the Contessa or attach myself to a wealthy benefactor. Eventually, it spelled an end for me at Madame Le Beau's. I was twenty-one but I looked twice my age. Madame Le Beau sold me to Angus MacGregor, a Scot whoremonger. His house was a far cry from Le Beau's, but still infinitely preferable to the street. The Scotsman had a lesser sort of clientele—merchants, barristers, even a smattering of tradesmen and servants from the better houses. One man I had become acquainted with during the brief period of my employment in Mayfair—a butler—became a regular customer. He was infatuated with me. He liked to say I had the manners of a lady, which appealed to him, and rather made me suspect he was in love with the lady he was employed to serve. He was like the rest of us, poor sod, trying to improve himself in the world without a clear idea how to go about it or, truth be known, much chance of making it out of his class.

"A time came when my caller didn't visit. This was strange, since it had been his habit to stop by every Monday evening, his regular night off, for a bounce on the bed. When he visited again, I could tell he'd been ill. He had a peculiar look in his eyes, as if he had a fever, and his skin was hot to the touch. It put me off a bit, to be perfectly honest. The worst thing that can happen to a girl who makes her living the way I did is to get a case of something catching. I know girls who've had their throats slit for giving one of their customers a social disease. Funny thing, though. He usually was keen to get to his business straight away and then talk a bit afterward, with a glass of whiskey. But this time he seemed to want to sit and talk.

" 'The most extraordinary thing has happened to me,' he said.

"I asked him what he meant, but he didn't say anything for the longest time. He sat staring at me, like the cat that ate the canary, silent as a mummy. I had a peculiar sensation in my stomach—a tingling, as if I was being pricked there by hundreds of tiny pins. I found myself sliding off the divan and getting onto my knees in front of him. He *made* me get on my knees like that, though I probably would have done it willingly enough if he'd asked me, because I was desperate for the money to buy a pipe of dreams. He got inside my head somehow and forced me to kneel in front of him.

" 'How would you like to have the power to make men do whatever you want?' he asked. 'To love you, to give you money, to do your bidding no matter what it may be?'

"I nodded. Who wouldn't like to have that kind of power?

" 'And would you like to live forever, Kate?' he asked. 'I don't mean in the other world, but in this one.'

"Who would not want to receive such a miraculous gift? To have power over men and immortality—to be like God. I nodded again. I don't know whether I realized what I was getting into. Of course, I *didn't* know. How could I? And yet on another level, in a way that it is possible to know something without knowing how you know, I had a sense of it. And still I nodded. Willingly, gentlemen. I was not forced into this. I somehow knew this would work where the other things I tried had failed, and that the result would be a magnificent flowering of all the passions bottled up in my heart, which not even years of prostitution and drug addiction had been able to kill. Perhaps passion is as immortal as the vampire, and it is the individual's sensuality that leads him toward its crimson secret, like a moth drawn to a flame, which is at once deadly and yet utterly irresistible.

"His hands were on my shoulders, drawing me to him. I remember feeling incredibly dreamy, as if I was heavily under the poppy's influence, though I hadn't had anything that night except a small absinthe. He pressed his lips against mine. My tongue felt something hard and sharp and out of place in his mouth, but I was unable to imagine what or even care. He kissed my eyes, my cheeks, my neck. I remember laughing softly as he sucked at the soft flesh in the hollow where my neck meets my shoulder. He blew on my moist skin there, his hot breath cooling me. I suddenly wanted him more than I had ever wanted a man. The dim outline of a melody floated through my mind. It was something I had not heard since those golden afternoon interludes with Dietrich Morse. It was Bach, of course, glorious Bach: the Prelude in C Major.

"I can remember wondering: What is happening to me? Magical, frightening, irresistible, sensual. It was all these things and more. Words do not exist to frame the pleasures and passions one enjoys with a vampire—and as one. Imagine hearing all the world's greatest symphonies at once, not as a jumble of noise but as a single explosion of bliss that fills you with total ecstasy. Your joy begins with the physical, but spills over into your entire being—your spirit, your mind—possessing you completely.

"There, trembling in the arms of a simple serving man, the universe was about to open itself to me. I was about to hear the music of the spheres, those first faint measures the tantalizing promise of what was to come.

"And then, without a word of warning or reassurance, he sank his teeth into my neck."

22

Retribution

SUCH LOOKS OF deliverance on your faces! Have you ever considered how little patience men have compared to women? This need to have what you want the instant you want it—with all due respect, it is your sex's most childlike attribute. Alas, it is not an endearing characteristic, in either little boys or men.

"I have reached the point of the story you wanted most to hear, yet do not forget this is my story. I shall tell it as I wish to tell it. Each of you has your own parochial interests. Professor Cotswold, you wish mainly to know about the process by which one becomes a vampire. It is the vampire's power that interests Lord Shaftbury. C.I. Palmer, you are concerned only about the criminal activity. Blackley, you, sir, are almost equally attracted and repulsed by the twisted nature of my tale, but more attracted than otherwise, I should think. Only Captain Lucian is completely horrified. Be forewarned about the remainder of my story. What has come so far is a lamb frolicking in the summer pasture compared to the rest of it."

(P. asks Woolf to name the man responsible for her becoming a vampire.)

"Unmask my benefactor, Chief Inspector? I am not at all sure I am prepared to reveal that part of my story. God knows I have inflicted my share of pain since making the change, but I see no reason to bring trouble down on someone who has given me a gift of inestimable value. But perhaps it would do no harm, for I am sure there is nothing you can do to hurt him. Let me consider it, and we shall see.

"You're staying to hear the rest of my story, Captain? Very well, then. I will continue.

"Unfortunately, Professor Cotswold, I cannot tell you in any great detail about the change that befell me after my lover sucked out my blood and the better measure of my life. At times, the individual involved in an experience is the least suited to describe what has happened. A baby knows birth firsthand, but we must leave it to others to detail the stages and actions that bring a child into the world. The birth of a fledgling vampire—for it is birth of a kind—is no different.

"I can tell you I was gripped by a terrible fever. For days I knew nothing of what was going on around me—neither where I was, nor how long I lay wasting away with my flesh on fire. I began to dream. At first my dreams made no sense, a jumble of images and fragments of scenes, the disordered product of a feverish mind. Imagine trying to extract the story from a manuscript made of random pages from a hundred novels. There was no pattern to the chaos of my fantasies, but with time a man emerged and gave a pattern to my fever dreams. I can see him perfectly in my mind—flowing black hair, full lips, a Roman nose, a strong brow, fierce burning eyes. At first he had only a face, but he gradually acquired a body. Though mostly hidden beneath purple robes, his form was as perfect as a marble statue. At length I realized he was no mere creation of my delirium but a guide to escort me as I walked along the edge of death on a path so narrow that one misstep would have meant my end.

"A hallucination, Professor? No, he was more than that. You are a man of faith. You believe in angels. This was my angel. Captain Lucian thinks I speak blasphemy. Then perhaps he was a fallen angel. Is your understanding of Creation too narrow to see the good and the bad are all part of the same vast clockwork devised by the Creator for His own unknowable purpose?

"My dark angel escorted me through the dangerous mountain labyrinth and down the arid passes, whispering poetry to me in a language I could understand only in my soul. I opened my eyes and found myself in the East End room my lover had rented for me to lie in during my change. You might think I would get up for a drink of water—I was *very* thirsty after who knows how many days of lying abed with the fever—or to look about me to reacquaint myself with the world. But I was too taken with the rich sensations washing over me to attend to mere physical concerns.

"Even someone completely indifferent to the passions of worldly experience—a monk, a nun, a Hindu hermit—would have been overwhelmed with the incredible richness and sensuality of what it is like to hear and smell and taste and see and feel as a vampire. Every sound, every color, the touch of a bit of velvet against my cheek—words are too small to describe how acutely we experience. This is what merely being alive in the world is like for a vampire.

"I knew then that I, an overly passionate village rector's daughter, had arrived at my destiny. And by such a strange and circuitous route! If it was not God's will, what was it?

"For the longest time I lay in bed, drinking it all in. The cotton sheet beneath my fingertips. The soft drum of the spider's feet against the bottom of the chair pushed against the far wall. The patter of rats playing in the wall. The conversation of people in the other apartments. The welter of cracks in the ceiling over my head in the dark room—I can see very well in the darkness, as all vampires can—the whole of the world around me was so much more complex and wonderful than I had realized. And touching, feeling, seeing, smelling—so sensual is the vampire's life that even these simple things are like making love.

"I also remember feeling a profound gratitude. I had been blessed with something very special and precious. My lover, my benefactor, my father in blood, how could I repay the kindness he had shown me? I owed him more than my life for he had given me more than life—an infinity of lifetimes was his gift, and the power to live them to a degree you mortals can scarcely comprehend.

"As I smelled food from the other apartments—potato soup, a bit of cold mutton from the rear of the building, an apple rotting in a desk drawer next door—I gradually became aware of my Hunger. I was ravenous. It was not ordinary food I craved but rather that most precious substance creatures of my sort require. This was my first experience with the Hunger. The headaches and nausea I felt if I went too long without my opium pipe were but an insubstantial whiff of wanting, a momentary craving, compared to the all-consuming need that filled me. The Hunger is more than a mere physical need. It was as if my immortal soul itself was in desperate need of sustenance. But still I do not come close to describing it! You cannot imagine the need, gentlemen.

"I sat up and swung my legs out of bed. I was as weak as a baby. Panic flooded into me. My Hunger was strong, but my body hardly had the strength to sit up: How could I hope to get what I needed to quiet the howling rising from within?

"There was a girl outside selling flowers. I could smell the fresh bouquets tied in fragrant bundles, gathered in a wicker basket. All of this I divined, gentlemen, without rising from my bed to look out the window. How did I know it was a child, a girl, with big brown eyes and a basket nearly as big as her? I *sensed* her, gentlemen, the way a hound apprehends the presence of the fox hidden in the covert, using mysterious perceptions designed by a God who created the tiger as well as the lamb.

"I got slowly to my feet, shaking, my balance uncertain, and looked about me, marveling that I could see so perfectly even though it was dark. My room was in what had once been a fine house. Now, the only signs of its former greatness were the decorative molding where the walls joined the ceiling and a fireplace with a carved marble mantel, cracked from age or misuse by an angry drunken tenant. How sad the remnants of former glory we find hidden within the dross and refuse of life! The wall next to the bed was pitted with holes my fists had made during my febrile seizures.

"I walked to the window and pulled back the moth-eaten curtain an inch or two. She was there—the flower girl—just as I had known she would be, importuning passersby to buy a penny's worth of flowers. Poor child. She was hungry, too, and the people ignored her offer to sell them a small handful of fragrance and beauty. It was then that I realized the sweetness I breathed in with every breath was only partly from the violet nosegays. It was her blood that smelled so sweetly to me—as fresh and new as flowers brought from the Haymarket less than an hour before.

"Merely sensing my craving was enough to cause the girl to look in my direction. She could not see me. I remained hidden behind the dirty curtain in my unlighted room, unsteady, hungry, filled with fear. I somehow knew I could use the power of my thoughts to bring her to my door to meet my need. Spare me the cold looks and even colder thoughts, gentlemen. I am not the monster you think me. I could have had the child into my room and drained her to the dregs in half an instant, but I resisted. For perhaps the first time in my life, I found the strength to resist the urge to surrender what would have been a most delicious experience.

"This, gentlemen, is the true measure of the power of the vampire. I did not kill the child, though I knew it would have brought me pleasure beyond anything I had ever experienced.

"I waited. I cannot say I waited patiently, but I managed to hold the Hunger at bay just a little bit longer while I waited for the sort of person to come along that I could drain of blood without regret. A most underappreciated emotion—regret. Is there a more persistent source of emotional pain than regret for what we did, or should have done but didn't?

"Fortunately, I did not have to wait long. I heard footsteps coming down the street. A great many footsteps, to be more accurate—men, women, children, fat, thin, young, old. The things you can tell about someone from the sound of their footsteps! These particular footsteps were quite familiar as I heard them enter the house and pound up the stairs. I somehow knew that my first communion as an immortal was in the process of delivering itself to me. I crabbed my way to the door. My head was pounding, or maybe it was just the sound of a big red fist beating upon the door. How my jaw ached! My blood teeth were pushing their way through the bone in my upper gum for the first time, splitting me from the inside out. The door swung open. It was not locked. And a good thing, too, because I doubt my fingers could have turned the skeleton key in the latch.

"Angus MacGregor, big as a house, angry as a bull, filled the doorway, side-to-side as well as up and down.

" 'Where ha' you been, ye bloody cow?' he roared.

"I was not ready when he hit me, though I should have been, for beatings were the chief type of authority Angus knew how to exercise over his girls. He caught me off balance—my balance was precarious enough—knocking me to the floor. He kicked me in the belly, sending me rolling toward the bed. Before I knew it he had grabbed me by an arm and thrown me against the wall.

" 'I wager you've been laying up here, hitting the pipe like a stinking Chinaman,' he said. 'You owe me, lass. You owe me for the lads you would have had, had you been at the house, making your living on your back proper like. You're going to work off the debt, but first you'll get the thrashing you so richly deserve. It'll help ye remember not to run off again, assuming you survive.'

"Angus's hands were huge, like the rest of him, with big scarred knuckles. He did not employ rough boys to keep the peace in his house, you may know. If there was anybody that needed being clobbered, Angus did it himself and saved the expense. He drew back his fist, fixing to knock me into next week. I think I was as surprised as he when my small hand shot out and grabbed his wrist before he could strike. That's when his eyes went cold and dead, like a serpent's. Whatever happened then was fair enough for me, because it was plain as the nose on my face Angus intended to beat me to death. As God is my witness, gentlemen, what I did to Angus Mac-Gregor, I did in self-defense. If he'd had the strength to turn the tables on me, I'd be sleeping in my grave now instead of him."

(Kate Woolf pauses and looks at Lord S., who finally nods, as if agreeing with the contention she is innocent of whatever happened.)

"So I stand there, Angus's great tree-trunk of an arm caught in my tiny fist. It took him a moment to recover, but then he tried to pull himself free. But his arm stayed put. Mighty Angus MacGregor, who had once gone forty rounds bare-knuckled in a heavyweight bout, lacked the strength to overcome me! Angus brought his head sharply forward, smashing his brow into mine, like a ram butting heads with a rival. I saw a moment of bright light but felt no pain. Angus MacGregor was somewhat the worse for it. If I hadn't held him up, he would have dropped like a felled oak. He recovered quick enough. His years in the ring had made him as used to getting beatings as giving them. He grunted and tried to pull free again, but he was caught snug as a badger in a trap. The harder he struggled, the tighter I held him, until the anger in his face became pain. I swear I did not mean to do it to him. There was a snap, a sharp snap, like someone breaking a piece of dry wood. That's when he began to howl. I'd broken his arm.

"It was then that I *saw* the other girls the whoremonger had killed—girls who crossed him badly enough, or had the misfortune of running afoul of him when he was drunk or in an ill temper. He'd beaten three to death. One he'd strangled. He'd slit another's throat. There were more, but I couldn't stand being in his brute mind long enough to find out. The desire burning within me was sharpened by a sudden taste for retribution.

"I threw him against the wall, filled with a sudden exultation. In that moment, I felt as if I were a part of God's own divine justice. The brute was about to receive his reward.

"My blood teeth came down out of my upper gum with a sort of click, Professor Cotswold. They are very sharp. I was careful to keep my tongue back so I didn't cut myself. My mouth was already filled with the warm, salty taste of my own blood.

"Angus begged me with his eyes, but by then I couldn't have shown him mercy if I'd had a mind to—which I most certainly did not. The Hunger had grown too strong in me to resist its insistent demand. I grabbed his thick red hair and jerked his head cruelly to the side, exposing the skin on his dirty neck.

"It was blind instinct that told me what to do next.

"I will not try to describe the ecstasy that flooded into me with the first taste of mortal blood. I heard Angus moan beneath me. I realized he was sharing my bliss, even though I was draining him of his life. I know, in the way that vampires know unusual things without understanding how or why, that I did not need to drink much of MacGregor's blood to satisfy my want. Yet the blood was so delicious to me, at once so exciting and deeply satisfying, that I did not want to stop drinking from the well of life. Why stop myself from enjoying the immortal wine that flowed from this fountain? I continued to drink swallow after swallow of Angus Mac-Gregor's blood as he slumped to the floor, drinking it even though I knew I was killing him a little more with each mouthful, drinking until there was nothing left to drink.

"When I was finished with him, I stood up, my body and mind singing as if the sacred vibrations of the planets and stars were alive within me and I in them. I looked down at Angus. His body had a sunken look around the eyes and a slight pucker to his thick lips.

"Perhaps you think Angus did not deserve to die for his crimes, at least not at my hands, with no judge to pronounce the verdict and a proper hangman to execute the sentence. Be that as it may, I will tell you what I think about the death of Angus MacGregor. I looked down on his crumpled body, only a few minutes earlier so large, so animated with life, and I felt exactly *nothing*. I felt no more remorse than I would feel stepping on a spider.

"And then, my dear gentlemen, I wiped the blood off my face and went out into the night in search of more."

23

Oranges

THUS I COMMENCED my career as a vampire in earnest. The rough life I'd lived in London provided the perfect education. I had the skills to be quite at ease with what I had to do. The streets have everything I need, and a pretty dress and an easy smile are all I use to get them. I did not return to Madame Le Beau's establishment. That, I feared, would have led to unpleasant complications.

"Professor Cotswold is wondering about my hunting practices.

"Dr. Van Helsing has you convinced I creep into bedrooms like a succubus to prey on the helpless as they sleep. Pure slander. Until the unfortunate episodes last night, when I reacted out of self-defense, I have never taken an unwilling lover—for they are lovers, the men who feed my Hunger. And I assure you they do not suffer. The vampire shares her bliss with her partner. I am particularly well qualified to testify on this point, gentlemen. While I was still mortal, I experienced for myself this most unique brand of intercourse. Had I not been willing to proceed to the deeper level and undergo the great change, I would have been no worse for the experience after regaining my strength—and in the bargain I had enjoyed a level of pleasure most humans never know.

"You know I am capable of killing. What happened last

night was, as I said, an act of self-defense. But I will not lie and say I have not killed before. Angus was the first. After that, I killed because I could not control the Hunger. The rush of ecstasy one gets is so incredibly intense—it is impossible to stop. As my strength grew, so did my will. I learned to slow the act, to savor it, to linger over the delirious pleasure each swallow of this immortal communion brought me.

"For the past week or two I have been experimenting with not killing the people who feed me. Though I feed at least once nightly, I let several of my lovers live as a way of proving to myself a vampire is not compelled to kill. Indeed, I have concluded it is unwise to kill. What Professor Cotswold is thinking is exactly right: The survival chances for a vampire who kills his or her hosts are not as strong as they are for the vampire who is discreet and quiet in his habits. I doubt I will continue to kill after last night."

(Vampire laughs, though it clearly is no laughing matter.)

"After all, gentlemen: You see where killing has gotten me.

"Ah, yes, Captain Lucian, your moral argument is also appropriate. It is indeed wrong to take another life. At first I could not help myself, but now I agree that it would put an indelible stain on my soul to continue the murderous behavior of my fledgling nights. What's that, Captain? My soul is already indelibly stained? Could you not say the same about us all? We are all of us sinners, since man's fall from grace. The difference is in grace and redemption. But perhaps I am beyond that. And perhaps you are, too. I pray that is not the case for either of us.

"To this I would only add, gentlemen, that we vampires are hardly the only ones who resort to lethal violence, depriving others of their lives. Only one lover have I given the change, bringing him across the border separating the world of mortal and vampire. A handsome man adored by many women in the London theatre world. The mob chased poor Edmund Castle into an abandoned house on the heath and burned him alive. So pray do not look on me with such an air of high moral authority, Captain. There are far more human killers abroad in the world than there are vampires.

"Professor Cotswold is wondering about the Hunger. It has never been very strong in me, except during feeding that first night, because I do not let it become strong. My benefactor told me I could go as long as a fortnight without feeding the Hunger, though I cannot imagine what would make me want to refuse myself the pleasure. Besides, one denies the Hunger at a risk. Left to grow too strong, it will take possession of me and, as its slave, I would behave without discretion. Far safer, I think, to keep it at bay.

"I have used my special abilities to attract beautiful lovers. Or men whose wallets are especially fat. I have not given up my dream of an elegant carriage and a beautiful house, though after this it will have to be in Paris or Venice. I already have enough for a wardrobe and first-class transport anywhere in the world. I will go where I am unknown and set myself up as a lady. None shall know my past or suspect me, and I will be able to live in high style and amuse myself as I see fit without anyone being the wiser. I may even take a gentleman in marriage, but only for a few years. My husband will grow old, but I, immortal, will remain forever young. And so I will move on again, perhaps in ten years' time, to another exquisite house in another exquisite city, surrounding myself with beauty and luxury and art and all of the things that are now mine for the taking. And who can say? I may actually fall in love. Perhaps I will share the gift with my husband, keeping him forever young, forever in love.

"Why, Captain Lucian, you surprise me! Hearing me speak of an undying love softens your heart a little toward me. You should let the world see more of your sentimental side. It's far more appealing than your pose as a stern young officer."

(C. asks for more detail about her ability to read minds and so forth.)

"Perceptive of you to ask about the other changes, Professor, for I have a very strong sense they are more significant than this unusual need to drink blood. I believe I am only beginning to see the outlines of the vampire's powers. I learned to read thoughts first. Then I learned to control bodies—to make people come here or there, to bend their head just so to give me easy access to their throats, or to look in the other direction as I slip by unnoticed.

"Recently, I have been learning to put thoughts *into* people's minds. A useful trick, that. To make Lord Shaftbury order me released from this prison, and to have him be convinced it is his own decision."

(Not bloody likely, S. responds.)

"Not today, but perhaps tomorrow—who can say for certain? It was easy enough to get out of here the first time. You must not hold my guards responsible, either for my first escape or the second, for which you will not have to wait long. You can look as stern and determined as you like, gentlemen. These pathetic steel bars cannot hold someone like me.

"You are aware our numbers are growing in London. Whatever is 'exponential growth,' Professor Cotswold? Mathematics was not my strong suit."

(C. doesn't answer, but the vampire nods as if she's stolen the information out of his mind.)

"Your concern is well-founded, but I think you greatly overestimate our population. We are only a handful. I had not thought we would become many, but then I do not think on grand scales, like Lord Shaftbury. You are right, sir: A congress of vampires would be powerful enough to usurp the control of entire nations, even of the world, although I am not sure whether it would be best to do this openly or to stay behind the scenes, pulling the strings of mortal puppets. I suppose it depends on what *kind* of vampire we are talking about. If you had the gift, Lord Shaftbury, no doubt you would want to make continents shake and tremble. But if Professor Cotswold were a vampire, he would probably sit back quietly, amassing great knowledge. As for me, I prefer to live for pleasure!"

(P. asks for details about the previous night's vicious crimes.)

"You have a tidy mind, Mr. Palmer," the vampire answers. "I admire that.

"I was walking down the street, fully satisfied. There were footsteps behind me, following me. It was old Bob, the grocer. I could see well enough what was on his mind. As fate would have it, his purposes and mine were neatly joined. You see, he had a taste for a woman, I had a taste for oranges, and it just so happened that old Bob had taken delivery on a barrel of Spanish oranges, which he was expecting to bring a good profit the next day when his vendors took their carts out into the streets. Yes, Professor, I do still require regular food. I allowed him to lead me to the door of his warehouse. And that's when he made his mistake. The fool grabbed me by the arm and attempted to take me by force. He didn't even intend to pay me for the use of my body. I'd had enough of the likes of him to last me a dozen lifetimes. You witnessed the aftermath of my anger.

"I compounded my rashness by leaving old Bob lying in the doorway while I went inside to enjoy an orange. It was delicious! I wish I had one now.

"A policeman happened along and found the grocer. It was just the policeman's bad luck, you see, for there was no way I could let him take me to jail. I did not count on the rest of you being so fast on his heels. You cornered me fair and square, although if I hadn't been trying to make up my mind what to do with the Reverend Clarkson, I would have been long gone. The rest of it, you know.

"Your revolver, Professor Cotswold, caused me considerable discomfort. Do not worry about it unduly. I will bear no malice to you when I am again myself, or toward any of you. You were just doing what you thought you had to do—which is only what I was doing myself.

"Some of you are wondering if I know anything about Dr. Van Helsing's whereabouts. The answer is no. Given the nature of his interests, it is entirely possible that he ran into trouble with another vampire. I do not know. Truly, gentlemen, if I had information about him I would share it with you. I swear to God I have never met the man, much less harmed him.

"Please ask Reverend Clarkson to forgive me for his collapse. I sincerely hope he recovers his health. I will pray for his recovery, and I hope he will be able to find it within him to pray for my redemption.

"That is all I have to say. If you have other questions, ask them now. With all due respect, gentlemen, I doubt I will be here tomorrow to assist further with your inquiries. I apologize in advance for escaping. I promise not to harm my jailers. Indeed, I somehow feel that I am beyond causing lasting harm to anybody ever again. Pray let us leave one another in peace."

(For the details of this foul creature's subsequent immolation and decapitation, see Lord Shaftbury's official report. Respectfully submitted, Algernon Turnor, Personal Secretary to Benjamin Disraeli, Lord Beaconsfield.)

I have been unable to obtain a copy of Shaftbury's report. Given the way things turned out in the end, I have come to doubt one was ever filed.

—*Posthumous Blackley*

PART VI

◆

Second Interregnum

24

Asprey House

The Reverend Christopher Clarkson correspondence. From the private letters of Archibald Campbell Tate, Archbishop of Canterbury, 1868–1883; Lambeth Palace Library, Sealed Collection.

March 12, 1880

Your Grace,

Thank you for inquiring about the state of my health and your warm expression of friendship.

I am pleased to report a fortnight's rest at Asprey House has had a restorative effect. Mrs. Simpson, the housekeeper and all-around majordomo here, nurses me with the zeal of a missionary newly sent among savages. The face staring back at me from the looking glass appears less and less like a cadaver as the days pass. Dr. Lattimore has granted me permission to take brief walks.

This evening I strolled as far as the village, where I attended evensong at St. Peter's, a Romanesque chapel predating the Conquest. Reverend Bartley, the vicar in Asprey and a fellow Oxonian, was anxious to hear the news from London, now that Her Majesty has dissolved Parliament. It is fortunate Dr. Blackley is not at Asprey House to hear the anti-Tory barbs that fly forth from the pulpit his family so generously restored. As for me, you know I find it impossible to harbor any ill sentiment toward Mr. Disraeli, having found the Prime Minister an eminently reasonable, capable, and wise leader of men.

I am deeply indebted to the brave Dr. Blackley for the use of Asprey House. It is a charming place. Think of a stone cottage but done up on a grand scale, not quite a manor house but only just. The house sits beside a stream nearly a mile beyond the village. The garden wants for care, but I plan to remedy that with my own two hands, as soon as Dr. Lattimore will permit it. We share a passion for gardening, so I know Your Grace understands the anguish I feel to see this lovely place go to seed.

And the Lord God took the man, and put him into the garden of Eden to dress it and keep it. (Genesis 2:15)

The front of the house is partly shaded by three old larches and given over to Granny's bonnets, forget-me-nots, and bluebells. Some Jacob's ladder would be a pleasant addition, I think. A stone wall on the east side of the property runs to the stream. White roses planted along the wall have been sadly neglected but will come back, if paid proper attention. Plum-colored *helleborus orientalis* planted in the shade would add a welcome bit of color.

I have begun organizing my thoughts on the recent business in London and made some preliminary notes on the London Vampire Panic. Dr. Lattimore has given permission for me to begin devoting an hour each day to writing my report. He suggested I undertake the work in serial installments, like one of Mr. Dickens's novels. He fears my heart still cannot stand the strain of prolonged work. I am not sure his concerns are warranted, but I will, with your indulgence, confine my efforts to the time my physician has allotted me.

It is impossible to know why God lets evil things happen. Rather, we must take refuge in our faith that it is all part of His divine plan.

I promise to record everything I can recollect in my report to you, down to the smallest detail. However, I see by my watch that I have quite used up my allotted hour of labor for today. My timing is good, for a delicious aroma is emanating from the kitchen. I have my appetite back, thanks to the efforts of Mrs. Simpson, who is an excellent cook.

Pray for my health, Your Grace, as I pray for yours, and for the Church and the world.

I remain . . .

Your servant in Christ,
Christopher Clarkson, Reverend

25

✦

My Dearest Olivia

The following facsimile, written out in Lucian's copybook, requires no explication.

—*Posthumous Blackley*

January 15, 1880

My dearest Olivia,

I am writing to suggest in the *strongest* of terms that you take young Andrew and leave London until the panic gripping the city is ended and public safety is restored.

Your continued skepticism about vampires is understandable but misplaced. Indeed, in the present circumstances it puts you at increased risk. I can confirm to you—in the *strictest* of confidence—these creatures *do* exist. I have seen the proof with my own eyes. Not even the most perverse imagination could sketch the outlines of these monsters and their horrific powers. It would be safer to lie down in a nest of vipers than remain in London while vampires haunt the night. We have kept it out of the newspapers, but the reign of violence continues to spread, both in geography and the range of victims. Men are being harmed now as well as women. No one is safe. I fear it is only a matter of time before some unfortunate child falls beneath the vampire's lethal shadow.

We *will* bring these fiends to justice, but until that happens, London is unsafe for you and Andrew.

The thought of something happening to you is simply too much for me to consider. During my visit to Moore House this evening, I did not have the opportunity to fully express my sentiments, but no doubt you have some sense of the *depth* and *intensity* of feeling that have taken possession of my heart. Had your policeman not intruded on us, my darling Olivia, I would have asked you a question that is very much on my mind of late. . . .

It is reassuring to know you are being watched over during these dangerous times. Still, a lone policeman would provide but little protection against one of these monsters. For all of these reasons, it is imperative you remove yourself and your brother to someplace safe until the London Vampire Panic is brought to an end.

I would be honored if you would accept the hospitality of my family's home in the Highlands. Kinloch Castle is a rambling old place high on a cliff overlooking Loch Lomond, but my parents succeeded in making the pile quite comfortable. I have taken the liberty of notifying the staff you might do us the favor of visiting.

My current work prevents me from accompanying you, of course, but you would find plenty to occupy you there. You like to read. Kinloch has an enormous library, ranging from musty old tomes—the oldest tower dates to 1100—to my own collection. My mother kept the nursery as it was when I was a child. It would be perfect for Andrew. My old nurse, Margaret Hillard, is still at Kinloch, although I expect you'd want Karol Janos to accompany you. She would be welcome, along with any servants you should choose to take.

You have but to say the word, my beloved, and Kinloch Castle will be a safe harbor to you and Andrew for as long as you care to use it.

With fondest affection,
Captain Charles Lucian

26

Death

Dr. Samuel Lattimore correspondence. From the private letters of Archibald Campbell Tate, Archbishop of Canterbury, 1868–1883; Lambeth Palace Library, Sealed Collection.

April 17, 1880

Your Grace,

I am writing with deepest regrets to inform you Reverend Christopher Clarkson died this morning at Asprey House.

I had called on Reverend Clarkson to listen to his heart and check his pulse and color. We had plans to have luncheon afterward. I promised to then advise him on a rose garden he was hoping to rehabilitate.

Mrs. Simpson admitted me through the main entrance a little after eleven. I accepted her offer of tea, thinking I would let Reverend Clarkson continue his work until midday. I went to the study a little before noon and knocked on the door. There was no answer. I turned the latch—it was unlocked— and found him slumped over the writing table. I knew the moment I saw him he was long beyond my assistance.

I estimate the time of death at a little past ten. I infer this partly from the state of the body and partly from the small progress he had made with his work since going into the room and closing the door at ten. Reverend Clarkson had written only a few lines in the neat script I have come to know and enjoy during these past months. The paper was labeled "London Vampire Panic," evidently the special report he was writing you. Unfortunately, he had knocked over the ink well, rendering the report unreadable. I instructed Mrs. Simpson to burn the paper in the grate, along with the rag she used to clean up the ink.

While Reverend Clarkson's death came as something of a surprise, it was not entirely unexpected. His heart had mended, but he failed to regain much vigor. During my previous visit, he complained of feeling old and seemed to have trouble recalling certain facts. I also noticed a certain childlike excitement when we took a brief turn around the garden. These last two things are common signs in a failing patient, though I had not expected the end to come so quickly.

At least I can tell you I do not think Reverend Clarkson suffered. Massive heart failure is over very quickly.

Mrs. Simpson and Reverend Bartley, the local vicar, have generously agreed to undertake the funeral arrangements. As Reverend Clarkson had no children and left no relatives that he knew of, I assume it is acceptable to bury him in Asprey. The little medieval church here is very picturesque; it is easy to see why he quickly learned to love it.

My other questions relate to Reverend Clarkson's belongings. I will write his solicitor in Oxford, inform him of the death, and suggest he contact you regarding any final disposition. Due to the nature of Reverend Clarkson's work with the Special Committee, I assume the wisest course is for me to gather up whatever papers and documents I can find and forward them to you. If there are any especially sensitive materials you need me to locate, please be so good as to let me know. If you could advise me of any particulars in this regard, I will do my utmost best to carry out your wishes.

Your obedient servant,
Dr. Samuel Lattimore

27

❖

Final Disposition

Dr. Samuel Lattimore correspondence, continued.

April 19, 1880

Your Grace,

Reverend Christopher Clarkson was buried today in the churchyard in Asprey. Reverend Bartley officiated. It was a simple ceremony, in accordance with Reverend Clarkson's wishes.

There were only a few people at the funeral: Mrs. Simpson, several elderly parishioners, the parish sexton, me. I made inquiries about the others, as requested. Reverend Bartley assured me that the old people present attended *all* the funerals. Dr. Blackley was unable to attend due to pressing business in London. He did send some lovely flowers.

I packed Reverend Clarkson's belongings in two wooden crates this morning, accompanied them to the station, and watched them loaded. If the wax seals bearing the "L" of my signet ring remain unbroken, you will know they reached you unmolested.

I also complied with your ex officio directives, extraordinary as they were.

I stayed overnight at Asprey House, so it was easy enough to come downstairs in the early morning hours to examine the body a second time, as per your instructions. I wore the crucifix you sent me outside my shirt. I examined the neck with great care, but found no evidence of wounds. I cut back the skin—I apologize if these details are distasteful—but I found no evidence of subcutaneous injury to the muscle tissue or blood vessels. However, since this sort of wound is reported to heal with unusual speed, even postmortem, I do not know whether my observations reveal anything one way or the other.

While I can neither confirm nor reject the possibility Reverend Clarkson was killed by a vampire, the facts argue that my original diagnosis was correct. Lacking any evidence to the contrary, it is my professional opinion Reverend Clarkson died of coronary thrombosis.

Nevertheless, I did follow the procedure outlined in your letter. I doubt circumstances justified it, but at any rate Reverend Clarkson was beyond being hurt by anything done to his body. Let us pray he is at rest in a better place. After driving the wooden stake through the heart and severing the head from the spine, I sealed the coffin for burial. You have no reason to fear seeing Reverend Clarkson again in this world.

I will leave it to your discretion whether to forward this information to officials in the new Gladstone government. It is my sincere hope this concludes the final chapter to this most disturbing affair.

Your obedient servant,
Dr. Samuel Lattimore

PART VII

✦

The Illusionist

28

Paris

THE FOLLOWING WAS taken from George Raphael's account of the London Vampire Panic. Omitted is the main part of his deposition, which adds little to my framing of the affair's early stages, or to the explication of the middle acts, which I reproduced from Cotswold's journal. (I have never been one to needlessly duplicate efforts!) Raphael throws an important light on his role in the vampire affair—and "role" is the appropriate term. After being interviewed by British and French authorities in Paris, he was detained in quarantine for two weeks to be certain he exhibited none of the vampire's tendencies. The incarceration gave him the opportunity to write a full and accurate account of his activities while in London, for which I paid him 1,000 pounds. After a fortnight in jail, he was allowed to travel to Italy, having been ordered not to return to France or Britain. Of course, George Raphael must be the same Mr. Raphael who fled the Hellfire Club's ersatz vampire attack the night I was there with Bertie and Duncan. I suspect the Contessa's macabre entertainment provided the germ of the idea for Raphael's subsequent felonies. It seems the criminal mind is as infinite in its variety as Shakespeare's Cleopatra. Little wonder the theatrical nature of Raphael's character comes through in his account.

—*Posthumous Blackley*

My denouement occurred in Paris on an idyllic winter day. No wind was necessary to keep the sky clear of clouds. The temperature was warm enough to make it pleasant for travelers to sit in the square and sketch Notre Dame Cathedral's west facade. The sun, seasonally low in the southern sky, was sliding toward the southwestern horizon and evening, casting sharp shadows on honey-colored stone.

I had myself gone to visit the famous cathedral. I wore a new suit from an excellent English tailor, with a black velvet cape and silver-headed cane. I was able to feel myself that day after being for too long in mufti. I was freshly barbered, every hair in place, my mustache meticulously trimmed and waxed. I am, I confess, obsessive about the neatness of my person, even if my profession sometimes forces me to temporarily adopt less fastidious habits.

The proper enjoyment of Paris begins on the Ile de la Cité in the midst of the Seine, I am convinced. This is where the city began, five hundred years before the birth of Christ. The island has been a place of ritual for more than two millennium, with the cathedral now occupying ground that is fairly soaked with history and mystical importance. Who knows what unhallowed acts took place on the Ile in the darkness of pagan times, when Druid priests sacrificed human victims to the gods of the forest. The ancient cathedral itself took two hundred years to complete after construction started in 1163—a long time for men to keep their gaze fixed upon a common goal; the human arrow seldom flies so straight.

But then, the miraculous cathedral was built because the archer was not man but God. After all I've done—and witnessed—I still have my faith, sinner that I am.

Notre Dame is a building of strange contrasts. The shimmering lightness of the stained glass seems to defy the density of the rock that cradles it. And yet the stone itself breathes with life. Like Michelangelo, who believed a statue lies sleeping within every rough-hewn block of marble brought down from the quarries in the mountains, the master masons of Notre Dame were blessed with the God-given talent to fashion buttresses and spires in a way that transcended the material's ordinary essence.

My favorite part of the cathedral is the west facade, with the statuary above the three arched doorways. Over the centermost, from which I had just stepped that day, is the Last Judgment Tympanum. Christ is in the middle, surrounded by the cross and symbols of his passion, sitting in judgment of the quick and the dead. At Christ's right foot is an angel—St. Michael, I think. Queuing up behind him are the faithful elect, their reverent faces upturned. Beneath Christ's left foot is Satan—misshapen, hideous, his scorn and hatred of Creation evident in his carved face. Behind the Enemy, a subservient devil drives the fallen into Hell. There could hardly be more contrast between the expressions of sorrow on their faces and the bliss seen in the faces of the chosen.

There is no escaping the evil, not even in the City of Light. I fear I will carry it with me always, now that it has brushed me. I pray it will not claim my life, but if it does, let me have a moment, God, to repent my many sins. My eyes lifting to the battlements, I saw the gargoyles, reminders of the fate that awaits the damned in Hell—and to the unfortunate victims of the *others* who walk the earth, their existence unknown to most mortals.

I turned from the end of the square and looked back at the incomparable Rose Window, which serves as a multicolored halo statue of the Madonna and Child. There was still time to repent my sins—but not before I saw Italy and Greece. There would be time to fully atone once my travels were over, after I had seen Florence and Athens and Egypt. Then I would buy a house in Tuscany and devote myself to good works, and collecting art.

I went to Le Bernardin, a café across from the Palais de Justice with a view of the Seine, as previously arranged. I found a table next to the window, where I could watch people coming over the Quai de la Tournelle from the direction of the Sorbonne. I had originally planned to go from London to the Netherlands, where I would spend as much time as I needed to view the Flemish masters, looking for one or two affordable but worthy intaglios for my collection. I only agreed to come to Paris when Sir Basil Worthy announced he would be in France on business and requested a meeting in a way that would have made it awkward for me to decline without damaging my prospects to do business with him in the future. Through our correspondence, Sir Basil told me he had spent the past five years in Africa looking after his mining interests. Now he wrote in a cable that he was interested in branching off into several other promising enterprises. That, needless to say, is where I came in.

I checked the time and slid my watch back into my vest pocket. I doubted my guests would be on time. Sir Basil would be prompt, of course, since he was British and had made his first fortune in railroads, where punctuality is not only a virtue but a necessity. However, the man he was bringing with him, Claude Bernard, was a French aristocrat. In my experience, the French have their own sense of time.

I was pleasantly surprised when Sir Basil and Monsieur Bernard appeared only a few minutes behind schedule. The Englishman presented me to Monsieur Bernard. We shook hands, exchanged cards, and took our seats. I sent the waiter for three glasses of wine. After a suitable period was devoted to pleasantries, Sir Basil asked me to outline for Monsieur Bernard the investment opportunity I had been telling him about in our correspondence.

And so I told Monsieur Bernard the story of the Anglo-American Transatlantic Cable Company. I spent some time describing the quality of our board of directors—"impeccable"—and the expertise of the firm's engineers—"without parallel." Monsieur Bernard appeared duly impressed with my news of the scientific breakthrough that would allow hundreds of telegraphic messages to be transmitted over a single strand of copper wire. The real importance of the new technology, I explained, would be realized when these capacious single strands were woven together into a thick cable that would be strung across the Atlantic, thus assuring our syndicate a virtual monopoly on transatlantic telegraphy for decades to come.

People say time is money, I said, but in the twentieth century the equation would change and information would be money—information about markets, business, politics, wars.

"We have the patent and own the technology lock, stock, and barrel," I told him. "No one will be able to compete with us when it comes to communicating across the Atlantic, first, and then within Europe and the United States. What we have is a virtual license to print money."

After that I sat back and waited for the possibilities to blossom in my two guests' minds. I motioned the waiter over and ordered mussels steamed in white wine. I had not eaten since breakfast and was famished. Unlike London, Paris is an excellent place to gourmandise. I'd already picked out the restaurant near the hotel where I would have supper at nine o'clock. I even knew what I was going to order: To start, *poelon de douze escargots aux noisettes.* For the entrée, *confit de canard aux pommes forestières.* And for dessert, *crème brûlée à l'ancienne.*

"How many positions remain in the syndicate for investment?" Sir Basil asked after a bit.

"At this point, I'm afraid none remain."

"Good God, man!" he sputtered. "Then why have you been leading us on?"

"I certainly didn't mean to do that," I said with a little shrug. "You're a businessman. You know how things are. When I began corresponding with you . . ."

I had been writing Sir Basil in Africa for six months, after hearing about his penchant for aggressive investments. I'd sent regular dispatches—scientific reports, surveys of the sea floor, forecasts on copper prices, important because of the cost in making the cable.

". . . the syndicate was only just forming. I would have been honored to have you on board, although I would never be so crass as to try to sell you on the project. Now, unfortunately, the syndicate is complete. The last share was subscribed only last week. I only wish we could have met together sooner to discuss the opportunity."

"Then there is no way to get a taste of this, Monsieur Raphael?" the Frenchman asked. "The proposition is sweet as the *crème vanillée*."

That reminded me of the gastronomic experience to come that evening, making me smile.

"Perhaps there is a way," I said.

The waiter delivered my mussels. An aromatic steam redolent of wine and garlic rose from the bowl, making my mouth water.

"One of our directors, a Mr. Hampton, suffered a recent financial reverse in the United States bond market," I said. "I think he could be persuaded to sell his share in the syndicate. I must warn you, though, that it will not come cheaply."

Sir Basil asked me to suggest a figure.

I plucked a mussel from its shell and regarded it on the tip of the silver fork for a long moment. I mentioned a number and popped the morsel into my mouth. I closed my eyes and chewed, thoroughly enjoying the experience, which I knew would be diminished by the astonished, even angry stares from the other men at the table. This is the decisive moment, I thought. I could almost hear greed prowling around the table, working its way into the men. And whichever way it worked out, I knew it did not matter. I had done far better than I ever expected in London. I could pay to go around the globe several times and still set myself up fashionably in a warm part of Italy when my wanderings were over. Besides, there were other fish in the sea besides Sir Basil and Monsieur Bernard. I had been sending the same bogus technical reports and dispatches to other potential investors.

"The figure you mention is astonishing."

I nodded to Sir Basil, agreeing he was right and pretending to be interested mainly in the mussels.

"Might we divide the share down the middle?" Monsieur Bernard asked.

"I suppose the papers could be drawn up, if it is also agreeable with the two of you to split the profit."

"An excellent point," Sir Basil says.

"But still, *mon Dieu,* the sum is quite extraordinary."

"I agree wholeheartedly," I said. "Fortunately, I was able to invest early on, when shares were much more reasonably priced. I could sell now and multiply my money almost a hundredfold."

Monsieur Bernard picked up his wineglass, turned it in his fingers, then put it down without drinking. "Such an arrangement would be agreeable with me, if it is with you, Sir Basil."

Sir Basil thought about it a moment, swallowed dryly, and nodded.

Monsieur Bernard took a wallet fat with bank notes from his coat. "You will accept a thousand francs in—how do you say?—earnest money until we can make arrangements to transfer the full amount? You can arrange the sale, I presume."

"That's unnecessary," I said, waving away the money.

"Please," Monsieur Bernard insisted, "I would feel better knowing we have an agreement."

"Very well, then," I said, and took the money. I was slipping it into my own pocket when Sir Basil grabbed my wrist.

"I'll take that, if you don't mind," he said. "These francs belong to Her Majesty's government."

I allowed the Englishman to take the bank notes from my hand.

"I am Inspector Charles Witherspoon of Scotland Yard."

"I *thought* you seemed a mite overanxious," I said. "And you, Monsieur Bernard? What is your real name?"

"It is Bernard—Inspector Bernard."

"And Sir Basil?" I asked. "I trust he is well?"

"He is very well, and I am sure he would thank you for

asking," Inspector Witherspoon said. "Sir Basil hired the Pinkerton Agency to verify your bona fides in New York when you first contacted him. The matter was eventually turned over to Scotland Yard. You've been corresponding with me for the past few months, Mr. Raphael. Or should I call you Mr. Buffet, as you were known in New York?"

"Why don't we stick with 'Mr. Raphael,' " I said amicably. "That's the name on my passport. It will make things less complicated. I was only Mr. Buffet for a short while. I've changed my name so many times that I'm not sure I can remember anymore who I really am!"

"I suppose we could even call you Professor Abraham Van Helsing," Inspector Witherspoon said acidly.

"I suppose you could," I replied.

29

✦

The Arrangement

HOW DOES IT feel to be bested at your own game?" Inspector Witherspoon asked.

There was something telling in the policeman's smile. And why were they not already dragging me off to jail? My highly developed intuition smelled opportunity.

"You have reason to be pleased with yourself, Inspector Witherspoon," I said, knowing policemen like to be appreciated. "I will not pretend it is at all pleasant to have you find me out. I may be a criminal, but I consider myself a professional."

Inspector Witherspoon glanced at Inspector Bernard, beaming.

"How ever did you connect me to Van Helsing? I thought I had pulled the wool over everybody's eyes."

"That was a bold stroke," Witherspoon bragged. "The police in New York were looking for a Mr. Buffet, who swindled J. P. Morgan out of $100,000. They had reason to believe Mr. Buffet, posing as a Mr. Rembrandt, booked passage to London aboard the HMS *Imperious*. But Mr. Rembrandt's baggage was sent to a hotel room booked by a Mr. Raphael, which was exceedingly curious."

"Indeed," I said, savoring the last of my mussels, insurance against the possibility that I might miss my supper.

"Even a more curious stroke was when a trunk was dispatched from Mr. Rembrandt's suite to lodgings in an altogether disreputable hotel belonging to a certain Dr. Van Helsing."

"I shall have to tip the porters more generously in the future," I said with genuine regret. "I presume you found Mr. Raphael in a similar fashion, working in the opposite direction."

"Just so. Van Helsing's trunk was delivered to a ship in Dover that had no passenger on its manifest by that name. My first thought was to look for a Mr. Rembrandt, but you were too clever for your own good when you decided to switch from Rembrandt to Raphael."

"I have a weakness for art," I admitted. "That is the real reason I came to Europe—to see the great masterpieces."

"Then the sensibilities of your criminal mind are not entirely depraved," Inspector Bernard said.

"I wired Inspector Bernard, my counterpart with the Parisian police, the moment I knew you were headed for Calais," Witherspoon said. "It did not surprise me to learn that Mr. Raphael had been in contact with a wealthy Frenchman, as he had been with Sir Basil. I will give you one thing, old boy: You are a planner."

"Thank you for the compliment," I said, and covered my mouth with the napkin. Knowing how easy it had been to follow my travels had given me indigestion. The ability for police to send telegraphs flying around the planet, requesting information about baggage and ship's passengers, had made the modern world a difficult place for those in my profession to do business.

"Let us return for a moment to the matter of your interest in art," Inspector Bernard said with a frown.

"I do not have a *professional* interest in art, Inspector. My love of paintings, sculpture, and architecture is entirely innocent, I assure you. I am, if I dare say so myself, a specialist, and rather good at what I do in my profession, the present circumstances notwithstanding."

"Is that what you call cheating people—a profession? Do all swindlers put on such airs in America?"

"Your distaste is understandable, Inspector Witherspoon. You are, after all, a policeman. I prefer to think of myself not as a swindler but an illusionist. I create illusions for wealthy people who are greedy enough to want to add to their superfluity of riches. I've never hit anybody over the head, held anyone at gunpoint, or jimmied a door lock. Furthermore, my illusions are educational. The people who give me money profit from a valuable lesson."

"You were hardly playing on people's greed in London," he said, and glowered.

"I admit I had no idea what I was getting myself into there," I said with an inward shudder.

"I have yet to meet a criminal who fails to concoct an elaborate justification for himself," Inspector Witherspoon said. "What of the dustmen and cooks you took money from in London for protection against the vampires? What sort of lesson were you teaching them?"

"Les vampires?" It was obvious this was the first Inspector Bernard had heard of the subject. Inspector Witherspoon had not given his colleague a full briefing, I realized.

"A pound here, a pound there," I said with a small shrug. "It is a small price to pay to be able to sleep at night. At the beginning of the sorry affair, when I did not believe in vampires any more than Inspector Bernard, I thought I was doing them a favor. Paying a quid to be told a garland of garlic hung over your bed will protect you from the vampires is cheaper and safer than drinking a draught of sleeping powder or sitting up all night, too terrified to shut your eyes. Besides, it wasn't the servants' money I was after but that of their masters and mistresses. Those were the real prizes."

I did not mention the gold Prime Minister Disraeli had paid me to consult with the government. If Inspector Witherspoon didn't know about that, I wasn't going to be the one to tell him. It would not have been in my interests.

"Are you saying, monsieur, that the people of London have a fear of *les vampires*?" Inspector Bernard asked, looking from me to Witherspoon and back. "I did not know the English were subject to foolish Eastern European superstitions."

I exchanged a look with Inspector Witherspoon, but as he showed me no sign that I should proceed, I elected to withhold further comment for the time being.

"It was good of you to let me finish my meal," I said. "I assume it will be a while before I eat so deliciously."

"That is a matter over which you have a certain degree of control, Mr. Raphael," Inspector Witherspoon said.

Bernard gave Witherspoon a questioning look, but there was nothing tentative about the English detective's manner. To broach such an offer, and with such authority, could only mean he was acting on behalf of his government. He knew of the committee's work, and he probably also knew that I had swindled the Prime Minister out of a fat trophy. Yet the fact that we were still sitting in the café, chatting almost amiably, meant I was not yet out of cards to play in this hand. Perhaps I knew something, or Witherspoon thought I knew something, of value to the government. Of course, it was also possible Witherspoon was merely concerned about keeping people from finding out how easily the British government had been gulled. It was amazing how often the wealthy and powerful preferred losing money to being embarrassed in public.

"What is it you wish to know, Inspector Witherspoon?" I said, raising the ante. "I will tell you anything."

"You could start by telling us where you have secreted the money the government paid you. We found nothing when we searched your hotel room."

"I apologize for misspeaking. I will tell you *almost* anything, although I am sure we could come to a certain agreement," I said, and raised an eyebrow.

"Steady on, Mr. Raphael," the regrettably honest British policeman said. His French counterpart, however, was disappointed that Witherspoon was not at all open to discussing a bribe.

"How may I assist your inquiries? I work alone, as you probably know. I have no accomplices to 'finger,' as we say in America."

Inspector Witherspoon leaned forward and spoke in a whisper. "The only information you have that is of any interest to me concerns vampires. Depending on how valuable what you have to tell me is, I may be able to look the other way on this business with Sir Basil."

"*Excusez-moi*, Inspector Witherspoon, but the authorities of my nation are not nearly so forgiving, especially regarding foreigners who cross our borders under assumed names to indulge in criminal enterprises."

"My instructions come from the highest office in Britain, Inspector Bernard. I would be very much surprised if Her Majesty's ambassador has not already delivered a letter to your government requesting cooperation in this matter."

"But I do not understand any of this, monsieur. You are prepared to let this professional liar go free in exchange for hearing fairy tales about *les vampires? Mon Dieu!* I have never in all my career heard of such a thing."

"I'm afraid they are not fairy tales, Inspector Bernard," I said. "Vampires exist. A plague of the monsters has descended on London."

"*Mais non!* What is this madness? Does it infect you both?"

"See what you think after you hear Mr. Raphael's story," Witherspoon said. "Assuming, that is, that Mr. Raphael prefers freedom to years in a French prison cell, followed by more time in a British prison."

I smiled and showed Witherspoon my upturned palms, an expression of surrender, of candor, of complete cooperation. "It is a small enough price you ask. I assume there will be no more talk about a refund of Mr. Disraeli's funds."

"Your future discretion is worth a certain amount, I suppose," Witherspoon said with the expression of someone swallowing a bitter pill. Bernard, for his part, gaped at me in amazement for having dropped the Prime Minister's name.

"Then we have an agreement," I said.

"I warn you, Raphael—or whatever your name is: I want the truth. Sir Basil is a gentleman and perfectly content to leave this up to the police. But the Americans you cheated— they are anxious to deal somewhat more roughly with you, if you get my meaning, should you happen to fall into their hands."

"I promise to tell the truth, the whole truth, and nothing but the truth, Inspector Witherspoon," I said, and snapped a fingernail against my empty wineglass to summon the passing waiter. "But first, I think, we must have three more glasses of the café's excellent Bordeaux."

30

The Greatest Challenge

AFTER BRINGING MY business in New York to a profitable conclusion," I said, "I decided the time had come for me to embark upon a grand tour of the Continent. I have always wanted to see the great treasures of art and architecture. These, you see, are my real interests."

"You are an American citizen?" Inspector Bernard asked.

"Canadian, actually. I grew up and went to college in Quebec. My father was a lawyer and my grandfather a banker. So I came by my profession naturally enough. On a lark I tried out for a part in the *Hamlet* my grammar school was putting on for its annual midwinter excursion into culture. I won the role, and to the surprise of all—but none more so than myself—acquitted myself quite well upon the stage. Throughout college I had leading roles in a number of productions. I learned all the actor's tricks of clothing, makeup, hair, and so forth, but those are merely the external components of taking on a character. This is the skill I learned to master—the taking on of another person's character, to become as real as that person, to become *more* real, regardless of the fact that the character is pure fiction. My real talent is in the theatre, although God forbid I should try to make a living at *that*.

"I also have a natural affinity for language. I grew up speaking not only English and French, as do many in Quebec, but also Hungarian. My mother, you see, was born in Budapest. I was surrounded by her family as a child, and they communicated with one another in the language of the old country. And so I picked that up, too. In school I learned Greek and Latin, which are a lot more useful than some might think, plus German and Italian. I can also hold my own in Spanish. After leaving the university, I worked for a time as a translator. All of that was a long time ago, and I am certain you are not interested in any more of my personal history than is necessary to provide the context to my recent experiences in London. Suffice to say that everything I had learned was put to work in my career as an illusionist.

"I arrived in London as Mr. Raphael, which you know. I checked into a good hotel, went to the theatre, visited the fashionable clubs where I'd arranged for invitations. My aim was to establish a certain veneer of respectable reality for Sir Basil by meeting and rubbing elbows with his friends. You have no idea how casual references to mutual friends can solidify one's credibility. You know the kind of thing: 'I had a drink with Lord Westmer, who asked if the African heat had improved your gout.' I did not guess at the futility of my work, that I was trying to establish a relationship of trust with a detective from Scotland Yard.

"I made several investments with Barclay's Bank and one of the older and more reputable trading houses. The accounts have since been closed."

"And the funds safely transferred to a numbered Swiss bank account," Inspector Witherspoon said.

I let that pass without comment. The money was beyond the policemen's reach, but there was no need to rub their noses in it. God bless the Swiss.

"While making the rounds in London, I began to overhear breathless horror stories about a vampire preying on the city's occupants. My mother was Hungarian, so I grew up knowing the legend of the *nosferatu*. One of my Hungarian uncles used to tell me the vampire would get me if I forgot to say my prayers before bed. The things people say to children! Still, I can assure you I never missed saying my prayers.

"The vampire stories I heard in London were linked to a series of grisly murders. I even saw a rather disgusting enactment purported to represent a vampire slaying a female at an upper-class brothel called the Hellfire Club."

The fact that I had been admitted there impressed Witherspoon.

"As a rational adult, I did not for one moment believe a vampire was responsible, my childish nightmares about *nosferatu* notwithstanding. Yet the murders were real enough, and so was the fear gripping the city. And with good reason. Is there anything more frightening than the idea of a vicious killer moving unseen among us, claiming his victims one at a time, evading the police with fiendish ease?

"Since Mr. Raphael had accomplished his bona fides in London, I decided to turn my skills in an entirely new direction. To be perfectly frank, gentlemen, I had grown tired of Mr. Raphael. He is, by nature, a supporting character, not a Hamlet or Caesar.

"As I sat in a concert hall one evening, listening to the great Hungarian pianist Franz Liszt demolish a grand piano with his pyrotechnics, the germ of an idea popped into my head. The more I thought about it, the more it grew: I would create the role of an itinerant vampire hunter from Budapest. My original assumption was that I would play the role more for pleasure than profit for a few weeks, then move on to Paris for my prearranged meeting with Sir Basil.

"The best basis for any theatrical character is a real person. I began with the memories of my uncle, who was notorious in my family of prosperous immigrants for his shabby dress. Then I appropriated the name of our kindly old family physician, Abraham Van Helsing. After a day of buying used clothing and collecting various props, Professor Van Helsing checked into the sort of down-in-the-heels lodging a wandering academic from Eastern Europe could afford.

"All of London seemed to have been awaiting the arrival

of Dr. Van Helsing. The commodities he had to dispense were hope and peace of mind."

"Which you sold at a tidy profit," Witherspoon sneered.

"You do me a disservice, sir. I never took more than the pittance offered me by servants and working people. When the masters and mistresses of the wealthy homes of Mayfair threw open their doors, too, I gladly accepted their invitations to drop by for tea and cucumber sandwiches. Yet the money to be had from the rich and the aristocrats was but the appetizer to the feast. I was mainly keeping my eye out for the main chance, without knowing when it would come, or if it would come, or in what form. That is the true art of my profession. Any cheap grifter can swindle the ignorant out of a few dollars, but only a true artist has the vision to recognize the outlines of an extraordinary opportunity taking shape. When opportunity knocks, gentlemen, you must be ready to answer the door.

"My supposed experiences in the Carpathian Mountains converted rather neatly into honorariums in some of London's best salons, but it occurred to me I might have the opportunity to advise some formal body—the city government, perhaps, or a club of concerned industrialists—looking to pay for the finest expertise that money could buy. And there were even bigger opportunities. Surely Lloyd's of London and other insurance concerns would suffer mightily if a vampire epidemic forced a quarantine that would shut down steamship lines and international trading and banking. Not that I thought such drastic steps would become necessary, mind you. But the merest shadow of a possibility for such an economic calamity meant that Dr. Van Helsing's expertise was very, very valuable indeed!

"I plied my trade, making new contacts, developing a clientele that was a little more wealthy and influential as the days passed. I showed my clients how to hang garlic at the windows. I advised them to wear crucifixes and place mirrors near their doors so they could see whether a stranger coming to call cast a reflection in the glass. If it made them feel more at ease, then all the better for it, I say.

"And then one day I found the mother lode, as I knew I would. One of Mr. Disraeli's secretaries turned up at my hotel with an invitation to visit Number 10 Downing Street. Politicians tend to be intelligent, shrewd, suspicious, and themselves masters of deception. If I accepted the Prime Minister's summons, it would be the greatest challenge of my career as an illusionist. It was one thing to pull the wool over a greedy banker's eyes, but to fool the entire British government—there was a challenge!

"Without the slightest hesitation, Dr. Van Helsing picked up his moth-eaten hat and battered valise and tottered off to Downing Street.

"It was, without a doubt, the biggest mistake of my life."

31

✦

Greed

AT DOWNING STREET, I was introduced to the Special Committee, as Mr. Disraeli called it. I knew of its members. Darwin was there, you know, with his young American proxy, Professor Cotswold, a hunter of dinosaur bones. It was obvious they both despised Van Helsing as a quack. If the nonscientists on the committee hadn't outnumbered them, I would have been quickly sent packing, saving me an infinity of grief.

"My only ally, among the professional men, was Dr. Posthumous Blackley, the prominent London society physician. Judging from his reactions to the reports about the vampire, it was obvious Blackley was a superstitious man, which seemed strange in a physician but played to my hand. He swallowed the poppycock I served like a hungry goose gobbling corn.

"On the general subject of vampires, the Prime Minister professed neutrality, but it was apparent Mr. Disraeli was sympathetic to old Dr. Van Helsing. His main concern was the threat a vampire panic posed to the social order. Mr. Disraeli feared undesirable political elements would capitalize on the mounting panic to bring about a period of anarchy and revolution.

"It was mentioned that Moore House, where poor Annie Howard had been employed, had on its staff a servant named

216

Karol Janos from Budapest. Everyone, of course, is aware that Sir Brendan Moore and his wife were blown up by anarchists in Hungary. Throwing myself a little too entirely into the role of Van Helsing, I told the committee we needed to interview Janos as soon as possible to determine whether she had any knowledge about the vampire's activities in London. It was a perfectly logical thing to suggest, since Janos was from Hungary, native land of the *nosferatu,* and closely associated with the first victim. I realized my mistake almost as soon as the suggestion was out of my mouth. I was only pretending to be Hungarian, but had put myself in a position to interrogate someone who actually *was.* The odds were greater that she would expose me than the reverse. Our old family physician, upon whom I had based the vampire hunter's character, Dr. Abraham Van Helsing, was from Budapest. What if Janos was acquainted with the Van Helsing family?

"That mistake alone should have alerted me that luck was running against me, but my pride—and my greed—wouldn't allow it. I was determined to pull off this illusion—my greatest illusion of all.

"My subsequent interview with Janos was unpleasant enough. I suspect she guessed I was an imposter, but she did not dare call me out. I was in the company of powerful men, and that has a way of intimidating simple people. Fortunately for me, Karol Janos's only real interest was Andrew Moore, a handsome little boy who is now the ward of his half sister, Lady Moore.

"Mr. Disraeli gave me free reign to proceed with the investigation, and all the rope I needed to hang myself. I don't really know how I came up with the ghastly idea—if you have ever had a prime minister stare at you, you know that it has a way of motivating you—but I told them it was imperative we methodically open each victim's grave and pound a wooden stake through the poor woman's heart."

"You *what?*" Inspector Witherspoon gasped.

I outlined the legend of the *nosferatu* to the policemen.

There was only one way to prevent a vampire's victims from undergoing the infernal metamorphosis. To prevent them from becoming the undead, to stop them from rising from the grave to feast off the blood of the living, a stake must be driven through each corpse's heart.

"And yet you have said that you yourself did not believe in *les vampires,* Monsieur Raphael."

"No, at the time, I did not believe. But everything becomes fuel for the illusionist's improvisation. My nimble mind almost instantaneously found a way to turn this grim task to good advantage—two ways, in fact.

"First, that evening I sent a note to Mr. Disraeli, informing him I was unable to remain in London. A vampire epidemic was raging in St. Petersburg. If I agreed to come to Russia immediately, the Czar had offered to give me the money to endow a program to eradicate the *nosferatu* from my native Hungary. As expected, the Prime Minister saw the Czar's presumed bet and raised him. I agreed to stay in London, of course.

"My second improvisation was keyed to the work I had set out for us the next day, opening the graves of the vampire's victims. The weather had been cold, which I hoped would make the job less awful than it would have been otherwise. It took no small amount of brandy to get me through it. Fortunately, I hold my liquor well."

"And did you see evidence of *les vampires*?" Inspector Bernard wanted to know.

"No. Nor did I expect to see any such evidence. The bodies looked as expected when the coffins were opened. This in itself presented a certain problem. If there really was a coven of vampires preying on London, one would expect to open the coffins and find the bodies strangely supple and alive-looking. I realized we wouldn't see this, so I took steps so that my illusion would remain alive even if the vampires didn't. This was my second improvisation."

I took a sip of wine and steeled myself against the policemen's reaction to what I was about to tell them.

"I found a pair of gravediggers in a gin shop," I said, "and paid them to steal the body of the first victim, Annie Howard, so she would seem to have risen from the grave."

Witherspoon called me a cur. Bernard labeled me "a cold-hearted wretch."

"No, sir, I am a professional, and a professional does what is required," I said. "Nothing more, nothing less."

Witherspoon, staring at me fiercely, demanded to know what they'd done with the body.

I told him I did not ask, that I presumed they put her in the ground with someone else.

He wanted to know the gravediggers'—the grave robbers'—names.

I said that I honestly didn't know. And I didn't. I didn't ask them their names, and I certainly didn't tell them mine.

"The girl deserves to be in her own grave," Witherspoon said to himself as much as to me. He was surprisingly bothered by the theft of Annie Howard's body.

The empty grave gave them all something to think about, I said, anxious to get past this difficult bit of road. It made believers of them all, except for Mr. Cotswold, who seemed determined to deny the existence of vampires no matter what the evidence.

But something most unexpected had already started to happen: I was beginning to wonder myself whether there might actually be a vampire in London. There had been nothing untoward about the victims' corpses, of course. But there was the odd matter of Maude Johnston, whose autopsy I was compelled to witness.

It was an ordeal to view the procedure. It is a terrible thing to see a human being dissected like a Sunday goose. But Blackley, who officiated, found something very strange indeed during the autopsy. Though I had tended to discount the previous reports, Miss Johnston had been drained of her blood, and Dr. Blackley could find no wound to explain how the blood left her body.

This was my first real inkling something truly bizarre was

afoot. On the way back to my hotel, I considered whether it would be best to pack it in and leave for Paris. However, the first installment of my fee was awaiting me at the hotel. I had the money locked in the hotel vault until I could arrange to have it deposited in my Swiss account the next day.

I could have left London at that point. I should have left. Yet I decided to remain, this time a victim of my own greed.

32

Nosferatu

ANNIE HOWARD'S EMPTY grave was my proof that the vampire coven was growing in number. Finding the fledglings' nest would be a difficult proposition, yet the sinister children of the original *nosferatu* would have to be stopped. It would require more resources—watchers, listeners, informants, and more money to pay them, the funds administered by the sole professional vampire hunter on Mr. Disraeli's committee. In the meantime, the killings were migrating toward the East End. That posed difficulties. I hardly need to explain to Inspector Witherspoon that the police are regarded as the enemy in the London slums. I could not have guessed that a vampire—yes, a *real* vampire—was about to be apprehended, and not by Scotland Yard or the Special Committee but by a group of superstitious old Irish women waving crucifixes.

Unbidden, the waiter delivered another glass of wine, which was excellent timing for I was reaching the part of my story that made my throat feel distinctly tight and dry, though my discomfort was certainly nothing like what the vampire's victims experienced. By then Witherspoon and Bernard were leaning forward on their elbows, their attention completely focused on my story.

Her name was Kate Woolf, I told them. She was not unlike countless other poor wretches one finds in Whitechapel—a prostitute, a habitué of the opium dens. She was caught in the act of killing an unfortunate girl named Mary Katharine McGuinn, happened upon while her teeth were still buried deep in poor Mary Katharine's throat. The women who discovered this stark tableau, Irish Catholics, like most of the people on that particular street, heard a ruckus and went to investigate, though God knows it must be dangerous to stick your nose into other people's business in Whitechapel. They arrived at the same time as a policeman, followed him up the stairs, and watched in horror as the vampire tossed the officer aside like a dirty bed sheet. The vampire then directed her attention to the women in the doorway, who were so stunned by the scene that it had not occurred to them to do the obvious thing—turn and run for their lives. The vampire, her face smeared with Mary Katharine's blood, began to advance on the women. Fortunately, they'd heard a thing or two of the *nosferatu* legend and brandished the crosses they wore around their necks to ward off the monster. The vampire hissed like a serpent, they said, and cowered behind the bedstead, terrified at the sight of their crucifixes.

Word arrived at my hotel that a vampire had been captured and taken to jail. It did not occur to me that Kate Woolf actually was a vampire. I imagined her nothing more than a pathetic madwoman whose delusions had led her to bite through the neck of an unfortunate urchin. London was on the verge of panic, the fear in the air so thick you could almost feel it. Little wonder it would push some unstable wretch over the brink.

The vampire was taken to a secret government prison called the Vicarage, I said, and drew a scowl from Witherspoon at my having mentioned the place in front of Bernard, thereby making it slightly less secret. As I traveled to the Vicarage, I considered whether I would be able to turn this new development to my advantage, or if it would make it necessary for Dr. Van Helsing to vanish into thin air. I was the first of Mr. Disraeli's committee to arrive at the prison. I was about to descend the dank well to the subterranean entrance when the figure of a woman appeared at the bottom of the stairs. I had no reason to think anything of it. Given what I'd been told about the Vicarage, I believed it to be virtually escape-proof. And yet in that instant, as my heart fluttered dangerously and my breath caught in my throat, I realized the deranged-looking creature was Kate Woolf, the supposed vampire.

She came up the stairs toward me, her eyes locked on mine. I am not a brave man, but I was not especially frightened. Even if she was a murderous madwoman, she was unarmed and seemingly not powerful enough physically to overwhelm me. I may not look very presupposing, but I am bred from hardy stock and as capable as most men of defending myself. I carried a razor in my pocket, since the neighborhood where Dr. Van Helsing's hotel was located was anything but safe after dark and not much better during daylight hours.

I had a number of options. I could stand aside and let Kate Woolf pass, thus avoiding or at least delaying possible complications resulting from me having to deal with her in front of the committee. Or I could apprehend her, playing the hero. It did not occur to me to try to destroy her the first chance I got—to slash her throat with my razor or push her down the long flight of stone stairs.

By then she was several stairs below me, near enough for me to see a weird fire burning in her eyes. I pulled my left hand out of my coat pocket, brandishing a crucifix, while my right hand remained around the razor in case things got out of hand. She stopped abruptly and threw her hands up as if to guard herself from the power of the cross, which had been used earlier to subdue her in her irrationality. But then she began to laugh and dropped her arms. It was the coldest, most unnerving laughter I have ever heard.

"The idea that crucifixes have power over a vampire is an old wives' tale," she said to me, advancing to the next step. "But then you know that, don't you, Dr. Van Helsing?"

She knew I was a charlatan. This woman, a product of the

gutters of London's vilest slums, had needed only one look at me to see through my illusion and denounce me as a mountebank.

I knew at that moment I was not dealing with an ordinary lunatic. I tried to pull the razor from my pocket but my body refused to obey my mind's commands. Mentally, I felt nothing to indicate I had been mesmerized, but that must have been what happened, for I was completely paralyzed. I couldn't move a muscle.

The vampire came up the remaining stairs and walked around me on the landing, looking me up and down as if she were trying to decide whether my blood was worth drinking. Sweat began to trickle down the back of my neck—a cold sweat of terror. The ship I had taken from New York was in a gale off Newfoundland that had most of us on our knees, sick and praying, certain we were going to die. But that was nothing compared to the fear I felt as the vampire looked me over, thinking about what she was going to do with me.

"It's passing strange how your mind can play tricks on you," she said. "I believed I could not bear the sight of a crucifix. That is what I had been told, so that is what I believed. And yet, as you can see, I am well enough. Look at this. See what I took off one of my jailers?"

There was a silver chain around her neck. She pulled it from her bosom to display for me the crucifix suspended from it.

"It's all a fraud, like you, Dr. Van Helsing. You're not really who you pretend to be."

My mind raced through everything that had happened in London since I'd walked into one hotel as Mr. Raphael and come out as Dr. Van Helsing. I thought of the places I'd been, the taverns where I'd bought whiskey, the people I'd met, the prostitutes I'd patronized. I had not run into her anywhere, I was quite certain. The only way she could know my name was if she could look into my mind and read my thoughts. It was at this point that she began to laugh again, all the confirmation I needed that she knew my private thoughts as well as I did myself. As she laughed, I saw the teeth descend from her upper jaw, fangs she would use to drain me of blood and leave my lifeless corpse lying outside the Vicarage for the others to discover. I told myself it would be no more than I deserved for the disreputable life I'd lived.

At the exact moment that I had that thought, the vampire stopped laughing.

"You aren't completely disreputable, are you?" she asked.

I was unable to respond, but of course I wanted to agree—to make her know that I was not without my redeeming qualities, that I loved beauty and worshiped art and had lived a life of crime as a means of financing my taste for travel and collecting.

"Perhaps you are capable of understanding the same is true of me," the vampire said. "None of us are completely evil or, I hope, beyond redemption, be we mortal or vampire. If I should ever happen to fall into the authority's hands again—which I sincerely doubt—I hope you will show me the same mercy I am about to show you."

I squeezed my eyes shut as she came to me, but I realized in the next instant that she was brushing by me, leaving me unmolested and alive. The vampire had recognized that we were both sinners, as we all are, and had graced me with her mercy.

In another minute or two I regained the use of my limbs. I went down to see if I could do anything for the guards. I was surprised to find them alive. They were in a sort of waking sleep, but they came out of it quickly enough when I spoke to them. I did not tell the others about my encounter with the vampire. After hearing what the guards had to say, I thought my own experience would add little to what we now knew about the vampire's powers. Besides, it would hardly do to admit that the eminent vampire hunter had proven helpless to defend himself against a fledgling *nosferatu*.

The next day, a séance was convened at the Prime Minister's residence. He was understandably furious about the vampire's escape. There was a debate over whether any future attempt should be made to capture a vampire, or if they should be exterminated on the spot when apprehended. Lord Shaftbury came down on the side of summary execution, which was greatly opposed by Professor Cotswold. The American paleontologist subscribed to the idiotic notion that vampires were some exotic new species we needed to study scientifically. I knew better. As much as I owed Kate Woolf for sparing my life, I had no choice but to come down on the side of exterminating the creatures, for I understood only too well their formidable powers.

The Special Committee determined to have a dragnet through Whitechapel and the surrounding neighborhoods that night to attempt to find Kate Woolf. I said nothing to the others on the matter, but that plainly spelled the end for Dr. Van Helsing. I couldn't risk Woolf exposing my illusion. Beyond that, I had no desire to meet up with her or any other vampires and lose my life.

33

Retreat

I RETURNED TO my hotel late that night and entered by a back entrance. In the morning, I bathed and disposed of Van Helsing's despicable rags. I dressed in one of my lovely new English custom-made suits and had a visit from the hotel barber. I dispatched my trunks to Dover and checked out of the hotel. It was time for Dr. Abraham Van Helsing to retreat into the mists of illusion.

I had a hack take me, now Mr. Raphael, to Victoria Station for the trip to Dover, where I would board the ship that would carry me across the English Channel and safely into France. I was alone aboard the train in a first-class coach. A porter tapped on the door and asked if I would mind sharing my compartment. Glancing past the man's shoulder, I said I was quite amenable to company. I never mind traveling with a beautiful young woman. There was something familiar about the woman. I had the sense that I had seen her somewhere in London, though I could not place her face. Or maybe it was an instance of déjà vu, that uncanny sense that you have seen or done something before.

The young lady and I talked about the usual things as the train left Victoria Station and made its way out of the city and into the countryside. The weather, the state of the gardens—the innocent topics of idle social conversation. We got onto the subject of the Gainsboroughs at the National

Gallery. She had a delightful knowledge of art. One of her relatives was the subject of one of the artist's better-known paintings, the portrait of Lady . . . *something*. I cannot recall the name. Ordinarily, this would strike me as odd, since I have an excellent memory for names.

We had a lively conversation about English and French portraitists. My companion was extremely well-read and cultured. She was charming company. Some beautiful women rely on their looks alone, but my traveling companion had not neglected to cultivate her mind. And, if I dare say so, I believe she found my company pleasant, too. I remember wishing that I were twenty years younger and twice as handsome. It was at about this time—we must have been halfway to Dover—that she asked if I wasn't the distinguished Abraham Van Helsing. I don't think Mr. Disraeli himself would have recognized me—shaved, barbered, dressed in decent clothing—but somehow she did. Alarm bells should have been peeling in my head, but somehow I was not bothered in the least.

I admitted it: Yes, Van Helsing and I were one and the same.

She asked me about the London Vampire Panic. Not wanting to worry her, I said that the hysteria was totally out of proportion, but that nevertheless she would be wise to stay away from the city until the authorities had the matter well in hand.

"You have been playing an extremely dangerous game, haven't you?" she said.

By that point I should have been alarmed she recognized me as Van Helsing. I should have been wondering how it was that she seemed to know Van Helsing's existence had been part of a game, an extremely dangerous game, as she'd said. And I should have been heeding the half-formed suspicion that she had followed me into the train car. Instead, I sat there smiling back into her lovely face. If I'd had anything to eat or drink since boarding the train, I would conclude I'd been slipped a narcotic. I was stupidly oblivious to the danger. No, that is not exactly right. It wasn't that I was unaware of the danger the lovely young lady presented to me, but just that I couldn't make myself care that my life was so plainly at hazard.

"There is an element of risk in everything," was my insouciant reply.

"You have not been playing cat-and-mouse with greedy rich men this time."

"I did not understand as much at the beginning, or I never would have begun the illusion."

"But now you know the danger."

I nodded.

"You could have stayed in London to help."

"I briefly considered it," I said, and I was telling the truth. There was no point trying to deceive her. She would have seen through any lie.

There were several problems with me trying to be of continued service to the committee. To begin with, I had learned all the things that were supposed to be of use in battling a vampire—garlands of garlic, crucifixes, holy water—were useless as weapons. Unfortunately, I hadn't come up with any useful information about what *would* stop a vampire. I didn't even know for sure whether a stake through the heart would kill one. I presumed it would, but as vampires were extremely powerful and intelligent, there seemed to be very little chance one would lie still while someone pounded a stake through its heart.

The other issue with me remaining in London to help battle the *nosferatu* was that it would have meant admitting I was a fraud. While I would have, with a very great reluctance, returned the money I'd bilked from Mr. Disraeli, I did not think my further assistance would have been welcome beyond that point. Besides, the powerful take being cheated especially hard. It is not the money as much as being made to look foolish that the high and mighty resent. If I stayed in London and came clean with the truth about what I knew about vampires—and the truth about Van Helsing—the chances were good that I would be the one locked up in the Vicarage.

And, finally, there was the matter of my own safety, and the well-being of anyone remaining in London while vampires still ruled the city at night.

"I do not know how this affair will work itself out," I said, "but I am not sanguine about the authorities being able to stop these creatures."

"That is because there is only one thing that can stop a vampire from killing," the lady said. She paused a beat, then added: "And that is another vampire."

I knew she was right. A human couldn't stop a vampire unless it was in a Hungarian folktale. The creatures were too strong, too cunning.

"I wonder if you would mind doing me a small favor," and she called me by my given surname, an appellation I have not used in many, many years. "I promise you will feel no pain and suffer no lasting harm."

And there it was, the awful truth of it. I was sharing my railroad compartment with a she-vampire, a creature who was utterly unaffected by the sunlight and, for all I knew, any possible defense I could have mounted, including hurling myself from the speeding train as my way of choosing one form of death over another. Still, I somehow knew she did not mean to harm me. I suppose now, looking back on that day, that this could have all been part of a fiendish guile, a way of seducing me into submitting myself to her strange and darkling need. And yet I decided to trust the vampire—an act of the most extreme lunacy.

I said I would be honored to help so lovely a lady in any way I could. I was already loosening my cravat and opening my collar.

I noticed that Inspector Witherspoon had stopped taking notes. He clutched the forgotten pencil in his hand.

One would imagine being bitten by a vampire would be something quite ghastly—like being attacked by a wild animal but all the more horrible because of the awareness and fear of becoming yourself a monster who preys upon the living. And it *can* be quite like that, I am sure. Consider Kate

Woolf, who on at least one occasion turned into a beast as soon as she had become intoxicated from drinking the blood of the living. My experience, however, was entirely different. Indeed, it was pleasurable beyond anything I can describe with mere words. Vampires are creatures of unsuspected and unimaginable sensuality—or at least they can be. I thank God the lovely vampire who kissed my neck before biting it was one of the gentler sisters of that race.

True to her word, she took only a small amount of my blood. There were no discernable aftereffects. I dozed off for a bit. When I awoke, the train was a little out of Dover. My traveling companion had inexplicably vanished. I cannot explain how she could have gotten out of the speeding train without breaking every bone in her body. The only evidence of the wound to my neck were two red spots that were slightly sensitive to the touch. By evening, not even these remained.

I have driven myself nearly mad trying to remember her name or even the features of her lovely face, but the particulars of our time together are lost to me. She did it to me, of course—she reached into my mind and rearranged my memory, protecting herself. The fact that she caused me no lasting harm speaks for itself. It is not necessary for vampires to kill to get the blood they require. I doubt the lady has ever harmed another living being. You certainly cannot say that what she did to me was hurtful. Quite the reverse.

As for Kate Woolf and the others like her, I can only think that they are not predisposed to properly manage the special powers conferred on them by their vampirey. If the committee and Scotland Yard are not able to bring the criminal members of the race under control—which I very much doubt—we can only pray the lady who shared my compartment for part of the trip from London to Dover and others like her will step in to help.

As the mysterious lady told me, only a vampire is strong enough to stop a vampire.

PART VIII

✧

The Lovers

34

The Orangery

COLLINGSWORTH SITS ATOP a knob of land, a bony protuberance rising up from the pastures and hedgerows, commanding a view of the surrounding countryside. The hillock has been a place of power for as long as people have been in Britain. A few remains of an ancient earthenware fortress built by the island's early tribes are in evidence behind the house. The Romans built a tower on the hilltop, which the Norman ancestors of the Collings family expanded into a castle.

The estate has been made over many times, becoming less warlike with each successive generation. Collingsworth drew near the perihelion of elegance when the Palladian mansion, designed for Richard Boyle, the third Earl of Burlington, was completed in 1750. Capability Brown added the final grace notes thirty years later when the formal French gardens were made over in the naturalistic manner that has come to be known as the "English" style. The genius of Brown's plan—which spared the remains of the prehistoric Brit earthworks—was that it appeared to be no plan at all. From its eminence, the house presides over a pastoral setting more natural than Nature herself could have made it. Still, the sweeping curves and seemingly random groupings of trees are no more an accident than the house's pedimented portico.

Attached to the house's southern wing is the Orangery,

newly built in 1879, a confection of glass and iron in a faux-Moorish style of Victorian provenance. The greenhouse was the last major addition to Collingsworth, with the minor exceptions of plumbing, electricity, and a central heating system. But for that, the seat of the Collings family has remained frozen in time since the late 1800s.

It was a brilliant winter day, so sunny that it was difficult to look out at the newly fallen snow dusting the countryside. Captain Lucian and Lady Olivia Moore sat side by side on a bench, not close enough to touch, and not daring to look at one another.

Lucian cleared his throat as if to speak but continued the uncomfortable silence. Olivia already knew what he was going to say. Any woman in her position would have. What she didn't know was what she would say in return. Never had she wanted something so much while knowing it was all quite impossible.

Olivia told herself she shouldn't have come to the Orangery alone with Captain Lucian. But Lady Collings, who had prevailed upon her to spend the weekend at the country house, was nowhere to be found that morning. It was but the latest complication in an already tangled social situation. Lord Beaconsfield had asked Lady Collings to invite Olivia to Collingsworth, as well as extending invitations to Lucian, Dr. Blackley, and Lord Shaftbury and his wife. Lady Collings told Olivia that even in his declining years, Mr. Disraeli loved to be in the company of lovely and intelligent women. Olivia suspected it was really Lucian who was responsible for the invitation, though that didn't make it any easier to refuse. Indeed, Olivia had surprised herself by agreeing to come, after Janos promised that Andrew would be well cared for in her brief absence.

Lucian shuffled nervously. Olivia knew he was looking at her with that worshipful gaze that made her feel as if she were melting.

A woman on horseback rode out of a covert at the bottom of

the hill. It was Lady Collings. She rode at full gallop into the woods and disappeared. A few moments later a man on horseback appeared—Dr. Blackley, riding hard in pursuit of Lord Collings's wife. How Dr. Blackley had lived so long without being ruined in public scandal was a matter of amazement. He had cast his wandering eye Olivia's way, though it was obvious he was more interested in experienced women.

Lucian again cleared his throat.

Olivia glanced up at him, filled with anticipation and at the same time dread. Why did things have to be so bloody complicated?

"You look as if you are about to say something," she said gently.

"I'm afraid I'm not very good at this sort of thing," he said, blushing in a way Olivia found most becoming.

"I hope you don't let that stop you." She gave Lucian an encouraging smile. She could not bear to see him suffer. The main reason Olivia had accepted the invitation to Collingsworth for the weekend was to find a way to ease poor Lucian's tormented heart, even though she did not believe they could achieve a resolution that would give them what they wanted—each other.

"You know that I care for you very much."

Olivia blushed.

"If unhappy circumstances had not deprived you of your parents, I would ask your father for your hand. I like to think he would have given his consent. I am laird and have come into my estate. I would be able to provide for you as well as any lady in the kingdom. I would also take care of little Andrew. You know how fond I am of the lad. I would watch over him and raise him as if he were my son."

"Then I suppose you will have to ask me."

Lucian looked at her and blinked.

"My father has gone to a better place. If you are going to ask someone for my hand in marriage, I suppose it will have to be me."

"By heavens, Olivia," Lucian said, grinning. Olivia knew

she was not like most girls Lucian knew. She was not demure, not unsure, and especially not silly—the trait she abhorred most of all in women.

The young laird got down on one knee in front of her and took her hand between his.

"Olivia, will you do me the honor of becoming my wife? I promise to love you and care for you and cherish you all the days of my life. And I promise to help raise Andrew, giving him every kind of support it is in my power to provide, and helping him grow into a fine gentleman."

Those words! Olivia had wanted to hear them more than anything else. He cradled her hand more tenderly between his, waiting for her answer. She bit the inside of her lower lip. She yearned to say the words Lucian wanted to hear, and yet she could not.

"I cannot give you an immediate answer, Lucian."

"Certainly you know I love you."

She nodded.

"And you know I have made a place in my heart for Andrew. It would be impossible not to. I have never known a brighter or more delightful little boy."

"I know."

"Then why do you not accept my proposal?" Lucian's face darkened though he did not release her hand. "Don't tell me it is *Cotswold*."

"No," Olivia answered with a small smile, "although he has made his interest known. As brilliant and dashing as Professor Cotswold is, I could never love him. Some girls might be content to marry men old enough to be their fathers, but I am not one of them. Sweet as he is, I could never love James."

"Then what is it? Please don't tell me you don't feel the same way about me as I feel about you."

"I am *very* fond of you, Lucian. You know that. There is nothing that would make me happier or more proud than to become your wife." She stopped and looked away, unable to continue meeting his eyes. "But there are things you don't know about me, darling."

"Is it your health? Are you unwell, my dear? Your hand is positively burning up."

"That's just the way I am. My fires burn more fiercely than most."

Olivia regretted the words as soon as they were out of her mouth, for it sounded as if she were talking about one thing but meaning something entirely different. She gently pulled her hand free and turned away.

"Listen to me carefully, Lucian, for I will not be able to tell you this more than once: Get up and leave me now and never look back. Forget me. Forget what you feel. In time, you will find someone else who might bring you a measure of real happiness. I fear that I can bring you only sorrow."

She felt Lucian's strong hands take her by the shoulders and turn her toward him. Their faces were nearly touching as she looked into his eyes. She looked away. It was the only way to stop Lucian from doing what they both wanted him to do—enfold her in a passionate embrace.

"I will never leave you, Olivia. Reject me. Spurn me. Send me away. It will make no difference. Nothing can break the bond tying us together. I want to be with you forever."

"Lucian, my love, you have no idea. What you want is impossible."

"Why? Do you not love me? If you don't, tell me now."

Olivia felt herself begin to shake. She could never tell him *that*.

"What is it that distresses you so, my love? We can beat it together, whatever it is. Share your burden with me. Your joys are my joys, your troubles are my troubles."

He took her two hands in his, a protective gesture, tender and gallant. In spite of the Captain's worldly experiences as equerry to the Prince of Wales, in some ways he was almost childlike in his naive goodness of heart. It was his most appealing quality.

"I want to know what is troubling you, Olivia. I *need* to know."

"Very well, then," she said at last. A strange relief flooded through her. Any secret confers a burden, and the weight of Olivia's was crushing. The decision to free herself of it brought relief so intense that for a moment she felt almost weightless. There was no way to know how Lucian would react, she thought, falling back toward earth. But if Lucian wanted the truth, she would give it to him. Then she would see if he loved her as much as he thought he did.

"Please get our cloaks so that we can go out into the garden. I do not want to be interrupted or overheard. And you must promise me to never repeat a word of what I am about to tell you."

"I promise never to breathe a word of it, my darling," Lucian said. "I swear it on my life."

35

✧

Prelude

"IT BEGAN WHEN Father was posted to Budapest," Olivia said.

The great Palladian mass of Collingsworth was already receding behind them on the hilltop. It was cold but the brilliant sun made it seem less so. The powder of new-fallen snow quieted their footfalls; Lady Olivia Moore and Captain Lucian glided silently over the ground, two kindred spirits wandering Capability Brown's idyllically reconceived English countryside.

"It was an adventure for me, traveling into the East, where everything was foreign and exotic. The deep forests, the mountains, the Orthodox influence on the architecture, Gypsy caravans—something about the very soul of the place was different. We saw forbidding castles where brave knights fought back the invading armies of Islam. Eastern Europe is a much fought-over place, the ground watered with the blood of many massacres and desperate struggles. Little wonder the area has given rise to so many strange things.

"The house we moved into in Budapest gave Mama the opportunity to come truly into her own. You know that my mother died when I was a baby in India. Cecilie was Father's second wife. There never was a kinder person than Mama, as I called Cecilie. Though there weren't many years separating us when she married my father, she slipped easily and naturally into the role of caring for me. She was gifted with an ability to take care of people. That must be why she was such a marvelous gardener. Plants, animals, and people seemed to thrive on her attention and care. When Andrew came along, I thought he would monopolize Mama's affection. But love is a miraculous thing: It does not divide but multiplies.

"Father's appointment to the ministry in Budapest gave Mama a chance to step beyond our house in Mayfair, with furniture and draperies my real mother had bought in London and India, and set up her own household, choosing the furnishings, hiring the servants. In Budapest our little family knitted together completely. To be blessed with a year of perfect love and contentment is more than many people know in this life. Still, it was hard to have end."

Olivia walked on a ways in silence, Lucian beside her, quietly waiting for her to resume.

"Budapest is a city of music. It is not as great a musical city as Vienna, but a close second. The symphony and opera are excellent. And, as you may have heard, it is known as the City of the Piano. Budapest is the home of Franz Liszt, the greatest living pianist, a man whose name is spoken of in the same breath as Beethoven, Bach, and Mozart.

"It seemed that the Fates were taking care of me in sending us to Budapest, although it ended up to be a good deal more complicated. Though I have been but little disposed to give myself to it of late, music has been the central force in my life."

"I had no idea until Lord Beaconsfield asked you to play after supper last night," Lucian said. "I have never heard anyone play with such emotion."

"Thank you again," she replied. She was accustomed to hearing effusive praise after getting up from the piano, but hearing it from Lucian was especially gratifying. "I have been an enthusiastic student of music since I was young. Father was always more interested in me becoming educated in the traditional way. All the time I was growing up I had tutors and governesses drilling Latin and Greek into me. If you would ever care to hear me recite long declamations of Homer and Virgil, I could do so without effort. And yet it was my musical studies that engaged me most fully.

"Mama encouraged me to pursue a real mastery of the piano. She helped me understand my ambition. I enjoyed playing for myself and my family in the parlor, or for my friends at parties, but without knowing it I had started to secretly yearn for more. There have been great women pianists—Clara Schumann comes to mind—but a profession is not considered desirable for a young lady. Would it scandalize you to hear me say that I hope one day this will no longer be the case?

"Mama arranged for me to have an audition at the Academy in Budapest so that I might continue my studies in a serious way. I was nervous as I sat down to play. The great Liszt was not there, of course, and a good thing, too, for I would have been too petrified to play. Attending me was Doktur Jutt, who as senior professor at the Academy was responsible for interviewing prospective students. I did not think I played well enough to be accepted, but when I was finished, Doktur Jutt told me when to come back to begin my instruction. I wanted to kiss the old German. There I was, in the City of the Piano, in Liszt's own school, accepted as a pupil.

"I threw myself into my studies. I was not presented to Liszt. He did not trouble himself with ordinary students. Yet I worked hard, harder than I have ever worked in my life, struggling to improve my playing to the point that I would deserve the honor of an introduction to the great Maestro.

"And then, over the course of several weeks, the happy part of my family's story drew to a close. There was something wrong with Andrew. Toddlers never stop moving, from the time they get up in the morning until the time they fall asleep, happily exhausted. You know there is something wrong when they become pale and listless. He had just started to walk, so it was natural that he would be subject to a certain degree of bruising. But he bruised easily, too easily, a light bump that should have left no mark causing instead a frightful black and blue spot."

"My God, the vampire," Lucian said in a harsh whisper.

"No," Olivia said with an abruptness that surprised him. "It proved to be something far worse, something without mind or capacity for mercy.

"A physician was called in. The diagnosis was arrived at quickly, the symptoms easily identified. Little Andrew had juvenile leukemia. There was no known treatment, no known cure. The physician told us he had, at most, six months to live."

36

The Maestro's Command

"THE CHILD IS dying?"

Lucian had put his gloved hand on Olivia's arm and stopped her, turning her toward him.

"Andrew is fine now, but he was a very sick little boy. Listen a little longer and everything will become clear.

"We each reacted to Andrew's illness in our own ways. Mama withdrew until the only thing in her world was Andrew. She spent every waking moment with him, playing with him, caring for him. Father threw himself headlong into his work. Neither of them could sleep. Mama would sit in a chair beside Andrew's bed, dozing fitfully. Father sat up late into the night in his study, reading dispatches and writing reports.

"I escaped into music. I spent my time in a practice studio at the Academy, working on the most difficult pieces I could find to occupy my concentration. One evening I was trying to play Liszt's La Campanella Number 3 in the Six Grand Études after Paganini. It is not a piece for small hands. In measure thirty-five there is a passage with sixteenth-note octave reaches that are physically impossible for me to play. But I tried. Again and again I tried. My frustration grew until I began to cry. It wasn't because I couldn't play the Étude, of course. I was crying for Andrew, and for my helplessness.

"I heard the door open behind me. A gentle hand pressed

itself against my shoulder. A handkerchief was proffered. It was a rich silk handkerchief monogrammed with the letter L. I turned and looked up to see Franz Liszt himself standing over me."

Olivia climbed the stairs to the pavilion overlooking the lake and took a seat, Lucian beside her. The trees on the far shore formed a ragged silhouette against the winter sun. The trackless snow on the frozen lake seemed to invite a wanderer's footsteps, although it was impossible to know whether the ice was thick enough to support someone's weight.

"The Maestro was—is—a gracious man. He pretended to believe I was weeping over the beauty of Paganini's music, not my inability to play it—or, as happened to be the case, for another reason entirely. 'I wept myself when I first heard Paganini perform in 1831,' he told me. 'Do you know his violin playing was so prodigious that people thought it inhuman? Some actually believed he had sold his soul to the Devil to achieve such genius.'

"Of course, the same thing has been said of the great Liszt.

"The Maestro's words soothed me and I was able to regain my composure. He does not speak English with a Hungarian accent, but rather a French one. He later told me his father had taken him to Paris as a young prodigy. He lived so long in France he literally forgot his native tongue and had to relearn it as an adult.

"As for the Études, he told me there were sections that could only be played by a man with large hands. 'I have been blessed with the ability to make unusual reaches,' he said, holding out his hands for me to see. His hands were unusually large, but the most remarkable thing to me was not their size but their appearance. They did not seem to be the hands of a sixty-eight-year-old man. The skin was smooth and blemish-free, not wrinkled and mottled with age spots. His fingers were long and delicate, tapering to perfectly manicured fingernails. 'I am embarrassed to acknowledge it now, but I have written music impossible for anybody but me to play correctly. When I was a younger man, I was very prideful. It was not a good use of my talents.'

"He pulled a chair up and on a blank sheet of music manuscript paper dashed off alternate measures for the most unplayable passages in the Number 3 Étude. I told him it was very kind of him to help me. 'Nonsense, child,' he replied. 'It gives me tremendous pleasure to assist younger pianists in developing their talent. Now, my dear, play something for me. Some Chopin or Beethoven would be especially lovely.'

"To perform for Liszt without practice or preparation—a terrifying idea, yet how could I refuse the Maestro's command? Liszt was a great champion of Beethoven. He once did an entire European tour to raise the money to build a monument to the composer. I chose the Moonlight Sonata. I began to think of Andrew as I played and quite forgot that Franz Liszt was sitting beside me as I poured my wounded heart into my playing.

" 'Bravo,' he said in a low voice when I finished.

" 'I remember when I met Beethoven for the first time. . . .'

"Those words—'when I met Beethoven'—made me feel faint, Lucian. Liszt is the greatest pianist of our time, maybe of all time. Through a chance encounter with him, I felt mystically connected, like souls reaching out to one another across time, to the greatest musical geniuses of all time.

" 'It was in Vienna in 1821,' he said. He told me he had worshiped Beethoven from the time he was a small child in Raiding. His father had taken him to Vienna, an eleven-year-old wunderkind. Some called him another Mozart, although the Maestro said that was rather much. For his first concert in Vienna, he played Hummel's Concerto in A Minor, and a fantasia he'd written based on Beethoven's Symphony in C Minor. The performance was a great success. He prevailed upon Schindler, a mutual friend, to take him to meet Beethoven. He wanted to play for Beethoven and invite him to his next concert. The encounter was anything but a success. Beethoven was already forgotten by the fickle public, whose infatuation of the moment was Rossini. The things Beethoven had read about Liszt in the papers, gushing confections about the brilliant young virtuoso, made him even more cross than he usually was. Beethoven was not, by natural predisposition, a happy man, the Maestro said.

" 'We were received coldly by Beethoven,' Liszt continued. 'He wouldn't allow me to play for him. He refused the invitation to my next concert. It was all the more exciting for me when I entered the concert hall for my next performance and found him sitting in the front row, so he could hear. He stared up at me with his baleful, unblinking eyes.'

"Liszt said he had never been nervous to play for an audience, but for the first and only time he trembled as he lifted his hands to play. As the crowd shouted with approval when he finished, there was only one person in the concert hall whose reaction mattered to Liszt. But Beethoven was not in his seat. He had walked out, Liszt thought with disappointment. Then he saw Beethoven approaching him from behind on the stage. He took Liszt by the shoulders and kissed him on the forehead.

"The Maestro got up to leave. I thanked him again for the courtesy he'd shown me. He waved it off as not worth mentioning, though it had been ten minutes I would remember and deeply cherish for the rest of my life. He stopped just before going out and looked back.

" 'Try not to be sad, Miss Moore,' the Maestro said. And then he was gone.

"The next day a package arrived at the house, a beautiful volume of Goethe's *Elective Affinities*. It was inscribed, 'To a promising young pianist,' and signed 'Franz Liszt.' One passage was neatly underlined in blue ink; I could not but help think the Maestro intended for me to pay special attention to the words. I remember them perfectly:

" 'The arts are the surest means of escaping from the world; they are also the surest means of uniting ourselves to it. Art is concerned with what is difficult and good. In seeing what is difficult performed with ease, we begin to think of the impossible.'

"I continued my studies with Doktur Jutt, who expressed pleasure at the sudden progress in my playing, which he attributed to his own good efforts. He did not realize that music had become my 'means of escaping from the world.' "

Lady Olivia and Lucian watched as a pair of ravens flew over the pavilion and landed at the edge of the lake. One stood with its eye cocked as its partner scratched at the snow and ice with its clawed foot. The birds, blue-black against the perfect whiteness, seemed displeased that the water was frozen.

"Two weeks passed. An invitation arrived for me to call on the Maestro for tea on Sunday afternoon. The note said he had just acquired two Boesendorfer pianos. One was new. The other had belonged to Robert Schumann. Liszt bought it from the composer's widow, Clara, one of my personal idols, who is teaching at the Frankfort Conservatory. The Maestro invited me to bring my family. Father was away on business, and Mama was reluctant to go, but she knew how important it was to me. It was a warm day, the sun bright in the sky, the air scrubbed by rain the day before. The fresh air would do Andrew good, we agreed.

"We began our visit with the Maestro showing us some of his treasures. In his library, behind the glass doors of a lawyer's bookcase, were autographed scores by Beethoven, Mozart, Bach, and Hayden. He also had a complete collection of Wagner's scores, addressed 'my dear friend' in the most affectionate terms. Of course, Wagner would have been nothing without Liszt's support. He was the first to recognize Wagner's genius, and through his efforts as patron ensured that Wagner's operas were performed until the world caught on to the new but brilliant Wagnerian ideas of harmony.

"It was a delightful afternoon. Liszt proved to be a charming host and conversationalist, entertaining us with stories about the world's musical luminaries and his many adventures as court musical director in Weimar. Even Mama forgot her troubles, listening to the Maestro weave a spell with his musical voice.

"After tea in the main parlor, he showed us the two pianos he kept in his study, an Erard and a Broadwood. The Broadwood was a sacred instrument. It had been Beethoven's. It was the last keyboard the great composer played before his death. Liszt said he played it only once or twice a year, gently touching the closed keyboard.

"The twin Boesendorfers were in the library, arranged so that the players could face one another. Liszt sat at one and invited me to find a place at the other. 'Clara's piano,' he called it. Upon each piano were transcriptions of an unfinished fantasia for two pianos. With his usual graciousness, the Maestro pretended that I would do him a very great service by playing through what he'd finished of the piece, claiming he needed to hear the two parts played at once to determine how well they worked together.

"I had to look over my shoulder to see Mama. She was in a window seat with little Andrew listless on her lap, where she would not be in my line of sight and distract me. She gave me an encouraging smile, no doubt suspecting the challenge before me in the untried Liszt manuscript.

"I looked back to the Maestro and nodded. We began to play.

"Since you don't play, Lucian, I should tell you that sitting down at a piano you've never played is a lot like getting on a horse you've never ridden. I always approach an untried piano at a recital with a certain degree of trepidation. One never knows what to expect. How will the keys be weighted? The action may be light or extremely stiff. And the sound—each piano has its own, and you only get to know it through experience. Some instruments are boomy in the lower registers and require a light touch with the left hand to keep the bass lines from overpowering the melody. With others, you must pound with all your strength to get anything out of the registers below middle C.

"I got no trouble from Robert and Clara Schumann's Boesendorfer. The instrument practically played itself. Which was fortunate, for the music before me was difficult. It was typical Liszt, beautiful but strange, the melodies drawn from the haunting Gypsy songs he remembered hearing as a child. I worked very hard to keep up with the music, and with my partner at the other piano, whose performance was at once effortless and sublime. As we progressed into the second movement, I moved into that magical realm of *otherness* one experiences when the music and the person listening to it seem to become one and the same. Perhaps you have had such a transcendent feeling in a concert hall. It is impossible to express in words. The music seemed to pour not from our hands but from our souls, an aria of shared bliss rising in the air. I had a vivid impression of what the music described— Gypsy women whirling around a campfire to the music of a bewitched violin, dark hair, dark eyes, colored silk ribbons, tambourines, and finger cymbals flashing in the firelight.

"We reached a point where my part rested for a measure and then ran to catch up. It gave me just enough time to glance up at the Maestro. I was struck by how handsome he was, even as an old man with long gray hair falling down either side of his face. His brow was high and as magnificently raked as his noble nose. His eyes were closed and he seemed lost within a spell. He didn't need to see the music; he knew it perfectly. He had somehow reached up to loosen his collar as he'd played. I had the sense that I was glimpsing into his past. As a young man, Liszt had been something of a Don Juan. There are still women who worship him. Listening to him perform, it was not difficult to understand why.

"My part resumed. We went on together a bit longer, until I turned the page and discovered the transcript suddenly ended. I must have looked startled, because the Maestro began to laugh. 'I warned you it was a work in progress,' he said.

"Mama clapped her hands and little Andrew mimicked her. It was so precious to see—and yet, in that single moment the terrible tragedy we found ourselves trapped within returned with all its dark force. Mama's face went from joy to agony within the single beat of a heart. I felt it come crashing down on myself, too. The chill was not lost on the Maestro, whose smile sank into a grave frown.

" 'I do not mean to intrude upon your private affairs, Lady Moore,' he said, addressing Mama, 'but I know of a physician renowned for his prodigious healing powers. He does not often agree to take on new patients, but perhaps I could prevail upon him to see your child. God willing, he might succeed where others have said there is no point in even trying.'

"Mama was starved for hope. She drank in the Maestro's words as if they were water and she had been lost for many days in the desert. With tears flowing down her cheeks, she said she would be forever in Liszt's debt if he could arrange for the physician to see Andrew.

"Liszt's offer brought Goethe's lines back to my head, the words striking me with an almost physical force: 'In seeing what is difficult performed with ease, we begin to think of the impossible.' But the impossible in music seemed an altogether different matter than the impossible in medicine.

" 'I promise I will do everything within my power,' he said.

"It had grown late. Andrew was sleeping in Mama's arms, the Maestro's words bringing peace to him, too. The time had come for us to go. At the door Liszt again promised to arrange for Andrew to have an audience with the great doctor. He gently touched the boy's head as Mama turned to carry him to the carriage. The child was smiling in his sleep, dreaming happy dreams, unaware of how precarious his purchase on life was at that moment.

" 'I cannot begin to thank you for all your kindness,' I said.

" 'The pleasure is entirely mine, Miss Moore,' he said, and bowed. 'I am no longer a young man, but being able to enjoy the company of someone so young and lovely is almost enough to bring back my lost youth.'

"While it may be scandalous for a proper young British woman to say so, I confess that at that moment I felt more than a small attraction for Liszt. The differences in our ages was too great for there to be anything more than an unexpressed mutual appreciation, yet even at his age, Liszt was a handsome, Byronic figure.

"I noticed something else as we said our farewells, something rather puzzling. Close to the roots of the Maestro's gray hair was a discernable darkening in color. I have seen older women and even older men who dyed their hair dark black or brown in the vain attempt to retain a simulacrum of youth. When they go too long between treatments, bits of gray become visible at the roots of their hair. What I saw in the Maestro's hair appeared to be just the opposite. Though nearly seventy, Franz Liszt apparently had been fortunate enough to retain his dark hair.

"Then why, I wondered, had the Maestro decided to dye his magnificent long locks a steely gray?"

37

◇

The Gate of Sighs

I DID NOT see Liszt for several days. I was in a rehearsal room at the Academy, playing the piano, and I had the uncanny sensation that the Maestro had come into the room and was standing behind me, watching me perform. I resisted the impulse to stop and look over my shoulder. I finished the piece. He was there, exactly as I'd imagined. I pretended to be surprised.

"I wanted to inquire whether he had been able to arrange an appointment for Andrew with the physician he had told us about, but I didn't want to be impolite. We made small talk until he suggested we take advantage of the beautiful day and go for a stroll. I happily consented, flattered at the great Franz Liszt's attention.

"We walked together through the streets, pausing to admire gardens and flower boxes. The Maestro talked of his friends Chopin and Berlioz. It was fascinating to hear his stories, not only because of my interest in music, but for what Liszt had to say and how he said it. I could not help but note again that he was extremely vigorous for a man his age. It was difficult for me to think of him as old. His eyes were bright and full of humor, his stride strong and certain. He stood up straight and tall, not hunched over, the way some people become as time and rheumatism bend their bodies and fill them with the aches, pains, and infirmities of old age. The golden-headed cane he carried lightly in his right hand was for fashion, not support, and from time to time he would use it to point out a particularly lovely or significant piece of architecture.

"We paused by a gate in the great walls that surround the old city. By then it was late in the day, not yet twilight, but close to it.

" 'Do you know what they call this?' the Maestro asked.

"I shook my head. I had been too engrossed in my piano studies and family concerns to spend time exploring Budapest. Liszt told me it was called the Gate of Sighs. As his eyes roamed over the heavy doors of scarred wood ribbed in iron and set into the heavy stone walls, he drew in a long breath that he exhaled in an extended sigh, as if the power of the place commanded him to feel and act out a portion of its drama.

" 'When I was a child, I would listen to the Gypsy violins play haunting melodies,' he said. 'Though my father took me away to Paris to study and perform, the music of my motherland lived on, whispering quietly in my blood. I was away so long I forgot my friends, I forgot my home, I even forgot my language. Still, the sad, strange music of the motherland was with me always. It was in me, a part of me. I am indistinguishable from it. The soil of the motherland is soaked in blood. For century after century my forebears fought to hold onto their homes, their faith, their lives. We have lived in a constant state of siege, the Germans attacking from the west, the Moslems from the south, the barbarian hordes of the steppes from the east.

" 'This gate,' Liszt said, and pointed with his cane, 'the Gate of Sighs, is where thousands died defending the city. Wives, children, and parents watched from the ramparts as the brave died by the thousands, but they held the city. In Budapest, at least, the streets did not run ankle deep in the steaming blood of the innocents. What desperate prayers were offered begging God for deliverance? How many long nights did the people of Hungary spend on their knees, begging for the power to save their families, their faith, their immortal souls? And their prayers were answered. Behold the evidence. The Gate of Sighs, where the tide was broken.'

"The Maestro asked if I was Catholic. I told him no. He considered this for a long moment. Liszt, somewhat infamous for amorous scandals in his earlier career, had grown to be a deeply faithful man. After a bit he asked if my faith was strong. I said it was.

" 'Life has its ways of testing one's faith,' he said. 'But you, my dear, will be tested more than others.'

" 'You mean with Andrew?' I asked.

"The Maestro nodded. He said he would take Andrew to see the great doctor, but indicated that would not necessarily be the end of our troubles.

" 'You need to prepare yourself,' he said.

" 'I know there is no guarantee of a cure,' I said, 'but at least we now have a reason to hope.'

" 'There is *always* hope,' Liszt replied a little sternly. 'You will have an important role to play in your brother's recovery. It will require personal sacrifice. You may well be required to care for Andrew for a great many years.'

"I said I would gladly agree to all of that and more.

" 'Saving your brother's life could change yours in the process.'

"I repeated that I would pay any price to help little Andrew. He took me by the arm and turned me back in the direction we had come.

" 'My best advice to you then, Miss Moore, is to pray to God for the strength and discernment to get you through the ordeal ahead. That is all I can say at this time. We leave tonight.'

" 'Leave?' I asked.

" 'The doctor who can save Andrew is a monk. He lives in a hermitage in the Carpathian Mountains.'

"I asked why it was necessary we leave that night. Father was away on business. It would be difficult, very difficult, to make the arrangements.

" 'Andrew has no time to spare,' Liszt said in a somber voice. I knew he was right. 'I have already attended to the details,' he continued. 'I will send a carriage in two hours to collect you, your mother, and brother.' "

" 'But Father—'

" 'He will understand your ability to act decisively when he returns to find his son's health restored and his life saved,' the Maestro said. 'Pack enough clothing for a week and bring plenty of books to read. The abbey is in a lonely place, and even with the fastest horses it will take us several days to reach our destination.' "

38

✦

The Abbey of St. Stephen

OUR DESTINATION WAS a tenth century monastery perched on the top of a remote mountain in a distant part of the country, a province that had remained depopulated since the time Suleiman the Magnificent put down an uprising by drowning the region in its inhabitants' blood.

"To reach the Abbey of St. Stephen, we traveled through the first night, all the next day, and into the following night. Fortunately, the Maestro knew how to travel in comfort. Our carriage had been built to his specifications, and was large and comfortable. We made good time while the roads were good, pulled behind a team of eight horses. We would stop at taverns and country inns along the way for meals and to stretch our legs. It was never long before we were back on the road again. The Maestro had arranged to have a fresh team of horses awaiting us at each stop. There were two drivers up top, and whichever one wasn't holding the reins would serve as footman and sleep between driving shifts.

"Liszt had been amazingly right about Andrew. His time was running out fast. He was comfortable when we were traveling, the motion of the carriage rocking him to sleep in Mama's arms. Whenever he awoke, the Maestro would begin telling him a Hungarian fairy tale, and before long he would be asleep again. Though he was too young to understand much of what Liszt told him, Andrew seemed mes-merized by anything our benefactor had to say.

"The rest of the time the Maestro either stared out the window, filled with a strange sadness, or read Shakespeare. He has a passion for books and art generally, which he likes to say have the power to refresh the soul. He once told me architecture is music crystallized, and music is the ethereal translation of the grace and symmetry of a beautiful build-ing.

"The second night of our trip, while Mama and Andrew were asleep, Liszt told me about our destination.

" 'The Abbey of St. Stephen is not the sort of place one thinks of in terms of a monastery of quiet monks,' he said. 'The original abbey was built a long time ago, when Chris-tianity came to what was then a pagan land. It was fortified during the wars. After much prayerful consideration, the brothers took the position that God did not want them meekly laying down their lives for Christ when only by fighting could they keep their faith from being extinguished in this part of Europe. They became a brotherhood of war-rior monks, blessed by God with unusual powers. They have returned to their quiet lives of devotion, but they remain keepers of secret blessings that came to them during times of utmost desperation.'

"Under most other circumstances, Liszt's talk would have disturbed me, but the only message I heard in what he'd said was that the brothers of St. Stephen would be able to cure Andrew, if only we arrived at the monastery while there was still time.

"The country became increasingly wild, the road narrow and rough. We stopped seeing other travelers along the way. There were no towns and only a few peasant cottages as the team of horses pulled us high into the Carpathian Moun-tains.

"My first glimpse of the Abbey of St. Stephen was by ragged moonlight as clouds began to blacken the sky. Even with the Byzantine cross atop the highest tower, the abbey was one of the most sinister-looking medieval fortresses I have ever seen. It stood alone atop a rocky peak blasted free of trees, a place so steep and forbidding that even shrubs and moss found it difficult to find purchase for their roots. The ramparts and gables were steep, in the style one sees in that part of Europe, especially in the mountains, where there is a need to resist the weight of heavy winter snows.

"The driver slowed the horses to a creep as we rolled onto a bridge crossing a deeply plunging gorge. In the moonlight, I saw the gears of the mighty engine that was used to raise the bridge, making access to the abbey impossible. We stopped before the gate, which remained closed. The horses pawed their feet and cried out, the way they do when they are anxious or afraid.

"A sudden agitation gripped Liszt. He jumped down from our carriage and strode past the horses. I put my head out the lowered window and saw him standing before the massive gate, staring up at it, the wind blowing his silvery hair and long black cloak about him. He did not call for the gate-keeper or pound his cane against the gate. Instead, he stood looking up at it, as if his impatient countenance could pro-vide all the force needed to open the massive gates and ad-mit us to the Abbey of St. Stephen.

"The sound of clanking chains behind the wall woke Mama, though Andrew continued to sleep. The gate groaned, as if seldom opened, and began to slowly rise. The Maestro got back into the carriage without a word of expla-nation as the driver snapped the reins and set the horses moving forward. The outer gate was but the first of several. After many more minutes we stopped, the door opened, and one of the drivers folded down the steps so that we might more easily disembark. The courtyard was much larger than I expected, meaning the Abbey of St. Stephen was even more massive than it had looked coming up the mountain. A single monk in a hooded caftan awaited us. Otherwise, the abbey seemed completely deserted. It was nearly midnight. The others were in bed, I thought.

"The monk attending us was of average height. Even beneath his hooded robe, one could see his broad shoulders and barrel chest. He drew back his cowl as he stepped forward to accept the Maestro's hand. He had a high, prominent forehead and eyes set deep beneath a ridged brow. He seemed strangely familiar, although I was sure we had never met. The other surprising thing about his appearance was his hair. Instead of being tonsured, as most brothers are, he had a thick head of long black hair, which he wore brushed straight back. I heard Liszt greet him as Brother Ludwig. It was plain from the look on Brother Ludwig's face that they were old friends.

" 'Welcome to the abbey, Brother Franz,' the monk said. *Brother* Franz, I noted. But then I recalled reading somewhere that the Maestro's late-blossoming faith had led him to take vows as a lay member of the Order of St. Francis. Even that seemed a bit out of kilter when I thought about it. The Franciscans took vows of poverty. The Abbey of St. Stephen appeared too warlike for the Franciscans, and, I thought, looking around me at the profusion of stained glass and elaborately carved stone ornamentation, entirely too rich for Franciscan blood. The citadel walls dated from the tenth century, the Maestro had said as our coach came up the mountain, which was two hundred years before St. Francis of Assisi's time, if I remembered my history correctly.

"The Maestro introduced Mama and me to Brother Ludwig. Though he was happy to see 'Brother Franz,' I was not so sure he felt the same about the rest of us.

" 'The sleeping child Lady Moore is holding in her arms is named Andrew. He is ill. Gravely ill,' Liszt added.

" 'I can see that,' Brother Ludwig said in German-accented English.

" 'We must help him,' Liszt said, giving the friar a look fraught with more meaning than was contained in his words.

" 'We will have to speak with the Abbot first.'

" 'Please, sir,' Mama said, sensing a certain reluctance in Brother Ludwig. 'I beg of you, help my child.'

" 'The Abbot is a compassionate man,' Brother Ludwig said. 'He will do what is best.'

"Liszt and Brother Ludwig stared at one another for a long moment. It was almost as if a communication without words was taking place, although that was, of course, impossible.

"The chapel bell began to toll midnight. The sound of singing, beautiful singing, began somewhere within the abbey walls. The Gregorian chant echoed against the courtyard walls, swelling louder and louder and louder. The monks emerged from a doorway overlooked by two menacing gargoyles. They walked two abreast, intoning a Latin chant that had probably been heard within those walls for more than eight hundred years, maybe longer. They moved in their double file toward the chapel for Mass. The higher voices of boys joined in. At least that is what I thought at first, but then I realized I was hearing *women's* voices. This was a very strange monastery indeed, I thought, with monks and nuns living alongside one another.

"One of the two brothers leading the procession broke away and came across the courtyard toward us. Liszt took a few steps forward to meet him. I could not hear the brief conversation, but the sharpness of the words—spoken in Latin, it sounded like—made it plain that there was disagreement. I guessed it was the Abbot the Maestro was speaking with. Surely he wouldn't refuse to allow the great physician who lived at the Abbey of St. Stephen to try to save little Andrew's life, I thought.

"Liszt turned and rejoined us, the Abbot coming with him. The monk drew back his cowl, the better to peer at us. He had a shaved head and a narrow, ascetic face. Though it was evident that our presence was not entirely welcome, he managed a small smile, which put us instantly at ease.

" 'I am Brother Michael, the Abbot here.'

"The Maestro introduced us. Brother Michael laid his hand on Andrew's head, nodding as if he understood everything perfectly. Andrew stirred a little in his sleep but did not open his eyes. It was beginning to rain.

" 'Bless this child, Lord, and watch over him so that he might walk in thy ways,' Brother Michael said, a benediction.

" 'Lady Moore, you must be very tired after your long journey,' he said to Mama. 'Brother Joseph will show you to your rooms. Your luggage will be brought up to you, along with hot water for washing and some hot soup, tea, and bread, if you wish it.'

"Brother Joseph seemingly materialized behind us when the Abbot said his name.

" 'You are very kind,' Mama said.

" 'We will talk in the morning,' the Abbot said. 'Now, you need to rest. God bless you.'

" 'And God bless you, Brother Michael,' Mama said, turning to follow Brother Joseph.

" 'A moment, if you please, Miss Moore.'

"I stopped almost before I could begin to follow Mama, Andrew, and Brother Joseph. They continued across the courtyard without looking back at me.

" 'I invite you to join us at chapel, if you are not too tired after your journey, Miss Moore.'

" 'I think I would like that very much,' I said. I wanted to thank God for bringing us as far as He had, and to ask Him to help Andrew get well.

"The Abbot regarded me closely for long enough that I began to feel uncomfortable.

" 'The three of us must have a long talk,' Brother Michael said, 'you, Brother Franz, and I.'

"I looked to the Maestro, expecting reassurance, but the expression of concern on his face did nothing to put me at ease. The rain had started to fall in earnest by then, cold against our faces and bare heads. In the torchlight, I saw that Liszt's white hair was now streaked with black. The dye he had used to color his hair gray was being rinsed out by the rain, running down the shoulders of his cape, staining it. The Maestro gave me a curious look, then understood what was happening. He touched his fingers to his hair and glanced at them with distaste.

" 'I should have used something more permanent,' he said.

"I hardly heard his words. I was too transfixed with what was happening to his *face*. His entire head seemed to blur as some strange metamorphosis occurred. I felt myself become faint. I was hallucinating. It was the result of exhaustion and worry, I thought. Or perhaps I was sick myself, standing there in the freezing rain.

"Brother Ludwig's strong hand took me by the arm, steadying me. I blinked to clear my eyes, but the illusion would not go away. I was looking at Liszt and not seeing the old man he was but rather the man he must have been thirty or even forty years earlier.

" 'You have no idea how difficult it has been to maintain this charade,' Liszt said with a sigh.

"I was grateful to feel Brother Ludwig's hand clamped onto my arm. At that moment, his grip seemed to be my only connection with the real world.

" 'You are not losing your mind, Olivia, although I certainly understand why you would think you are,' Liszt said.

" 'Perhaps we should forego the chapel and have our talk now,' Brother Michael interrupted. 'The Lord will understand if we miss Mass. Come. We must get the young lady out of this cold rain before she goes into shock.' "

39

The Abbot's Laboratory

OLIVIA AND LUCIAN had gotten up from the pavilion and walked around the frozen lake, turning back toward the house. The majestic Palladian facade of Collingsworth was in front of them in the distance. Olivia thought it good that Lucian have something solid to fix his eyes upon as her story became increasingly unreal.

"We have become so civilized that it is difficult for us to accept that something beyond the commonplace is possible," she said. "Yet my brother's illness had pushed me to a place where the impossible was what I prayed for. The world is a much larger place than we think. Strange things happen in distant lands. When we hear of them, we think they are fairy tales, because we have become incapable of folding our minds around the fantastic and magical. Think of what I am about to tell you as if it were a fairy tale, Lucian. If you love me even a little, do not be too quick to think I have lost my mind."

Olivia glanced up at the man who had only a short time ago asked her to marry him. He was looking down at her with an expression of tender concern. She hoped he would understand. She had no choice but to continue. She had told him too much to stop now.

"We reached the Abbot's office and I realized Brother Michael and I were alone. The others had turned off somewhere in the monastery's winding corridors, leaving us to have our talk in privacy. We were in one of the abbey's more ancient wings, and yet Brother Michael's office was anything but inhospitable. The central chamber sat in the midst of six vaulted alcoves, most of them apparently filled with books and obscure scientific apparatus. A rich Persian carpet covered the stone floor, and a fire burned in the fireplace, which was large enough to walk into, making the Abbot's lair somewhat more comfortable than it otherwise would have been. The main part of the room, centered around a massive table covered with books and manuscripts, was bright from the light of what seemed like a hundred candles. I noticed Brother Michael's medical gear in one alcove—an examining table, a fearsome array of surgical tools in a glass cabinet on the wall, and, fading into the distance, shelves containing medicines, herbs, and drugs. For some reason, perhaps the Gothic setting, it put me in mind of Mary Shelley's *Frankenstein,* but I pushed such thoughts out of my head.

"He took my cloak and put a shawl around my shoulders to keep me from catching a chill.

" 'I am sure you are unaccustomed to spirits,' he said, handing me a glass of brandy, 'but as a physician I urge you to drink this.'

"I took a sip. The liquor burned my throat, but had its desired effect.

"Brother Michael said he could tell that I was curious about Brother Franz, as they called Liszt, but that I should leave those questions for another time. Of greater importance to them all was Andrew's well-being. 'He is gravely, gravely ill,' the Abbot said in a sepulchral tone. I nodded.

" 'Can you help my brother?' I asked in a beseeching voice. 'Are you the great healer the Maestro has told me about? Please tell me you will use your skills to save little Andrew's life.'

"Brother Michael's lips made a tight, straight line as he looked at me in an almost fierce way. I was certain he was going to refuse my request. We were seated next to one another on a pair of heavily carved, high-back wooden chairs. Looking at him, the cold authority in his face, made me feel as if I were facing a judge about to condemn me to the gallows.

" 'I will oversee the boy's treatment . . .'

" 'Oh, thank you, Brother,' I interrupted. He held up his hand, cutting off my gratitude midstream.

" '. . . but only if you decide you wish to pursue the treatment, once you understand the ramifications. The child has leukemia. I wish that I knew a cure for such a disease. I don't. One doesn't exist.'

" 'Then there's nothing you can do to help?' I said, so weighed down with disappointment that I could hardly speak.

" 'I did not say that,' Brother Michael replied. 'This abbey has been here for many centuries. Through the grace of God we have managed, in all modesty, to collect most of what little wisdom there is to be had in this world. We are a brotherhood of mendicants and scholars. And yes,' he added, 'the other thing you have heard about us is also true. We have been warriors, when forced to defend the faith, but it has been a long time since we have had to take up our swords in defense of the Lamb. In recent years we have been left at peace to devote ourselves to the various arts, some practical, some better suited to celebrating the beauty of God through music and art. My own pursuits have been, as you can see, of a scientific nature.'

"He indicated the laboratory he maintained in his office. I expressed my interest, thinking perhaps Brother Michael had made some medical discovery that would help Andrew, even if it wouldn't cure him. The Abbot smiled at me for the first time. He was proud of his achievements and keen to share them. I followed him into a darkened alcove where there was a worktable beneath the low-vaulted ceiling cluttered with tools, boxes, and scores of tiny gears. He turned on a lamp, illuminating the scene, but it was a lamp unlike any I had ever seen.

" 'This is called an incandescent light,' Brother Michael explained. 'Do you know much about electricity? Electricity is the energy you see expressed in lightning during a thunderstorm. It is possible to make electricity by various means, mechanical and chemical. By combining the proper chemistry in a barrel I keep on the roof, I maintain an electrical charge to power this lamp. The light is created when an electric current passes through the carbon-filament fiber within this curiously shaped little bell jar made of thin glass. The interior of the bell jar is an airless vacuum. I perfected the technology a few years ago, but continue to tinker with the design. I am working on another design where light results when the electricity passes through a gas medium instead of a carbon filament. Such a lamp might have a longer life.'

"I was impressed and said as much.

" 'Just wait,' Brother Michael said. 'My invention is going to shake things up. I've been sharing my ideas about incandescent lights with a bright young man named Edison I correspond with in the United States. Mark my words, Miss Moore: The incandescent light is going to have a profound impact on the world. Homes and cities will be more hospitable and safer during the nighttime in the years to come because of the incandescent light.'

"In one corner was a box emitting a low hum. This was an invention that collected moisture from the air, which Brother Michael called a 'dehumidifier.' It, too, was powered by electricity. He said the device pumped compressed gas through copper tubing, causing it to cool. Moisture in the air then condensed on the coil and dripped into a pan. Brother Michael used the collected water for the plants in his greenhouse. He had installed several of the units in the abbey to remove the unpleasant dampness that often permeates stone buildings.

" 'I wish all of my inventions were a success, but alas they are not,' he said. As if to confess the limitations of his ability if not his imagination, he showed me a box about the size of a large concertina, with numerals written on the keyboard. It was a mechanical abacus.

" 'You press in numbers you wish to add, subtract, multiply, or divide using the keyboard. When this lever is pulled, the answer to the simple arithmetic problem is displayed here. Try it.'

"I manipulated the keys to multiply seven times seven. The answer—forty-nine—was displayed in rotating numbers on the top of the box.

" 'But it works,' I said. 'How clever!'

" 'Only for simple operations,' Brother Michael said. 'To be truly useful, my calculating automaton would need to do square roots, tangents, and so forth. Unfortunately, higher functions are beyond the capability of a mechanical device of this sort. It would take a machine the size of this room and a tremendous amount of energy to operate it to solve each problem. But I am not beaten yet. For a calculating automaton to work, it would have to be electrical and built of miniaturized parts, using not gears, as my first model, but perhaps electrical impulses powering tiny switches to perform computations. The switches themselves would be electrical, not mechanical, and would count by remembering their charge. Since electrical energy moves with the speed of light, such a machine could be tiny enough to hold in your hand, yet it would be capable of crushing the most enormous equations in fractions of a second.

" 'But,' he said, as if waking himself from his technological dream, 'none of this is why you traveled all the way to the Abbey of St. Stephen.'

"I followed him back into the other room. We retook our chairs. He made a steeple with his fingers and rested his chin against the peak, looking at me intently.

" 'Medicine,' he said, after remaining silent for nearly a minute, 'sometimes uses fire to fight fire. Substances that are quite toxic in large doses—arsenic, mercury—can be used to treat certain diseases and illnesses. Sometimes embracing a potentially deadly substance is the only way to counteract an equally lethal pathology.'

" 'Are you saying the treatment carries its own risk?'

" 'There is always risk,' Brother Michael said. 'In this case, the risk would not be so much to Andrew as it would be to those around him.'

"I had no idea what he meant by that, but I waited to hear the rest.

" 'If you decide you want us to treat Andrew, we can defeat his sickness, but only through giving him a sickness of another sort. This one, however, poses little threat to Andrew. Indeed, it is the only disease under the sun that confers certain benefits. It will give him great physical strength as he grows older. It is a jealous disease and will let no other sicknesses infect him as long as he is its host. It will enhance his mental capacity to an extraordinary degree. He will be able to read one of Kant's dense philosophical tomes in an astonishingly short amount of time and remember each word.

" 'But,' Brother Michael said, pointing his index finger at me, 'there is a cost. In physics, we say that for every action there is an equal and opposite reaction. The benefits do not come without their price. We can only defeat Andrew's disease with another disease. And a disease is never a pleasant or harmless affair. The particular disease we will use to defeat Andrew's leukemia will change the boy in small but significant ways and leave him forever dependent upon one peculiar and undeniable need.'

"Brother Michael stopped. He leaned back in his chair and stared at me, as if it were up to me to continue the discussion.

" 'What is it that Andrew will need?' I asked.

" 'Every fortnight he will need to drink a few ounces of fresh human blood.' "

Lucian stopped as if he'd suddenly reached the end of a long chain tether. He stared at Olivia, his lips parted as if he had been struck momentarily dumb. She could see the confusion in his eyes, and behind it, horror.

"If you love me . . ." she said.

He nodded dully.

"Brother Michael then said to me, 'This brings up the matter of how you fit into the equation of Andrew's treatment, Miss Moore. None of this can happen without your complete cooperation.'

" 'If I must agree to provide Andrew with a transfusion of my blood every two weeks, you needn't even wonder if I will give my consent,' I said. I would have done *anything* to save my precious brother's life. Anybody in my position would have, even you, Lucian.

"Brother Michael lowered his head, looking at me through his eyebrows, and said cryptically, 'I am afraid that it is somewhat more complicated than a simple matter of transfusions, Miss Moore.' "

40

✦

The Miracle

AFTER THE TREATMENT, Andrew fell into a delirious fever."

"But—"

"Kindly allow me to tell the story my way, Lucian," Olivia interrupted. "All will be made plain in the end. Besides, I can only tell you some things by inference. I was not present for the treatment, although I was to learn everything soon enough.

"While Mama and I feared the worst, judging from Andrew's condition, Brother Michael did not appear to be unduly concerned. I prayed—oh, how I prayed—that the physician-monk was not merely making a good show of it. Time proved Brother Michael correct in his optimism, thank God. Mama and I were sitting beside Andrew's bed one evening—I was pretending to read, Mama was staring at the child with the stricken expression that had not left her face since Andrew's treatment—when he opened his eyes and sat up in bed. His eyes were clear, his color good, his smile radiant.

" 'Mama,' he said and put out his arms.

"Brother Michael had worked his miracle.

"We stayed on at the Abbey of St. Stephen so Brother Michael could observe Andrew's progress and help us all adjust to his special circumstances. The monks and nuns, while unaccustomed to little ones, were very accepting of Andrew. Though the members of the order had undertaken a penitential vow of silence around the time of our arrival, Brother Michael had given them leave to speak to Andrew, and many of them seemed to take special delight in his company. Andrew was given free run of the place, and his insatiable curiosity and tireless feet took him all the places there were to visit, invited or not. Brother Michael encouraged Mama and me to let the boy go off with the others in the abbey for hours on end without our supervision, though one of the brothers or sisters was always with him. This served as a tonic for us all, he said; people, like plants and animals, need room to breathe. Andrew's illness had necessarily kept him from interacting with others and exercising his young wits as well as his body. And Mama and I had made it our business to never let the child out of our waking minds for a moment, whether we were in the same room with him or merely nearby.

"Mama lost her care-worn look, although I had exchanged one burden in my heart for another that, while less heavy, was onerous enough in its own right. Still, it filled me with joy to see Andrew running through the abbey like a healthy child, singing or laughing. It was during our time at the monastery that he began to talk, and not just a few mispronounced words and broken phrases, but in complete sentences that evidenced his increasingly complex grasp of abstract things that should have been beyond the knowledge of so young a toddler. Mama was delighted with her precocious little boy. As was I, though my delight was tempered with the understanding that his rapid intellectual development would soon present its own challenges.

"The main consequence of Andrew's treatment, at least at the first, was that his new condition left him unusually sensitive to light. In time he would learn to overcome this, Brother Michael said. Again, he was right. Brother Raphael, one of the monks who was especially fond of my brother, helped Andrew train himself to gradually overcome his sensitivity, to the point that he learned to go outside in the direct sunlight and suffer no discomfort.

"One of the most curious things about our stay at the Abbey of St. Stephen was that I did not see the Maestro. Brother Michael would only say that Liszt had gone into seclusion at the monastery to do special penance. I gathered the penance, like the order's overall vow of silence, had something to do with his bringing us to the abbey, thus permitting mere outsiders to become privy to the hermetic brotherhood's greatest secrets.

"I finally saw the Maestro a week before we were to leave. I was in one of the abbey's many small chapels. I had gotten in the habit of going there to pray before bedtime, asking God for strength for what lay ahead. I heard someone come in. I looked around and there was Brother Franz, smiling in the doorway. You must be wondering *which* Liszt I found myself regarding: young or old. It was young Liszt, in appearance if not years. I got up from my knees as he slid into the pew beside me. I regarded him carefully in the flickering light of the altar candles. It would have been easy to be deceived in such light, but he was as near to me as are you. This was no illusion. Franz Liszt appeared to be no older than thirty. Such was the power of the brotherhood's secret. It had saved us the grief of laying Andrew out in a tiny coffin and bathing him in our tears; it had saved the Maestro from the ravages of his old age.

" 'I would have never imagined it possible to cheat time,' he said. He seemed to read my thoughts, for he added, 'I have been given special leave of my vow of silence to speak with you. You're wondering about the way I look.'

"I nodded. He seemed to know *exactly* what I was thinking.

" 'It has erased the years in my face and body. I did not believe it was possible.'

" 'Will you become older, then, as the years pass?' I asked. 'Is the condition permanent, or has it only given you a second start in life?'

" 'I will not age outwardly. Not in my physical body. Only in here.' He touched his heart.

" 'But Andrew will grow into an adult?'

" 'Brother Michael has assured me of as much, although no older.'

" 'And the others here?' I asked.

" 'We all have several things in common,' Liszt told me. 'Our faith, our dedication to knowledge and art, and the peculiar circumstances of a condition we all share.'

" 'Then Mama and I are the only—'

" 'There are the peasants who live behind the mountain in a small village. The brotherhood has watched over them for generations. We take care of them and they take care of us, if you understand my meaning. You might be surprised to learn they have no idea of their importance to us. We can be very subtle.'

"I touched my fingers to my neck without realizing what I was doing until I saw the Maestro's stricken look. 'I would never touch you without your permission,' he said. 'None of us would.'

" 'Of course not,' I said, embarrassed that I had hurt his feelings. I tried to cover the moment by asking him about the others' ages.

" 'Most of them are a great deal older than I, thanks to the gift. I am but a babe compared with Brother Michael and Brother Raphael.'

"I thought it odd for him to call it a *gift*. Brother Michael always referred to it as a disease with certain benevolent side effects. But in many ways it was a gift, or would be, if its power could be carefully contained.

" 'Like us, Andrew will never know the ignominy of old age. There will be no lines in the corners of his eyes, no wrinkles in his cheeks from smiling. His back will not hurt or his joints begin to ache from rheumatism. The ravages of time will not touch him. He will be like an angel—perfect, beautiful, ageless. And like an angel he must devote himself to improving humanity, to making the world more beautiful, to celebrating the joy of God's creation.'

"The Maestro put his hand lightly on my shoulder, and as he spoke I knew he was giving me a solemn charge.

" 'You must ensure Andrew grows up understanding these things, Olivia. You bear a tremendous responsibility. As the child grows, so will his capacity for good. Channel his interests and powers in the right direction. Teach him to resist the Devil's temptations. God gave all of us free will to choose between good and evil. For the ordinary mortal, his eternal soul hangs in the balance. So it shall be with Andrew. But because of his special abilities, he will have the power to influence countless other souls. It is up to you to make sure he grows up working for the good of man and the glory of God. The alternative is unspeakable. Do you understand what I am telling you, my dear?'

"I said I did, and promised the Maestro I would not disappoint him and the others.

" 'The years that must be devoted to the child's upbringing is why the *Illuminati* Council here at the abbey chose you over the child's mother as his guardian. While the task will require the constant care a mother might best provide, the job is better suited to someone with fewer worldly entanglements, shall we say. It will be far easier for an older sister, someone blessed with intelligence, talent, devotion, and more than a little courage to look after the child until he has grown.

" 'Your responsibility will not end until Andrew has grown up straight and true and can return to the Abbey of St. Stephen to claim his rights as a full member of the brotherhood. At that time you, too, will be welcome to join us, if you so choose. Do not look so alarmed, my dear,' he said. 'You would not have to remain cloistered here. Most of the *Illuminati* live out in the world and return here only for periods of rest and contemplation. We can do the most good living amidst humanity, not here behind the abbey walls.'

"I started to ask a question about returning to Budapest,

but he stopped me and said he would not accompany us when we left.

" 'I must remain here to continue the penance assigned for bringing Andrew to the abbey without receiving approval first. It is a small price to pay for saving the child's life. There wasn't time for the formalities. Brother Michael and the others understand that, even if the boy does not fit the criteria the *Illuminati* have developed to decide who to help in that way. That is an issue on which I have to part company with my brothers and sisters, though I concede the principle. There's something off-key about a law that declares the life of an old pianist worth preserving, but not the life of a beautiful little boy. I promise to visit you in Budapest if I can, but I do not have much time left for Franz Liszt. The time has come for me, as an ordinary mortal, to make my exit from the world's stage. Brother Franz will not really be dying, of course, but his old identity must. It's the way of this life, you see. Perhaps you could bring Andrew to Bayreuth. I hope to be there to hear *Parsifal* performed. Dear Wagner: His immense genius towers over everything. Next to you and Andrew, dear girl, his *Nibelungenring* is the sun that illumines my summer sky. In the meantime, the solitude and meditation will do me well. Maintaining the illusion that I appear as aged as I should is a tremendous drain on my energy.'

"I started to tell him I didn't know how we would get along without him. He'd become a part of my family.

" 'Then we must say goodbye when the time comes but not farewell. I promise you one day we will sit down together at the keys of Beethoven's Broadwood and play duets. Brother Ludwig would love to have that piano back from me, but I can't bear the thought of parting with it.'

" 'Brother Ludwig?'

" 'Oh, my goodness, yes. You didn't know? You *are* in for a treat. You must pay your respects to old Beethoven before you go. Brother Ludwig may look a bit formidable, like a thunderstorm in the form of a man, but he positively melts when he meets someone who admires his music. Ask him to play you his new sonata. On second thought, you won't have to ask. It would be impossible to get him to *not* play it for a pretty admirer! It's very good, you know, though unfortunately no one outside the *Illuminati's* little circle will ever get to hear it.'

"Liszt leaned forward then and did something that very much surprised me. He took my head in both his hands and kissed me on the forehead. The way his eyes fell to my lips just before he did it made me think his original intention was to kiss me full on the mouth, but he apparently thought the better of it.

"And then, before I could react, he was gone."

41

✦

Interlude and
Recapitulation

WE RETURNED TO Budapest and were very happy
for a time. My best memories are from this period.
Papa and Mama went about in a state of bliss, now that their
golden child's health had been restored by our visit to a
cloister of odd, secretive monks.

"Of course, Andrew's well-being was conditional upon
one peculiar need being met. That was taken care of every
two weeks with a minimum of trouble and certainly without
causing any lasting harm. One of our servants would experience a strange, pleasurable dream, nothing more. Brother
Michael, Brother Gabriel, and the others had done an excellent job of teaching us how to handle the process with a minimum of disturbance and no lasting effects for the
benefactors.

"I returned to the conservatory, where my teachers soon
determined it was time for my first public recital. I performed mainly Beethoven, out of homage to the Maestro,
who remains to this day at the Abbey of St. Stephen, as far
as I know. I caused something of a sensation at the end of my
performance by impulsively adding a piano interpretation of
the final section of Wagner's opera Gotterdammerung, de-
parting from the text of the music—I was playing without a

score, at any rate!—for a long, improvisational exploration of tonal and harmonic colorations. The audience—which included Archduke Rudolf, the son of Franz Josef, King of Hungary and Emperor of Austria—applauded until I thought the concert house would collapse. They would not be satisfied until I played an encore. I choose Liszt, of course—*The Mephisto Waltz.*

"Both of the pieces played as mere impulses—*Gotterdammerung* and the *Mephisto*—turned out to be prescient. Although it was hardly on the magnitude of *Twilight of the Gods,* my family's brief interlude of happiness was about to come to a crashing end, not with the glorious immolation of Siegfried, but in the explosion of an anarchist's bomb. The trouble that followed us home to London has been nothing but one prolonged waltz with Mephistopheles, though I will tell you more about that soon.

"But for that brief moment, I had my triumph. The reviews in the next day's newspapers proclaimed an incomparable genius had been transferred from the vessel of the teacher— the great Liszt—into the smaller, younger, prettier vessel of the student. One review proclaimed that I was the first woman since Clara Schumann to have completely distinguished herself at the keyboard. This was heady stuff for a girl who had just turned eighteen and had not yet been presented to London society. The future seemed blindingly bright for a brief, shining moment, even with strains of *Gotterdammerung* and the *Mephisto* echoing in my head.

"And then, like the light when you blow out a candle, everything golden was gone, except for dear little Andrew.

"Andrew and I returned to London with his governess, Karol Janos, buried Mama and Papa, and took up residence in Moore House. I did not go near the piano. But for my brother, the light had gone out of my life. I rather thought the Maestro might write, especially after my parents' death, but there was nothing. Brother Michael had told me the *Illuminati* would have no contact with us until we proved we were worthy of the gift that had been bestowed. Only then, for better or for worse, would they reach out to us. How I dreaded what that might mean as London cowered through the worst of the Vampire Panic. Though we were not directly responsible for any of *that,* I have lived in fear that one of their avenging angels would call on us to take back the gift over which we had proven to be imperfect stewards.

"I need to make one thing perfectly clear: I take responsibility for the terrible things that happened. If the authorities were capable of dealing with the truth, I would have gone to them at the first. But where would that have left Andrew? He would have become an instant object of fear. Under the circumstances, I had no choice but to deal with things as best I could.

"But I get ahead of myself.

"On the night of November first this past year, I had the unhappy occasion to attend a friend's funeral, leaving Andrew at home in Janos's care. The tot has developed a passion for Homer, of all things, an interest his governess indulges but does not share. Janos fell asleep in the nursery, reading the *Odyssey* to Andrew, although not in the original Greek, of course, which is what he loves best. The boy got up and found his way to Annie Howard's bed. She was always one of his great favorites, probably because she had a passing resemblance to poor Mama. He snuggled up beneath the covers with the girl, with a child's natural and innocent affection. But the blood speaks powerfully to someone who has made the change. It was very nearly Andrew's time, and the Hunger called out to him. The child did not mean to harm Annie. But without me there to help him control the appetite for what his body craves most, there was a regrettable accident. I am embarrassed to admit that we moved poor Annie's body to the kitchen to make it look as if an awful intruder were responsible for the attack.

"As if that wasn't tragic enough, something else happened about this time that was to have even greater consequences.

Unbeknownst to me, Janos was letting Andrew use her to satisfy his Hunger at odd intervals. These feedings weren't necessary, mind you. They were comfort feedings, the way you might give a child a glass of milk and piece of cake before bed to make him feel full and satisfied. The consequence of this was that she became weakened enough for the change to take hold in her.

"Janos did not share her secret with me. I could have easily seen it in her, and I should have, but I was too distraught with grief and guilt and fear that we would be found out after what happened to poor Annie that I didn't pay much attention to anything during those first dangerous weeks.

"Left to her own devices, Janos made an unfortunate mistake. The first was to lose control of herself with her friend Fannie Turner, the first time the Hunger called to her. Janos had no idea what to expect or how to control herself. The result, as you know, was tragic. That was the second death on my conscience.

"Janos fell into a black mood after that, as you might well expect. I feared she would try to take her life. I managed to educate her about what I had learned from Brother Michael, and advised her that the only way to make amends for what had happened was service, prayer, contrition, and atonement. She was able to turn the corner, thank God. I don't know what I would do without her.

"Unfortunately, Janos made one more mistake. Our man Ballantine had formed a certain attraction to Janos and had been pursuing her, although this also came as a complete surprise to me, when I found it out. There is far more to running a London household, I have discovered, than ringing a bell when it is time for the servants to bring in tea. Apparently, Ballantine's affections were not entirely unrequited. Unfortunately, when all was said and done Janos had unwittingly passed the gift on to Ballantine.

"Despite the mask they present to the world, some people are basically good in their hearts, and others aren't. Ballantine belonged to the latter category and immediately gave himself over to the worst possible excesses. Lady Margaret Burke was the first woman he pleasured himself with."

"That cur," Lucian said.

"In doing so, he proved himself lecherous, murderous, and guilty of having designs far above his station. As the Prince of Wales's boon companion and equerry, Lucian, I need hardly tell you that His Royal Highness had maintained an intimate friendship with Lady Margaret Burke."

Olivia glanced at Lucian and saw he was blushing. Apparently he did not entirely approve of Prince Edward Albert's merrymaking.

"Ballantine was also a fool. He could hardly have picked a more dangerous person to prey upon. Her death aroused not only Scotland Yard but the attention of the government. As you know, it took no time at all for Lord Beaconsfield to impanel the special investigative committee to swoop down on Mayfair to protect our next king's reputation, if need be, and run the malefactor to the ground.

"My suspicions about Ballantine were not aroused until the terrible killing spree in the East End on New Year's Day. Only then did I overhear the servants whisper that he was in the habit of patronizing the fallen women who haunt the streets, gin mills, and opium dens in that part of the city. I would have never imagined that a servant in our household could take perverse pleasure in inflicting pain and death on these poor creatures, but when I looked at Ballantine—when I really looked at Ballantine—it all was immediately self-evident. I called him and Janos into the parlor, shut the door, and asked them both some very impolite questions. It didn't take many minutes for me to get the truth—the bloody, horrifying truth."

"What did you do about Ballantine?"

"What could I do, Lucian? By the time all of your eyes were scrutinizing Moore House, I was so distraught I could scarcely draw a breath without twin blades of anxiety and guilt stabbing into my heart."

Olivia stopped and gripped Lucian's arm the way a floundering swimmer might cling to a rescuer. For the first time since beginning her story, her carefully maintained composure began to desert her.

"What else was I to do in the end, Lucian?" she cried. "I had no choice. Ballantine had passed the gift on to one of the prostitutes he frequented. The killings were spreading out in a circle I could not control. The city was on the verge of open panic."

Olivia felt Lucian's gloved hand beneath her chin, raising it until their eyes met. They were almost back to Collingsworth. The house's portico framed Captain Lucian's body, making his shoulders seem even more broad and strong.

"What happened?" Lucian asked in a flat, controlled voice.

"The police couldn't stop Ballantine. I mean no disrespect, Lucian, but the government couldn't stop him. Cotswold, with all his knowledge of science, couldn't stop him. And Van Helsing—well, surely you realize by now he was a complete fraud. He couldn't stop Ballantine."

"So what did you do? Or did you do nothing?"

"Janos wanted to try, but I doubted she would be a match for him. The old Magyar steel is still in her eyes, but she has come close to breaking down over everything that has happened. Still, something had to be done. Ballantine had gone completely insane with his power. For someone like him, blood is the most powerful of drugs. He could not resist it. He reveled in it, in the perverse exultation it gave him to subjugate and torment those he took it from, draining them until their hearts stopped and their empty flesh grew cool beneath his touch. He was a monster, Lucian. I had to do something."

"You mean you . . ."

Olivia drew herself upright and looked at Lucian directly, toe-to-toe, face-to-face, eye-to-eye.

"I killed Ballantine."

"Good God!" Lucian gasped.

"I committed murder, but as terrible a deed as it was, what

choice did I have? Certainly the courts would have condemned him to die. I only did what they never would have been able to do. And I did it before he was able to claim another life. I burned the body and scattered the ashes. No trace of the fiend will ever be found."

He gave her a hard look. "Are there other vampires in London?"

The question made Olivia's heart sink. It sounded as if he had decided his ultimate responsibility belonged to his Special Committee. The Captain was a military man, she thought, a man of honor sworn to do his duty, a proper Englishman.

"At this point, I believe the beacon of your attention need shine no farther than Moore House."

Lucian nodded gravely.

"But there is yet another problem," Olivia said. "And a very serious problem at that."

"Can I help?"

Her face brightened. Maybe he hadn't decided to despise her for her complicity and her crime. "It is Lord Shaftbury. He has shrewdly worked it out that Moore House is the epicenter of the London Vampire Panic. It might surprise you to know he employs a private cadre of spies. They brought him information he did not share with the rest of you."

That made Lucian frown, though Olivia could tell it did not entirely surprise him.

"If Shaftbury plans to arrest you, I cannot prevent it," Lucian said. "The most I might hope to do is help you get across the Channel with Andrew and Janos."

The words brought a rush of hope fluttering back into Olivia's heart. "That you still care for me enough to consider such a thing is more gratifying than I can possibly say, dear Lucian. But the situation is more delicate than it appears. Shaftbury does not want to arrest me. Not if he can get me to help him."

"Help him how?" Lucian asked slowly, sensing he was about to learn something he would just as soon not know.

"Lord Shaftbury is not interested in justice or the public's safety or even revenge," Olivia said with a bitter smile. "Certainly you know as well as I that Lord Shaftbury is a lustful, ambitious man. Beneath his pose as a virtuous public servant lies a man interested in only one thing: power. He lives it and breathes it. He *worships* it the way the Israelites in the desert turned away from God to pray to the golden calf. Shaftbury has seen the vampire's power. More than anything else he covets this power for himself. And he will stop at nothing to possess it.

"After supper last night you saw us having a tête-à-tête by the backgammon table. I could tell by the protective look in your eyes you suspected Lord Shaftbury was making an improper suggestion to me. And he was, but not the kind you think. What Shaftbury was saying, in the low, whispering voice he uses to make offers and threats, is that he wants me to give him the *gift*. He's blackmailing me, Lucian. If I refuse him, he vows to have my entire household, including myself and Andrew, arrested and executed in secret without trial."

"Then the man is a complete blackguard!" Lucian said with anger. "He thinks he can force you into having Andrew or Janos change him into a vampire?"

"No, my dear, he wants *me* to change him."

Lucian stared at Olivia with stunned incomprehension.

"When we were at the Abbey of St. Stephen, I promised Brother Michael I would watch over Andrew as he grew into manhood, teaching him to respect and fear his powers, and to put them to good use for the service of mankind. But the only way I could ever hope to keep up with the child was by making the change myself, Lucian. During Andrew's feedings, I let him slowly introduce the disease into my blood. I was very sick for a long time, but it was a sacrifice I was willing to make so that I could take care of him. Although I have proven inadequate to the job, I will do better in the future, if we can just get past the present trouble."

"I never could have imagined . . ." Lucian said, and

stopped, as if unsure he'd really heard all that had been confessed to him.

"The other complication in this matter is you, dear heart," Olivia said. "I had not counted on falling in love. I had fully intended to turn you away, to forego any chance of real happiness in my life, the better to care for Andrew. I also wanted to spare you my private horror. I have done you a very great disservice in telling you these things, but I feel as if I had no choice. I am very much in need of your counsel, Lucian."

Lucian nodded, his mind beginning to catch up with it all.

"What am I to do about Lord Shaftbury? That Mephistopheles is the last sort of person on earth who should be given this power. If you can still find it in your heart to love me even a little, please tell me what to do."

"And what you say is true? You are really one of them?"

"Yes, my love," Olivia said as gently as she could. "I am a vampire."

PART IX

✦

Terminus

42

1920

NOW IT ALL ends, forty years after the London Vampire Panic, with my intense private satisfaction to finally understand what happened. God knows that is a rare enough occurrence in this world. The older I get, the greater my sense that life is an impenetrable mystery.

I have just been sitting here, staring out the window at the rain, wondering about why it is that some events become notorious and famous, while others are forgotten. I doubt a year goes by that the papers don't carry some lurid recount of Jack the Ripper's spree of disembowelment and cannibalism. There are no like stories about the London Vampire Panic. In 1880 the government still had the authority to keep distasteful things from being reported in the press. The Vampire Panic, infinitely more chilling in its details and implications than the Ripper's brief career, has been virtually forgotten.

Lord Beaconsfield, as Disraeli was styled after being made a peer, lost the election to his old enemy Gladstone. When he went into retirement, his Special Committee simply ceased to be, along with countless other supernumerary committees, study groups, and investigations.

I am one of our group's two last surviving members, now that Cotswold is gone, killed by the fever last summer while digging fossils in Africa. (Of all the damnable things to be doing at his age!) I will be the last to go. Shaftbury, the pompous old devil, was first, killed in a fall while horse-back riding that weekend we were all last together at Collingsworth.

There never was a definitive close to our committee's investigation into the London Vampire Panic. Had the murders continued, no doubt the investigation would have gone on, but they stopped as abruptly as they had started, and with as little explanation. Bit by bit, like winter easing into spring, the Vampire Panic dissipated and we went on to other things, none quite so horrific.

How strange, then, in my eightieth year to have the sum of it all presented to me, tied up as neat and tidy as a package as I sat one morning at the desk in my study, drinking a cup of coffee and reading the *Sunday Times* before putting the finishing touches on my memoirs. There it was on page one, the final bit of the puzzle. The *Times*'s Paris correspondent filed a report on the return of tourists to the City of Light in the aftermath of the war. The photograph accompanying the piece showed a crowded café on the Champs Elysées. Sitting at one of the tables, oblivious to being photographed as they looked lovingly into one another's eyes, were Lady Olivia Moore and Captain Lucian—Lord Lucian, I should say, since he's succeeded to the lairdship of his family's vast estate in Scotland.

The delicious Olivia and Lucian were married in the spring of 1880 and went off to Scotland together with Olivia's young half brother, Andrew. I was at the wedding. It was a smallish affair held—I looked this up in an old date-book—March 28 in St. Agustin of Canterbury Church. Until I sat down to work on these memoirs, I had not thought of Olivia and Lucian for years. One knows so many people in London society. They come, they go, and one loses track.

And now, after not seeing them for forty long years, there they were, Lord Lucian and Lady Olivia, sitting in a Paris café, obviously still very much in love. This was astonishing enough, since love and marriage tend to be mutually exclusive terms in the upper tier of British society. But what stopped me stone-cold was the fact that, in the Paris photograph, neither Lucian nor Olivia looked one day older than when I last saw them at their wedding, or the time before that, at the weekend house party at Collingsworth, when Lord Shaftbury fell off the horse and broke his damn fool neck.

Lucian had to be close to seventy, Olivia in her sixties. And yet from the look of the photograph, they had not aged a single day in four decades.

I got out my magnifying glass straightaway and inspected the photo closely, thinking I had to be mistaking some other couple for my "old" friends. I then went rummaging about my private archives, flipping through the scrapbooks and photo albums until I managed to locate a picture of Olivia and several of Lucian. But there was no mistake. The couple in Paris *was* Lucian and Olivia.

I made some discreet inquiries after that. The resulting letters sit before me on my desk. Lucian, Olivia, and Andrew have not been home to Lucian's ancestral castle in many years. They have become avid world travelers, I learned, their life an endless series of cruises and treks to distant lands. I am told Andrew has grown up to be a fine gentleman. After Oxford, where he took firsts in all of his exams, he went off to the Far East. He has not been home to Britain in years.

I have no proof of it, but I think that Lucian and Olivia must have somehow learned of my inquiries, quiet as they were. One day, not long after I'd received the last of the letters reporting that Lucian and the others had vanished into the world, I woke up possessing the stunningly clear memory of the events reported in the previous section of this memoir.

I will not attempt to explain how I knew something that was impossible for me to know, something that must surely strike you, dear reader, as a hallucination. I will only say that the recollection—for that is what it seems to be—is far too detailed to be the product of senile dementia. I can only think that Lucian must have confided to me at Collingsworth, and that either he or Olivia were able to make me "forget." I am unable to explain why the buried memory has only now come to the front of my mind. Perhaps Lucian, realizing I had discovered the truth by independent means, freed the lost fragment, wanting me to understand, at least in my final days, what happened when we were all together that weekend in the country.

There can be no doubt what Cotswold called the "epidemic" was linked to Moore House. From there it probably extended back to Hungary, where Olivia and Andrew had lived for a time. Though I do not know for certain, it is logical to assume that the boy was the start of all the trouble in London. As a child, Andrew would have been incapable of understanding the consequences of his actions. Whether he was personally responsible for any of the deaths—although perhaps he had something to do with the demise of Annie Howard, their servant—I rather much doubt. Instead, I suspect he unwittingly spread the condition to others, who had as much trouble controlling their impulses as the wretched creature that Cotswold beheaded in the cellar of the Vicarage to keep it from killing us all.

I can only assume, judging from their appearances in the photograph, that Lucian and Olivia are, for want of a less hysterical term, vampires. And Andrew, too. Of course, I do not believe Lucian or any of the others is capable of wantonly killing people by draining them of their blood. An English gentleman would not stoop to so foul an act. And since I have heard no more accounts of vampires killing people, I presume there are other quiet, nonlethal ways to accommodate their needs. Perhaps the condition is, as Cotswold believed, a medical condition that can be controlled with careful maintenance.

Yet there is one mystery remaining: Shaftbury.

As I recall, it was Lucian who asked Shaftbury to go for a ride the afternoon of the fatal accident. Shaftbury was a reptilian character, and I always doubted he was truly a gentleman. One can easily imagine the disagreement, with Lucian taking Lady Olivia's side as her protector, against Shaftbury, who wanted to possess the powers of a vampire for himself. Perhaps Shaftbury lashed out at him with his riding crop. Lucian, the best of horsemen, would have easily parried the blow, resulting in Shaftbury taking the unlucky fall that cost him his life.

I am certain Lucian did not murder Shaftbury to protect Olivia—though if not for the timely accident, who can say how things might have turned out? Lord Shaftbury would have made the very *worst* of vampires.

I have arranged to have these papers locked away by my solicitor until the next century. By then, even Lucian and Olivia will be beyond caring if the world learns the truth about the London Vampire Panic. My other secrets will be burned. There is no point in leaving behind personal correspondence to embarrass surviving husbands and children. I have kept so many letters, written out in delicate feminine hands, tied with ribbons, some still bearing faint traces of perfume. I have so many; burning them all will take days!

My story is ended, but not my life. I may be a hoary old man without much time left, but I am not beyond enjoying certain pleasures. My new Irish cook is not unmindful of the graces a concupiscent and attentive young girl can bestow on an aged man of the world.

And now I put down my pen, its long labor concluded, to wander off toward the kitchen wing. Although the craving comes to me less often than it did when I was a young rake, I still often have an appetite for a delicious slice of peach pie.

VAMPIRE HUNTER

by
Michael Romkey

Entombed for almost a century in the corpse of the "Titanic" at the bottom of the icy North Atlantic, the Vampire is finally released by a treasure-hunting expedition—that never makes it back alive. In a small South Carolina town, a stranger calling himself Charles Gabriel seeks desperate help from a beautiful psychiatrist. But while irresistible sexual passions are stirred by supernatural powers, the town falls victim to a horrifyingly rampant surge of unearthly evil.

I, VAMPIRE

Living forever, he dwells among the
mortals. Connoisseur of the finest in life—
beautiful women, well-aged wine, and
classical composers—he has no need of
guilt. For he is neither good nor bad,
neither angel nor devil. This is his story.

THE VAMPIRE
PAPERS

An invitation to study the life of the
Vampiri, those creatures who are joined by
blood and cursed to live out their days in
lonely immortality.

THE VAMPIRE PRINCESS

Come aboard the ultraluxurious Atlantic Princess's maiden voyage and cavort with a glittering array of millionaires, movie stars, and royalty, all with their own dark secrets. But not one of them has a past as evil as the ravishing Princess Nicoletta Vittorini di Medusa's. And not even you will be able to resist the siren call of the deadly ecstasy she offers. . . .

THE VAMPIRE VIRUS

The mysterious death of an archaeologist lures disease-control researcher Dr. Bailey Harrison deep into the jungles of Costa Rica. There, in the hot zone, an unknown and potentially devastating new virus has made its first lethal appearance. Yet a more horrifying evil awaits Bailey at the end of her quest. For in a lavish estate carved from the savage wilderness, an extraordinary man rules, the master of a forbidding world. And he himself is slave to a centuries-old hunger.